WHERE THE
LEY LINES MEET

FINAL CHAPTER TO THE CLAIRE SAGA

TOM McCAFFREY

Black Rose Writing | Texas

ISBN: 978-1-68513-399-3 (Paperback); 978-1-68513-427-3 (Hardcover)
PUBLISHED BY BLACK ROSE WRITING
www.blackrosewriting.com

Printed in the United States of America
Suggested Retail Price (SRP) $22.95 (Paperback); $27.95 (Hardcover)
Where the Ley Lines Meet is printed in Garamond

Cover art by Richard Lamb of Inspired Lamb Design

*As a planet-friendly publisher, Black Rose Writing does its best to eliminate unnecessary waste to reduce paper usage and energy costs, while never compromising the reading experience. As a result, the final word count vs. page count may not meet common expectations.

PRAISE FOR

WHERE THE
LEY LINES MEET

"Fearless character arcs, razor-sharp dialogue, gut-wrenching tenderness and action that makes *Top Gun* look like a toddler's bedtime story—buckle up for McCaffrey at his best…"

–Joe Barrett, award-winning author of *Managed Care*

"Buckle your seatbelt—or better yet, allow AI Jayney to cocoon you in safety as you dive into this latest offering in Tom McCaffrey's sci-fantasy series, *The Claire Saga*. In *Where The Ley Lines Meet*, all of McCaffrey's "mystical misfits" are back in an action-packed page turner of high jinks and high stakes, culminating in an ending you won't see coming. As we have come to expect, McCaffrey's humor and his heart are on full display in his loveable, wise-cracking characters, including—as always—Claire the beloved mule."

–S. Kay Murphy, author of *The Dragon Singer* series

"Sci-fi spectacle, gut-busting laughs, intergalactic reunions, ass-kicking heroism, and tear-inducing goodbyes. *Where The Ley Lines Meet* is not only a perfect ending to the beloved Claire Saga, but it expertly showcases the anarchy of brilliance we've come to expect from Tom McCaffrey."

– David Buzan, author of *In The Lair Of Legends*

"WTLLM is a compelling tale about love and family – transcending bloodlines, species and galaxies. Hang on tight as McCaffrey delivers a fast-paced, emotionally-stirring, thrilling and satisfying conclusion to his unique series, *The Claire Saga*."

–E.H. Wilde, author of *The Memories of Eskar Wilde*

THIS BOOK IS DEDICATED TO
DR. STEVEN GREER
(A TRUE VISIONARY)
AND
THE DISCLOSURE PROJECT
HTTPS://WWW.FACEBOOK.COM/THEDISCLOSUREPROJECT

AND
TO PETE FLANAGAN
AND HIS "DOG-ASS METS" RIP

WHERE THE
LEY LINES MEET

FORWARD

I met Tom McCaffrey like most people meet him; he struck up a conversation with me. Instantly, he was a part of my life, sending daily encouragement, checking in on life, and being a friend. It wasn't until I read *The Wise Ass* that I caught on to his gift. McCaffrey doesn't just build community; he writes it into existence. He's so good at it, in fact, that he can tie an entire universe together, and in his latest novel, *Where The Ley Lines Meet*, we get the full breadth of his reach.

From the first page to the last, the action is gripping, weaving a line through the tales of each of his beloved characters. The pacing of the chapters flows seamlessly, especially for such a large cast over a massive setting. It's easy for readers to connect, if not fully find themselves within the storyline, whether in space or on Earth. I found myself tearing up in every scene yet still enjoying the adrenaline of the action. The idea of family plays a huge role in understanding the motivations behind each hybrid, human, and Centaurian character, and McCaffrey gives us a beautiful glimpse into their backstories while creating a sense of urgency in his writing. There is the warmth of familiarity and the fear of losing it as the characters we've loved for a long time face imminent danger. In true McCaffrey fashion, there's enough humor to laugh through the crying.

The most poignant part was the reintroduction of Casa Claire. For all who know Tom McCaffrey, this powerful image is not imagined. He has created this space within his family and community to house our spiritual connection as universal beings, and he does so through his Celtic roots. Claire is a spiritual guide who symbolizes love, protection, and direction for Jimmy and the rest of us. Because to say that Tom McCaffrey is just a writer would be a gross understatement. For his readers, he's a lighthouse, a safe zone, a place to come and pour a glass of whiskey, hold it high, and say *sláinte*!

-Kerry Fryar Freeman, Author of *Sedona: A Novel*

PROLOGUE
(Bless Me Father)

Peter "Buck" Sheridan pulled his classic 1968 Chevy Camaro into the clergy parking lot behind the Shrine of the Immaculate Conception rectory and parked in the reserved space designated "Monsignor." It was Saturday morning, so Buck knew Monsignor Delahanty would be playing the back nine at the Army Navy Country Club, using the passes he provided him each March. Buck hit the remote kill switch he had his cousin install in the red monster that once belonged to Buck's grandfather. It disabled the Camaro's engine and prevented even the most creative car thief from hot wiring the only thing of value his father had left him. *Trust but verify.*

Buck whistled softly and a tricolor Jack Russell leapt from the back seat onto the leather shotgun seat of the car. Buck slid a leather vest with the words "Service Dog" embossed on both sides over the dog's relatively broad shoulders and fastened the buckle snuggly beneath his chest.

"C'mon Fergus," Buck said, opening the car door.

"Let's go unburden our souls."

The dog effortlessly leapt over his large caretaker, clearing the curb on the driver's side, and then scrambled onto the walkway that led to the side door of the old church.

Buck loved this old church. It reminded him of his childhood in Pearl River, New York, where he first attended St. Margaret of Antioch with his family, and later, on his own. Buck was a very religious man, and while a young teen considered entering the priesthood, until Mary Jane McLoughlin stole his heart and his virginity the night of their senior prom. *Wonder what MJ is up to?*

Despite his lifelong enchantment with the opposite sex, Buck never married. Instead, he entered the army as a commissioned officer right out of Manhattan College and spent the rest of his nomadic life stationed at posts in almost every country while he steadily rose through the ranks by his hard work, devotion to the military, and his enduring faith in God.

Buck had served with distinction as a young officer during postings in hot spots throughout the middle east and Africa. He earned the first of two Purple Hearts when, as a green second lieutenant fresh out of college, he was wounded saving a young girl when his platoon took rebel fire while protecting a progressive Muslim school in the local town that had the audacity to admit young women.

Over the past thirty years, during Buck's steady rise to his present rank as a Four-Star General leading NORTHCOM, his unwavering moral compass, fine mind, and sense of fairness, had earned the devotion of the soldiers who served under him, as well as the respect of the revolving hosts of politicians from both parties that inhabited the true seats of power. Buck had little time for the latter.

Buck's lifestyle and focus on his professional advancement was not conducive to long-term relationships. But that did not mean there weren't enough short-term relationships to satisfy his desire for female company. Unfortunately, most of his favorites moved on to the security of marriage to others once Buck moved on to his next posting.

Buck had traveled the world and prayed in the most beautiful cathedrals left in existence, but he found smaller local churches offered him his strongest connection to his Lord. ImCon, as Buck liked to call this church, had the added bonus of being the temporary home to one of Buck's younger cousins, Father Jack Lawlor, a Harvard grad and rising star in the Catholic Church, and whose name already had been whispered in the *Palazzo Apostolico* in Rome.

Buck scanned the nave of the church and spotted an elderly woman rise from a pew towards the front and quietly slide past the curtain of the closest confessional. A tiny red light appeared over that stall. The rest of the church was empty.

Buck went to the rack of votive candles along the back of the church, slid a twenty into the poor box and then lit a pristine white candle with one of the wooden tapers retrieved from the box of sand at the edge of the candle rack. After offering a silent prayer for all of his deceased family, friends and fallen comrades, Buck looked down at his loyal companion by his feet and said out loud, "And God bless Fergus. Amen."

Fergus wagged his unbobbed tail appreciatively.

The red light above the confessional stall went off and, a moment later, the now forgiven old woman slid out from behind the curtain and proceeded to the altar rail. She then knelt to carry out the Our Father and five Hail Mary's she would need to complete her confession for swearing at her neighbor during a heated exchange over the latest political scandal rocking the current administration.

Buck left her to her prayers and slid into her spot in the confessional, pulling the curtain closed and positioning his large body as comfortably as possible on the worn kneeler. Four years as a starting Jasper linebacker had wreaked havoc on his knees. Fergus remained directly outside the curtain, standing guard.

Buck heard the latticed screen slide open with a soft thud and reflexively responded, "Bless me father, for I have sinned. It's been three weeks since my last confession."

A deep and somber, disembodied voice cut him off. "Forgive him Lord, but Buck you're full of shit. I haven't seen you for three months."

"Hello, Jack." Buck said.

"Father Jack to you," came a voice colored with mock curtness.

"What's this I hear of a potential posting in a Vatican dicastery?" Buck replied.

"What's this I hear of a definite appointment to Commander of Space Force Command?"

"I guess each gets us closer to God." Buck said.

"Tell me your sins, my son, and say your Act of Contrition, so we can get out of this musty cubicle and grab a cup of Mrs. Stucki's coffee in the rectory."

Five minutes and a penitential decade of the rosary later, Buck and Fergus followed Jack through the sacristy and into the back passageway that led to the rectory. Fergus, knowing from experience that a piece of Adrienne Stucki's delicious crumb cake awaited his arrival in the rectory kitchen, raced ahead of the two men to claim his prize.

By the time the two men entered the kitchen, Mrs. Stucki had two cups of coffee with corresponding slices of crumb cake waiting before their respective seats at the kitchen table.

"Good morning, General." Mrs. Stucki said softly.

"Good morning, Adrienne," Buck replied in his best faux flirtatious manner, "that crumb cake looks almost as tempting as you."

"That will be another ten Hail Mary's, General." Mrs. Stucki said with a smile, as she turned back to the stove and busied herself preparing the afternoon lunch for the three visiting priests from Chile. "And congratulations on your promotion."

"I haven't accepted the job just yet, Adrienne." Buck responded.

"Why not?" Jack asked.

"Because, if rumors are true, given that there are no secrets in Washington, I'm not sure I'm ready to learn definitively that we are not alone in the universe." Buck answered, this time with all seriousness.

* * * * *

"With all the recent news broadcasts showing military videos of UAPs," Jack said as he licked the tip of his middle finger and rubbed it along the edge of his plate, capturing the lasts of the crumbs there before sliding them into his mouth, "it has made me wonder how Mother Church was going to handle the possibility of the existence of other life forms."

"That's the problem," Buck said. "If I accept this promotion, I'll be read into some pretty classified material. I'm not sure I can assimilate those possibilities into a faith that has guided me since I said my first prayer."

"Don't worry about the things you cannot change," Jack offered in his best homily delivery. "You handled accepting Darwinism just fine without missing a genuflection. The Good Book didn't cover that possibility."

"Sure, but that evolution took place on this planet." Buck replied. "And Jesus waited until we were hairless apes before he gave us his take on God and heaven. He never mentioned sharing the Celestial Kingdom with ET."

Buck poured himself the last of the coffee from the French press carafe Mrs. Stucki left for them, before heading off to the church to arrange Sunday's flowers . "How would you, who is clearly destined for a crimson, and possibly white, Mitre, someday, explain it?"

Jack stood and walked over to the window, closing his eyes as he basked his face in the warmth of the morning sunshine. Feeling God. Buck studied his contemplative cousin, who once was a four-year starting point guard on his Crimson varsity team and resembled a young Gregory Peck. The Irish curse of salt and pepper hair had not yet taken hold in his thick black mane. With those central casting good looks and intelligence, it was no wonder he was destined someday to hold the papal ferula.

After a few moments, Jack turned back to Buck, smiled, and pointed to Fergus, who was sleeping quietly at Buck's feet.

"When I was growing up, the nuns used to tell me that animals don't go to heaven." Jack said. "But I believe that all creatures have a soul. Especially Fergus. All souls are welcome in Heaven. Fergus and ET alike."

"I hope you are right, Jack." Buck said, as he reached down and softly stroked his sleeping companion. "Because if Fergus doesn't get into Heaven. I'm not going either."

"Let's not get ahead of yourself," Jack replied with a smile. "It's not Fergus' admission through the pearly gates that I'm worried about."

CHAPTER ONE
(Reservation)

"Helen. . ."

"Helen, honey..."

Helen LaLousis did her best to ignore her partner, Bobbi Angelini's voice and rolled over to the far side of their king-size bed, fighting to retain the last vestiges of the dream she was having.

"Helen." Bobbi stage whispered, this time shaking Helen's naked shoulder. "There are noises coming from the kitchen."

Helen rolled over, wiping the sleep-cobwebs from her eyes.

"You sure it's just not ghosts?" Helen said hoarsely as she tried to get the moisture working in her mouth and throat. "Those McCarthy brothers love to break your stones."

Bobbi closed her eyes and telepathically scanned the house.

"No," she said. "These noises are corporeal."

Bobbi continued to shift her face slowly from left to right.

"And whoever's doing it is preventing me from accessing their thoughts."

At that moment, Eddie Angelini, dressed in a form-fitting blue jump-suit, materialized on Helen's side of the bed carrying a large bed tray ladened with two orders of Belgian waffles coated with melting ice cream, two glasses of orange juice, a steaming French press, coffee cups and utensils.

"You ladies still take your coffee black?" Eddie asked matter-of-factly, then winked at his sister.

"Holy shit!" Bobbi bellowed, causing an alarmed Helen to bolt up in bed, naked to her waist. This knocked Eddie, the tray and all of its contents, flying. But before Bobbi could slide out of her side of the bed everything in the room froze in place, including the airborne breakfast and Eddie Angelini.

"Helen sure has a lot of ink." Mark Lenahan said, materializing in a similar outfit beside Eddie. After collecting the tray and all of its contents from their frozen positions in the air and carefully resetting the breakfast down at the foot of the bed, he licked his finger tips and exclaimed, "Now, that is fucking delicious."

Helen's hooded bathrobe levitated off the chair in the corner of the room, crossed to its owner and wrapped itself around Helen's shoulders, covering her many tattoos and everything they rested on. Just then two tall figures with long burgundy hair materialized on Bobby's side of the bed. The female's hands were glowing while the male's hands worked the air before him like a maestro as they orchestrated Helen's arms into the sleeves of the robe, closed the front and then caused the robe's belt to tie itself into a nice bow.

The female flicked an index finger in Eddie's direction, and he immediately continued his original trajectory, landing for a moment on the floor before reappearing on his feet instantaneously with a smile and the rest of his dignity intact.

"I told you we should have called ahead." Stella, the tall female, said.

"I just wanted to surprise her." Eddie said, sheepishly. "And, after twenty years, I wanted to cook someone a meal again."

"C'mon sis," said the tall male standing beside Stella. "Unfreeze these lovers. Let Eddie have his reunion."

"As you wish, Apollo." Stella responded, as the glow from her hands started to dim. "Lenny, you may want to hold Helen, so she doesn't fall out of bed. Eddie, grab Bobbi."

The two men appeared beside their charges, as instructed, and firmly held Helen and Bobbi by their shoulders as the two women reanimated.

Bobbi's eyes brimmed with tears as they immediately focused on her brother.

"Frozen or not, my mind heard everything before you even said it." She wrapped her arms around her brother's waist and pulled him onto the bed beside her.

Helen, reanimating while still in a frightened mode, went to shove Lenny reflexively as she continued her leap out of bed. Lenny deftly avoided the move and reappeared behind her, wrapping her in a bear hug until she could get her bearings.

"What the fuck?!" Helen shouted as she stared at the broad arms that held her and struggled in vain until her eyes set on the now materializing figure with thick white hair that appeared directly before her. He was popping the last of a buttered scone into his mouth.

Helen stopped struggling and stared until that flicker of recognition kicked in.

"Whitey?!" Helen exclaimed. The man broke into a broad grin.

"What did I miss?" Whitey said, licking a dab of the butter off his lips as he looked around the room. "Besides these home-made English scones."

* * * * *

After hugs all around, the Centaurians collectively transported from the bedroom and rearranged the Oracle's breakfast dining room by sliding two smaller tables together, surrounded by seven chairs, before Helen and Bobbi, now both in their bathrobes and slippers, arrived downstairs from their living quarters in human fashion.

Stella, sitting at the head of the table, directed Helen and Bobbi to the two empty seats to her immediate left and right.

"I trashed the waffles, they got cold," Eddie declared as he appeared through the swinging doors from the kitchen effortlessly carrying a large silver serving tray with enough steaming breakfast fare to feed a firehouse.

"You know," Eddie said as he distributed the plates around the table in a blink of an eye, "I miss my kitchen."

"Jayney may be excellent at everything she creates for us on Proxima b," Whitey added, digging into his plate, but she never quite mastered the hash brown. You really need to share your secrets with her, Eddie."

"Finely shred and mix those potatoes and onions in equal measure, add just a drop of olive oil to the skillet and flip until crispy on both sides," Eddie said.

Everyone in the group dug into their meals, except Bobbi, who sat sipping her coffee while assessing her returning friends. No longer human, they looked younger than the last time she saw them, the night all hell broke loose.

Helen looked up from her breakfast and smiled at her partner. Despite their best, Helen, like Bobbi, showed her age.

You know we couldn't risk coming back or even contacting you. Petrichor forbade it.

Stella's voice continued to intrude upon Bobbi's thoughts. Bobbi was impressed, given that Stella was simultaneously carrying on an aural conversation with Helen.

Father was afraid that whatever AI those two twins had conjured up would be used by the government to set a trap around those, like you, that stayed behind.

We all played dumb, Bobbi responded telepathically, while sipping her coffee like a mental ventriloquist. *And that lawyer your dad hired, Jack Vaughan, did an amazing job of selling the plausible deniability to the feds. After a few tough interviews, they left us alone. Never even questioned the kids. The men in black never actually uttered a word about it, but boy, their thoughts showed me that they were pissed over the ass whooping you guys threw them in Oregon before you left. Especially killing the evil twins.*

Stella laughed as if in response to something Helen said but glanced over at Bobbi just long enough for their eyes to lock.

"Hey, no mental whispering during meals, sis," Apollo declared from the far end of the table.

"Helen," Whitey interjected, "How are the kids doing? How's Lucian?"

"Amazing," Helen responded. "Scarlett and Savanna have been mastering the craft under the tutelage of their darling Aunty Bobbi, and Lucian just retired from the Navy. He's still living in the house you left him."

"And the other properties?" Apollo asked.

"Eileen is still living at Everett and Michelle's home. Retired. A constant gardener, she's kept that back yard looking amazing." Helen replied. "Blue and Maeve crossed the veil a few years back. They are buried by Claire and Mr. Rogers."

"But they are always around." Bobbi added.

"And speaking of final resting places, how's the family home?" Apollo asked.

"The girls share it when they are stateside. Jack Vaughan hired a local couple as caretakers to keep it up when they are overseas." Helen answered. "Janice and Brian Erickson. They seem really nice."

"Where overseas?" Lenny asked.

"Savanna is finishing up her second doctorate at the London School of Economics, and Scarlett is a lecturer of Art and Design at the Sorbonne in Paris." Bobbi replied.

"But they both come home every June. They've never missed the Solstice." Helen added.

"What month is it here, anyway." Lenny asked. "Been so long, I've lost track."

"Summer." Whitey responded, sniffing the air. "Oh, how I want to run through the woods and howl at the moon again."

Lenny nodded, then explained to the Terrans. "There's no moon on Proxima b."

CHAPTER TWO
(Home Again)

"Mudda fucka?!"

Brian Erickson stared at the floor of the stall area of the barn. Those were definitely large hoof prints in the wood shavings. From the size difference, they were two separate sets. They looked fresh. He stepped out of the barn and looked around the side paddock. Nothing. Having just run the electric John Deere mower over the back section of the property, he knew the perimeter fencing was intact, so there were no equines or other visitors.

Brian hated the silence of the electric lawnmower. It made him feel alone. It also didn't hold its charge long enough for him to get anything done in a timely manner. And he hated being here any longer than he had to. There was just something spooky about the place. But a job is a job.

There was one particular spot in the back property that Brian avoided like a Yankee fan at a hometown Red Sox game, where the riding mower battery repeatedly died, even if it was freshly charged. The same thing happened when he tried to use the electric weed whacker. The power drained instantly before the first stalk was sliced. Brian found an old scythe in the storage shed, but he wasn't going to chance stepping into the area, which was probably full of rattlers. They loved the high grass. As a result, a perfect ten-yard circle of tall wild vegetation stood in the center of the large open field, rippling in the Northern Colorado breeze, like an inverted crop circle.

This place is weird.

Brian plugged the mower into the barn's exterior outlet for the second time that day and headed back into the house to check on his wife. Hopefully, Janice would be done giving the place the once over in preparation for the owners' return in a few weeks. Maybe she'd have the coffee pot brewing.

Janice never seemed to mind coming to this house. She spent most Saturday mornings there on her own. During the winters, when the two sisters that lived there were overseas, she'd stop in whenever the weather got tricky, just to make sure that the heat was working and there were no leaky pipes or storm damage. Once a week, she would drive into town and collect whatever mail had accumulated for the two sisters. If something looked important, Janice would forward it to France or England. Otherwise, she left it in a box in the small office area off of the kitchen.

Brian came by to handle the snow shoveling in the winter and the lawn and shrub maintenance in the nicer weather. Sometimes he repaired the fences or gates if they succumbed to the weather or wind. He painted the exterior of the barn and that other studio at the back of the property a few years back. He stayed clear of the bat house, whose once black paint was now worn down to its natural wood. Those critters gave him the creeps.

Overall, Brian didn't mind the work. He was still in decent shape, especially for a retiree. And he liked to stay busy. Plus, Janice enjoyed the added responsibility. She said it broke up the monotony of early retirement.

It was good money; a generous weekly retainer was directly deposited into their joint account by some legal office back east. In fact, that income, along with their social security, was more than enough to live comfortably on. They didn't need to touch their 401K.

There was one spot on the outdoor property Brian didn't mind being around; a pet cemetery where you first entered the large open field in the back. Two larger graves were marked by two large wooden crosses with the words CLAIRE on one and MR. ROGERS on the other. Two smaller graves and crosses with the letters B and M sat on either side of the larger ones. Janice had mentioned something about two mules and a couple of family dogs, being buried there. A trio of older women who came by regularly to visit the sisters during the summers when they were home, often stopped by throughout the rest of the year to place fresh flowers on the graves.

Brian always had a strange sense of calm and well-being whenever he was in that area. It was always the first place he mowed on the weekends.

It took Brian ten minutes to walk back to the house, so he knew there was another fifty minutes to kill before the mower would be fully charged. He still had the side and front property to do.

Brian had time enough to drive into town and pick up a couple of burgers from A&W, and maybe a shake. If Janice was finished, maybe he could talk her into coming along for the ride.

Brian removed his boots and left them outside the sliding glass doors that opened off the back yard and into the basement.

"Jan?" He called out. Nothing.

He listened for the sound of the vacuum, but the house was quiet.

He called out again. Again, no answer.

Brian wondered if his wife had gone into town. He decided to go upstairs and make himself a coffee while he waited for her return. As he climbed the stairs, he decided to text her and ask that she pick up those burgers while she's out. When he reached the top of the stairs, he heard the text chime from Janice's phone coming from the kitchen.

"Jan," he called out again.

"In the dining room," she called back. Her voice sounded strange.

As Brian turned the corner, he froze. There, at the large dining room table, sat Janice and five strangers. Janice had a nervous look on her face.

"Brian," Janice said. "We have company."

When the young woman with burgundy hair sitting beside his wife placed her hand gently on Janice's forearm, Brian knew something wasn't right. Janice wasn't a touchy-feely type of person. Brian quickly reached behind him to draw his hand gun from its hip holster, but the gun wasn't there.

"That's a fine little weapon," came the deep male voice from behind him. Brian spun and came face to face with Mark Lenahan, now standing a few feet away, carefully examining the handgun that Brian never felt leave his holster.

"Can't go wrong with a Glock 42," Lenny said.

Brian's racing mind had not even registered this first sleight of hand when a tall burgundy haired male materialized in the living room right beside the man holding his handgun.

"Fawk!" Brian exclaimed.

"Is that a Southie accent?" Lenny asked.

"Brian," the tall man said. "We need to talk."

Lenny deftly ejected the cartridge from the handle of the weapon, caught it with his free hand, and, before Brian could blink his eyes, had emptied it of all six bullets with the blur of his thumb.

He snapped the magazine back into the gun's handle, tossed it gently back to Brian, then raised both palms to the bewildered caretaker and smiled.

"Brian," Lenny said just a little too excitedly, "I've waited a long time to say this to someone and actually mean it... Wait for it now... Ready..." Lenny leaned forward and extended his empty upward palm as he performed a chivalric bow. "We come in peace!"

CHAPTER THREE
(Taking The Reins)

Buck took the stairs all the way up to his new office on level 5, Wedge three of the Pentagon. He enjoyed watching his security detail huffing and puffing as they tried to keep pace with his two-stair approach to ascension. Buck made a mental note to move his operations to one of the Colorado bases. He believed that sitting too long in an office made you soft, and the thin Colorado air would be the best way to train everyone's body to be ready for anything. After all, there is no oxygen in space.

Buck was also a little superstitious, and after September 11, 2001, rumor had it that this section of the Pentagon was rife with spirits of the heroes that died that day. That explained why the newest office with the best view in the building sat empty. It was bad enough Buck was going to have to deal with ETs, but ghosts as well?!

Buck had instructed his number 2, Major Douglas MacArthur Corry, whom he brought with him from the Army, to hand-pick a group of loyal men and women for his support staff. He told him to pull them from the other services and separate details, so there would be no competing loyalty to anyone but Buck. Buck trusted Mac with his life.

Buck's new staff was waiting for him in his way too large conference room that housed the latest and greatest technology. This included holographic, cloud based smart boards that appeared along the center of the beautiful mahogany conference table, where thirty people could sit comfortably. It was almost full now. They all stood and saluted as he entered the conference room. Buck marveled at the diverse group of young faces that peered out from beneath their saluting right hands.

There was one older, attractive woman, a blonde Lieutenant Colonel sitting beside Mac. What appeared to be an iPad on steroids sat on the table before her.

"As you were." Buck said as he took the open chair at the far end of the conference table.

"Let me start by introducing myself." Buck began without waiting for them all to return to their seats.

"My name is Peter Sheridan. You can call me General. . . Sir . . . or those that are more daring, Buck."

That broke the tension and brought smiles to most of the young officers around the table. But the Lieutenant Colonel didn't surrender her poker face.

"I was as surprised as I'm sure you all were to learn that I had been tapped for this post." Buck continued. "I never got above a C in any of my science courses in school and never even flew a plane, although I have leapt out of a few and crawled away from a downed CH-53 chopper in Somalia. So, given the choice, I like to keep both feet firmly planted on the battle fields of terra firma."

Buck made eye contact with each member of this new group. He could always read a person by the way they responded to his locked gaze. That was his strength as a military leader. The ability to assess instantly the people he engaged, including his opposition.

"That means I'm going to have to rely on each one of you to help me not look like an asshole."

That drew a few chuckles from some of the more confident players at the table.

"So, learn your roles, and make sure this old guy never steps on his dick when he is in public, especially when testifying before those morons in Congress."

Did I just see a Mona-Lisa smile on the Lieutenant Colonel's lips?

Mac did a great job selecting this group. All had their lights on, and everyone was home.

"Now, I'm going to begin our new working relationship by giving each one of you a choice." Buck continued. "It will be the last choice you get to make as long as you are serving in my command."

He gave them all a moment for this to sink in.

"Some of you can come with me to what will be my choice of our new base of operations at the Buckley Air Force Base in Aurora Colorado. However, those that wish to stay within spitting distance of the heart of our government are welcome to remain stationed here, in this office."

Buck gazed at the hands of the men and women around the table and guessed that those with wedding bands on their left ring finger were more likely to stay put. He hated to force families to uproot and leave their schools and communities if he could avoid it. To do otherwise was to start off by poisoning the feelings of spouse and children. And that eventually floated up to the affected officer.

The Lieutenant Colonel didn't wear any jewelry on her hands. Buck watched as her nicely manicured nails rapidly typed something onto the screen before her.

"Okay," Buck said, standing up. "Major General Corry will handle your initial assignments, and I'm sure some of you will be managing your change of station arrangements. Dismissed. "

"I have PCS fact sheets for anyone who needs them," Mac added before the rest left the conference table. "And you can find all the other information you need at 'militaryoesource.mil.'"

With a final soft salute, Buck exited the conference room through his private door into his spacious office, while his staff filed out the other exit into the main hallway. A moment later, he heard a knock on the door he closed behind him.

"Enter." Buck stood at the window staring down at the Pentagon Memorial on the west side of the building. He made a note to stop in at the Chapel on the ground floor below him, before he moved his office to Colorado.

"General," came the confident voice of a woman from behind him. He spun and locked eyes with the Lieutenant Colonel, still carrying that iPad. She extended her hand as she crossed the room.

"Buck, I'm Dr. Renee Clarke," she said, receiving Buck's reciprocal hand and shaking it with a firm grip that telegraphed that she was used to commanding professional equality.

"I'm your Chief Science Officer."

"Well, Dr. Clarke," Buck said with a smile. "You've got your work cut out for you."

CHAPTER FOUR
(All Roads Lead To Rome)

Fucking binary.

01001010 01101001 01101101 01101101 01111001

00100000 01110111 01100101 00100000 01101110

01100101 01100101 01100100 00100000 01110100

01101111 00100000 01110100 01100001 01101100

01101011 00101110

"Jimmy, we need to talk."

Moments later, Petrichor materialized in the cabin of Jimmy's personal spacecraft, which he dubbed Shadowfax, after Gandalf's stallion. Tolkien's Lord of the Rings was one of the few series of books Jimmy had actually enjoyed reading as a teenager. Jimmy was returning from a reconnaissance mission of the Ophiciuchus Constellation, where he liked to explore the planets in its Goldilocks zone.

While Jimmy enjoyed his post human life within the AI protected artificial interior of Proxima b, he enjoyed visiting nearby planets where he could walk on their surface without fear of the sun's radiation. Most of all, since he left Earth, Jimmy missed the feeling of the wind blowing through his hair, which, since his evolution as a Centauri-Terran hybrid, now hung full and thick from the top of his head to his shoulders.

Proxima b's ubiquitous AI, "Jayney," (named by Jimmy's Centauri best friend, Everett, in response to the headlights on the Earth's human Blonde Bombshell from Earth's 1940s, Jayne Mansfield) generated options that coincided with Jimmy's ever developing ability to control Centauri spacecraft. Jayney recently offered Shadowfax access to a series of wormholes that provided Jimmy with easy entrée to this closest galactic neighborhood. Normally, Jimmy traveled on these ventures with his wife, Gina, who, like Jimmy, made the molecular transition from an Italian American Earthling to Centauri-Terran hybrid through the involuntary application of a golden beam from the Centauri Hadron Distributor. But ever since Proxima b's heirs apparent, Stella and Apollo, Jimmy's children, returned to Earth with Claire and some of the original members of the mule's Berthoud crew, Gina and Michelle, Everett's spouse, had been drawn into the Centaurian queen bee, Petrichor's, close circle of advisors on the ever-evolving life of the Centauri people.

Jimmy didn't mind the occasional solo expeditions, since Gina, who seemed to have evolved at a faster rate than Jimmy, liked to control Shadowfax during their joint sojourns. In all fairness, she was a much better pilot. She also embraced all the technology and absorbed all the new science their forced emigration to Proxima b had provided. Jimmy remained a relative luddite, by choice, relying on Jayney and the lifelong voices in his head to provide the minimal information he needed to get from point A to point B. A little alone time with Shadowfax gave Jimmy a chance to play catch up.

Jimmy had just maneuvered Shadowfax out of the mouth of the return wormhole and could now see his adoptive planet through the transitioning translucent skin of his spacecraft. He executed a perfect barrel roll just because he could.

Suddenly, a tall, voluptuous goddess, with flowing blonde hair that seemed to highlight her flawless porcelain skin, appeared before Jimmy, standing just on the far side of Shadowfax's holographic control panel.

"Speak of the devil," Jimmy said aurally. "hello, Petrichor."

Despite his devotion to Gina, Jimmy could not help but be thrilled that Stella, Petrichor's daughter with Jimmy, had gotten her mother's looks, except for her burgundy locks, vestiges of the variant "Ginger-Gene" that ran through Jimmy's Celtic bloodline.

Petrichor, the most evolved Centauri and that planet's chosen leader, softly cleared her throat before speaking.

"So, we're going to do this in English, are we?" she asked.

"When in Rome," Jimmy replied, gesturing to his surroundings.

Jayney, assume control. Petrichor commanded telepathically.

The control panel disappeared, and Jimmy suddenly found himself sitting across from Petrichor in matching holographic captain chairs. Petrichor, as always, was beautiful.

Just because I bought dessert, doesn't mean I can't look in the bakery window.

"Why do Centaurians even bother with space ships?" Jimmy asked, determined to change the subject before Petrichor rifled through his mind. "After all, we can pretty much transport where we want, when we want."

Petrichor thought this over for a moment.

"First off," Petrichor responded in her naturally sultry voice that still sent erotic chills across the best parts of Jimmy's body, "despite the Centaurian genetic homogeneity, we each remain individuals and develop our skillsets accordingly. Not all of us can physically handle transversing great distances."

Jimmy thought that over. He realized that since his evolution to an intergalactic hybrid, he limited his own spontaneous transportation to within a few miles of his existing location. In fact, he often enjoyed covering the distance physically almost as quickly through his enhanced hybrid biological abilities. Why miss the scenery?

"And we still are not sure of the capabilities of hybrids." Petrichor added, reading his thoughts.

"Did I just hear a little condescension in your voice?" Jimmy teased. *Must remember to put that toilet seat down.*

```
01010111  01101111  01110101  01101100  01100100
01101110  00100111  01110100  00100000  01101001
01110100  00100000  01100010  01100101  00100000
01100101  01100001  01110011  01101001  01100101
01110010  00100000  01101001  01100110  00100000
01001001  00100000  01100100  01101111  01110111
01101110  01101100  01101111  01100001  01100100
00100000  01110100  01101000  01101001  01110011
00100000  01101001  01101110  01100110  01101111
01110010  01101101  01100001  01110100  01101001
01101111 01101110 00111111 00001010
```

Wouldn't it be easier if I download this information? Petrichor asked telepathically.

"My ship, my rules," Jimmy responded resolutely.

"Fine. Secondly," Petrichor continued, with a hint of exasperation in her tone, "we need to be able to visualize where we are transporting to, so if we previously haven't been to a place ourselves, we must be able to see it in the mind's eye of another. Someone who is at the location in question. That's how I found you just now."

Jimmy assessed this idea against his own experiences and realized that with his own application of this skillset, he actually kept it pretty limited to transporting to where he could see or remember.

"And finally," Petrichor concluded, "the most direct path between two points is not always the most enjoyable."

Jimmy's mind was suddenly flooded with Petrichor's very tactile memory of their first close bedroom encounter on Proxima b. Even though they didn't consummate the deed, it was an exciting near miss. In the end, Jimmy's swimmers were technically directly transported to Petrichor's fertile gene pool by the creative Dr. Nim, and their amazing daughter, Stella, was conceived.

"One sometimes enjoys the scenery along the longer path."

Jimmy's face fully flushed at the memory. He was surprised to see a little corresponding crimson rise in Petrichor's porcelain cheeks.

"So, my liege," Jimmy said, again changing gears to move away from this dangerous diversion, "to what do I owe this unexpected pleasure?"

"I've been summoned before the Intergalactic Federation," Petrichor responded, all thoughts of pleasure vanishing from her face.

CHAPTER FIVE
(Shanghai Express)

At Stella's direction, Brian quietly sat in the chair she vacated without any apparent movement and joined Janice at the dining room table. He reached beneath it and clutched his wife's hand protectively. Lenny and Apollo returned to the last of the empty seats. Stella then began to physically circle the table, lightly tapping the left shoulder of each person she passed like the "It" contestant in Duck, Duck, Goose.

When she reached Brian and Janice, Stella tapped them both simultaneously, and left her now glowing hands on their shoulders for an extended period. In that moment, Stella uploaded everything about them, individually and as a couple. She learned of their respective professions, he was a mechanical engineer at a robotics company, she was a grade school teacher. Stella learned how they met, how their grown son, who they had successfully raised to adulthood, and still loved with all of their heart had moved with his own family across the world when the couple retired to Colorado. She learned of the love and care Janice had shown this home in their absence and understood Brian's anxiety about the property, including around the circle out on the back field, where the ley lines meet. Most of all, Stella learned how much they loved each other, and how both, in that moment, were willing to sacrifice their own lives for that of their spouse in the face of this unknown. Stella knew they were good people.

Stella, in turn, downloaded to Brian and Janice all of her visual childhood memories of her time on Earth, especially those growing up around this home. She shared the intensity of familial love that she felt for this planet and most of the people who inhabited it. She shared her memories of Claire and Mr. Rogers, Blue and Maeve, both in living and spirit forms, and those of the rest of the family of misfits, including the mystical humans who stayed behind and the hybrids that now sat around the table with them. Stella shared glimpses of her mother, Petrichor, and life and wonders on Proxima b. Stella shared her reasons for returning and how the fate of the Earth now hung in the balance. Finally, Stella shared her willingness to trust these two humans and, out of respect for their free will, offered them a choice.

"I'm in." Janice shouted out loud.

"And if I'm not?" Brian asked, more concerned than defiant.

You'll both wake up, sitting in your idling car in the driveway of your lovely home on the far end of the estate, without any memory of ever having stepped foot on this property or meeting anyone around this table. Those memories and those just shared would be suppressed forever. Apollo answered telepathically.

As Brian gazed around the table, the rest of the hybrid crew, who had mentally witnessed the entire exchange, all nodded in agreement.

Brian suddenly felt his wife's hand intensely squeeze his own beneath the table.

"Don't fuck this up for us, Bri," Janice whispered. He turned to his wife and saw that determined look he first fell in love with when she was a young bartender at The Field Pub in South Boston. "One last big adventure, together."

His eyes welled up as he felt that love for her all over again.

Brian nodded almost imperceptibly, smiled at his lovely wife, and whispered in his cumbersome Southie accent, "I'm in."

A moment later, an excited Lenny stood beside the table, gazing appreciatively at the dusty bottle of Macallan in one hand, a cluster of shot glasses, finger-tipped locked over his head in the other.

"A boisterous toast to Jimmy Moran for leaving behind his stash of fine whiskey!" Lenny proclaimed.

A moment later, a topped off shot sat in front of each chair at the table.

"And to the newest additions to our misfit crew." Whitey added.

"You may want to go easy on that, Stella and Apollo," Eddie warned the siblings, they don't serve this nectar on Proxima b."

Eddie, Whitey, and Lenny all looked at each other and tossed down their shots in unison, while the others watched. The three friends all closed their eyes and silently let their bodies appreciate the warming of their souls.

"Not to worry, we share our father's DNA and I remember all of those dinners I witnessed back in the day." Apollo responded before tossing down his shot. With a responsive shake of his head, through clenched teeth, he hissed, "so, we're traditionally and genetically predisposed to enjoying it."

Janice raised her shot glass to Stella. "*Sláinte mhaith,*" she toasted before tossing it back and banging her empty glass twice on the table. Brian followed with his own "*sláinte agatsa,*" before downing his own with the repeated double tap of his empty glass.

"*Sláinte chugat!* Stella responded with a Gaelic phrase she pilfered from her newest friends' memories. She tossed back the shot as she had seen the others do and felt the immediate pleasant burn follow the whiskey down her throat as her tongue flattened against the roof of her mouth, her chin reflexively tightened and her eyes instantly watered.

Any race that can create this drink is wonderfully crazy and worth saving. Stella shared it with the hybrids.

"Welcome to the crew." She hoarsely whispered to the humans.

CHAPTER SIX
(I Know What I Don't Know)

"So, what kind of doctor are you?" Buck asked, as he gestured for the Lieutenant Colonel to take one of the overstuffed leather chairs on the far side of his way too large desk. He, in turn, made himself comfortable in the captain's chair on his side.

"I received my bachelor of science from Purdue in Astronautics Engineering Technology, and then my Ph. D. in Astrophysics from MIT's Kavli Institute, all on Uncle Sam's dime," Renee responded rotely.

Buck was beginning to wonder whether the person sitting across the desk was a product of one of the secret government labs he had heard rumors about. He waited a moment to see if she had any more to add, then realized she wasn't the sharing type.

"How long have you been with Space Force?" Buck asked.

"Just over ten years," she replied.

"Those must have been challenging times," Buck prompted.

"There was a steep learning curve for everyone, which was to be expected, given the sudden responsibilities over everything above 50 miles in altitude," she responded. "But I believe we have held our own in maintaining our country's advantage in the last great frontier."

"Did an excellent job establishing our country's permanent moon base," Buck said.

"Yes," she responded. "I was stationed at the Artemis Base Camp for most of last year."

"Impressive," Buck said, meaning it. "I hope to visit there during my tenure," this time without conviction.

Buck had pretty much shot his load concerning his anecdotal knowledge about the projects he was aware of in his new command. After all, the military branches were proprietary, and information was rarely shared between them in any meaningful way. Buck would have to wait until he was "read-in" to everything that was happening during his team's transition period. He knew he could rely upon Mac to navigate the political and administrative land mines he would be facing, but he knew he needed to be able to tap into the minds of officers like Dr. Clarke, if he was ever going to lead this branch into the future. He knew he had to win her over.

"So, you have been around for this most recent increase in public hysteria over the flying tic-tacs?" Buck asked, looking to lighten the conversation.

"Yes, sir," she replied, her voice a little guarded.

"What do you make of it all?" Buck asked.

"I can volunteer that there has been a direct correlation between the steady increase in UAP sightings and Congress' tripling of our service's research and development budget," she responded.

"That must give me lots of great toys to play with," Buck said facetiously, hoping to draw some human emotion from his new subordinate. He would have settled in that instance for her Mona-Lisa smile.

The Lieutenant Colonel studied the General for a moment. Buck suddenly felt like a lab rat about to be sectioned.

"Sir, may I speak freely?" she finally asked.

"Please," Buck replied.

"There were three other officers with your rank available from the other branches of service who were up for your position, all of them with well-documented credentials in math or science," she stated.

"I believe you are correct," Buck responded. "All solid candidates."

"I have checked your record," the Lieutenant Colonel continued. "You graduated from a smaller Catholic University with a bachelor's degree in political philosophy. You minored in religious studies."

"Right again," Buck replied. "A Jasper until my last breath."

"Then you spent the last twenty years rising slowly and steadily through the commissioned ranks in the army," she recited.

"You are on a roll, Lieutenant Colonel," Buck rejoined, worried that he may have given her a little too much leeway. But at least he was sensing some passion in her voice.

"So, with all due respect, sir, how did you get this job?"

Now it was Buck's turn to study the Lieutenant Colonel. He guessed she was in her early forties. He noted that her blonde hair was tightly pulled back in a neatly controlled bun but he could tell that it was thick and long in its natural condition, probably shoulder length. She wore a minimum amount of makeup that leaned in towards androgyny, but that did not disguise the natural beauty of her features. The slight symmetrical crow's feet were barely perceptible around her eyes, which were jade green, and her lashes were full and her own. Same with her lips, which glistened with clear lip gloss, more likely coated for protection from the elements than adornment. There were no smile lines framing her mouth, but Buck guessed that was from lack of opportunity, or desire, rather than Botox.

The Lieutenant Colonel was tall, about 5' 9" and had the body of a onetime competitive athlete, college level, possibly a swimmer, maybe a skier. Buck guessed that she probably maintained her fitness on her own schedule these days through late evening runs around the base or through the neighboring streets or parks near whatever post she found herself. She was a loner, not a gym rat. There was nothing soft about her.

After a minute of awkward silence, Buck leaned back in his captain's chair and made a big production of slowly placing his right foot up on the closest corner of his desk, and then carefully resting his left foot on top of it.

He pointed to his shoes.

"Lieutenant Colonel," Buck began, "are those your size 12 shoes on my desk?"

For the first time since he met her, his subordinate looked confused. She gazed back and forth between Buck's highly polished black Bates Oxfords and his Irish blue eyes. Given the six feet expanse between his two features, she was forced to turn her head to execute the move. He could feel her mind racing as she tried to get ahead of where Buck was taking her.

"No, sir," she responded after a moment. "Those are definitely not my shoes."

"So, Lieutenant Colonel," Buck continued, "you've never walked in them?

"No, sir."

Buck now slowly removed his feet from his desk. He sat up as tall as he could muster and gazed directly into his subordinate's eyes.

"Well, Dr. Clarke," Buck continued, all the fun drained from his tone, "until you have marched a least a mile in my size twelves, preferably during a firefight, don't ever assume to judge me, or my abilities."

He raised himself to his full six-two height with his back straight and his shoulders back, and never broke gaze as she took his cue and stood up reflexively in attention.

"I don't need you to tell me what I don't know, Lieutenant Colonel." Buck said tersely. "Your job, assuming you wish to remain as my Chief Science Officer, is to tell me only what I need to know before I need to know it. Is that understood?"

"Yes, sir." She responded with a little less confidence in her voice.

"Good," Buck replied, his face softening. "So, assuming we meet again at my command post at Buckley, be ready to tell me everything I need to know."

Dr. Clarke nodded, a hint of more respect in her eyes.

Buck gestured towards his office door.

"We're done here, Lieutenant Colonel," he barked. "Please tell Major Corry your decision on the job offer on your way out."

CHAPTER SEVEN
(An Unexpected Journey)

In the moments it took Jimmy to materialize in Petrichor's chamber from the ship docking station, she had downloaded her binary instructions to the two females sitting on the nearby holographic settee.

Welcome home, sweetie. Gina Moran shared with everyone in the room telepathically upon his arrival.

"*Everett was very upset you went to the Ophiciuchus Constellation without him,*" Michelle added. Michelle was an older, pure Centaurian, who was Gina's best friend and the extraterrestrial responsible for Gina's conversion into an intergalactic hybrid while still on Earth. Michelle was also the spouse to Jimmy's pure Centaurian best friend, Everett, who was responsible for Jimmy's post-death resurrection and hybrid conversion back on the blue planet. The Centaurian couple took their friendship and their roles as progenitors to these once humans very seriously. Jimmy and Gina would have given their lives for Everett and Michelle.

"I found this great super-earth in the Goldilocks zone around its binary star, Alpha Ophiuchi. It has a comfortable atmosphere, lush vegetation, and large bodies of fresh water," Jimmy responded. "Too bad Everett didn't come, because some of those lakes looked like they might have fish in them."

"Don't tell him that." Michelle replied. "That would kill him. Do you know that he had Jayney create a G. Loomis NRX+ fly fishing rod from his memory?"

"Is there anything our Jayney cannot do?!" Gina responded.

"Ev insisted that it be made out of graphite and resin, even though we have far better materials here on Centauri. He even had Jayney create a running stream for him to practice his casting."

"He showed it to me." Jimmy chimed in. "Quite authentic."

"I told him he should have Jayney stock the stream with fish next time," Michelle continued.

"Jayney already did," Jimmy responded. "Ev just sucks at fishing."

I heard that! Everett said as he materialized in Petrichor's chamber wearing a set of green waders and a straw hat and carrying a whicker creel and the fishing rod in question. Water ran from Ev's waders onto the holographic floor and pooled around the soles of his boots.

Jayney, can we dispense with the water? Petrichor pleaded. The liquid disappeared.

Jimmy materialized beside his friend, flipped the lid off the creel and shook it upside down. It was empty. "I rest my case!" Jimmy declared in his best lawyer voice.

A moment later, Ev's waders and gear disappeared, and he was dressed, like the others, in a comfortable unitard. Ev looked dejected. Jimmy placed a comforting arm around his friend's shoulder and gave him a brotherly squeeze. "You'll get 'em next time, big guy."

"You think so?" Ev asked hopefully. "Maybe I'll have better luck on that super-Earth you just mentioned."

Jimmy smiled and shook his head. "Nah, . . . you REALLY suck at fishing."

`Everyone, including Petrichor, had to laugh at that line. In the big scheme of things, laughing audibly was still somewhat new to the Centaurians, although there had been an increasing level since the hybrids arrived. Ev and Michelle had mastered it from their time down on Earth, but their brethren back on Proxima b, including Petrichor, still looked a little uncomfortable in the performance.

"On a more serious note," Gina interjected, "Petrichor has just filled us in on her upcoming trip to the IF."

"The Reptilians have lodged a complaint against Earth over the alleged downing of one of their drones." Michelle added.

"They are our protectorate," Petrichor continued. "We have to answer for it."

"The Reptilians had no business being anywhere near Earth," Everett stated, with a lot more emotion than expected.

"Be that as it may," Petrichor replied, "the Terrans did us no favors by being so witlessly aggressive."

"Said the woman that single handedly whipped a lot of Terrans asses, including its military, if I recall." Jimmy responded.

"They were threatening our children!" Petrichor declared, matching Everett's tone in intensity.

"I'm going to need you to download a complete background on the Reptilians before we face the inquest," Jimmy stated.

Petrichor shook her head.

"I'm not sure the High Council of the Intergalactic Federation is ready for Jimmy Moran. The invitation was for me, alone."

"Tough shit." Jimmy replied. "Guess who's coming to dinner."

"As the resident Centaurian expert on Earth and its inhabitants, I'm coming along, too." Everett interrupted.

"Why not?!" Jimmy stated. "You can take second chair at the hearing. I'm not taking that asshole Aldor with me."

"May I join this party?" Gina asked. "I can keep Jimmy in line. Last time he argued before an alien counsel he almost got himself de-animated."

Petrichor smiled as she telepathically shared her memory of Everett's historic Centauri trial in an instant. Everett laughed audibly at the memory of Jimmy breaking Aldor's nose.

Jimmy noticed Petrichor omitted their "bedside" encounter outside the chamber to spare any awkwardness with Gina.

Petrichor shook her head. "I need you and Michelle to stay here and act as my regents. It's the only way I will be comfortable being absent from my duties here on Centauri. You two are my most trusted advisors."

Gina took a moment to let this sink in. She glared back and forth between Petrichor and Jimmy. Jimmy knew that look. Jimmy tried to peek at her thoughts, but her mind was locked. He knew Gina wasn't convinced. After a moment, she nodded. "As you wish."

"Jayney, pack my toothbrush," Jimmy commanded the Centuarians AI, before Gina could put up a Sicilian argument. "Road trip." He turned to Petrichor. "Your ship or mine?"

"Neither. We can't get there by ship."

CHAPTER EIGHT
(God's Country)

Buck insisted on driving his Camaro cross country to his new post. Fergus wasn't a big fan of flying, and Buck wanted to take the few days without human company to consider all the things he knew from experience he needed to anticipate before assuming a new command. Mac Corry was already at Buckley handling the details for Buck's arrival. Buck wanted to hit the ground running.

"Don't know what to make of that Lieutenant Colonel, Fergus." Buck said, looking over at his loyal furry co-pilot riding shotgun beside him. Fergus was napping in the warm sun coming through the passenger window but thumped his tail rapidly on the leather at the sound of Buck's voice.

Buck was surprised that Dr. Clarke accepted the post after their encounter at the Pentagon.

Buck was traveling the most direct route on I 70 West directly from DC to Colorado. In his younger days he would have driven the straight twenty-four hours and crashed once he got there. This time Buck broke the trip up into two legs and stayed overnight at the pet friendly Towne Place Suites By Marriott near Columbia, Missouri. He felt the urge to actually "see" the land he had been protecting for close to four decades.

Buck loved to drive through "Flyover country" as the DC wonks liked to call it. Despite his New York roots, he had little love for either coast of his beloved nation. He knew from first-hand experience that, historically, most of the blood shed to protect it from harm came from the often-fatal battlefield wounds of the young men and women of its interior states. The citizens of "the Coasts" maintained a constant air of elitism that rubbed his middle-class, Irish Catholic genes the wrong way.

Buck did his best to keep his head down and his nose out of politics. In his humble opinion, there was plenty of blame to go around as between the two major political parties, who really didn't give a shit about their constituents.

Buck rationally believed there was truth to the rumors that multinational billionaires controlled the purse strings for both parties. A pox on both their houses. It was all about the money. In return the billionaires compelled bad political decisions that caused division among the citizens, and a destabilized world that always resulted in conflict between people, tribes, and countries. Every one of those billionaires siphoned substantial income from the war machines in every country. Technology, information, pharmaceuticals, manufacturing, fuel production, energy and even agriculture all supported and thus drew some sustenance from mankind's continuing creative capacity and desire to kill one another. Didn't matter if the killing occurred on the streets or the battlefields. Discord must be fomented.

At the same time, these billionaires flew their private jets to remote enclaves and gathered under visually exciting banners containing altruistic acronyms for a luxurious week of fine dining, entertainment, and spa treatments. There they could discuss the future of mankind and dictate how the common folks would need to continue to sacrifice for the good of the global economy. Occasionally, they trotted out some young, recently discovered media darling to demonstrate the democracy of their viewpoint, in a similar fashion to the nameless narrator in Ralph Ellison's *Invisible Man*. After all, these Masters of the Universe had to show that the present world was unsustainable, and the unsuspecting plebians needed to hear that from one of their own. Priorities must be reset, and existing national political and monetary systems and geographic boundaries discarded and reformed.

But no matter what happened, their wealth would continue to accumulate.

Many of his peers that Buck had served with over the past three decades in the military had succumbed to the temptation and entered the military industrial complex as soon as they retired from active duty. Each went from lower middle class to country-club wealthy overnight.

Buck felt just a bit hypocritical whenever he criticized those retirees for cashing in on the blood money. After all, it was that blood money that supported the military. Without the steady flow of money that went into the dark recesses of research and development, Buck's soldiers would still be fighting within eyeshot of one another with swords, muskets, and trebuchets. Death, up close and personal. Money funded modern technology that reduced wartime murder to the emotional equivalent of a video game.

Buck gazed out over the endless wind farms that littered the open prairies on either side of the interstate where thousands of cattle used to graze, and wondered when the last time was that he ate a cheeseburger that wasn't created in a lab. Over the past decade alone, countries had culled their domestic cattle numbers to a third. He wondered where PETA was when those mass slaughters took place.

Still, Buck was thankful he didn't have to cover his monthly food or energy bill, or he would have to take one of those high paying lobbying positions just to make his nut.

The only thing Buck still could depend upon in today's complex world was the men and women who served under him. The only thing he could control was how he led them. The only thing he could rely on to fulfill his leadership duty properly was his experience and his integrity. And his integrity was formed and guided by his faith.

But, at that moment, Buck was only praying that he had enough gas in his tank to maintain his Camaro's 85 mph cruising speed on this final twenty-mile straightaway along the last leg of the Kansas I70W. He knew that there were still a few mom-and-pop petrol stations just on this side of the Colorado border. Fuck REEVs, FCEVs or even PHEVs. No Chinese batteries for this old soldier. Buck had seen the young children mining conflict minerals during his last tour in Africa. He had given up wondering why US scientists hadn't come up with a more feasible alternative energy source. Every panel, bolt and piston in this anachronistic road warrior was machined and assembled by Union Labor here in the U.S. He trusted it to get him where he needed to go in all weather conditions. He'd just put his $15.00 a gallon fill-up on his government credit card as a moving expense.

And he had all the petrol he needed at Buckley, on Uncle Sam's tab. The military still needed to move its planes, helicopters, and tanks reliably around the globe. And its Generals. Rank had its privileges.

CHAPTER NINE
(Homecoming)

Lucian Benson silently flew up 23 North on his mat-black VERGE TS ULTRA and took the turn onto Meining Road without braking. He loved this bike, one of the toys he treated himself to when he retired from the Navy. He loved its simplicity, its sleek, modern, hub-less design, low center of gravity and its speed. No clutch, no chain, no belts, no cooling systems, no maintenance. The rear tire was its engine and all he needed to focus on was the throttle. He could charge it at home in a half hour. He loved that the only sound he heard on his rides was that of the wind coursing around his helmet.

He often took his bike twenty minutes north on Colorado 103 into Wyoming where he could navigate its interstates at a cruising speed of 80 mph without worrying too much about exceeding the bike's maximum range capabilities. He particularly enjoyed driving at night. The visual blur of the passing, oncoming headlights heightened the sensation of speed. The feeling reminded him of his time in the U.S.N. Fighter Weapons School, and later, the F-38C's he flew off the USS Gerald Ford, just before both he and that aircraft carrier were decommissioned. Both vehicles provided him with that G-force sensation that was always immediately followed by an endorphin rush. Lucian lived for the rush.

He slowed to a snail's pace once he entered the quiet side street out of respect for the safety of the families that lived on this estate and the wildlife that often sprinted across the roads without warning. He curled left onto the back end of Beverly Drive and then followed its serpentine course to the last property before the foothills. Home.

Lucian loved this home, his only one since his siblings sold the family farm after his parents' sedan was crushed by an 18-wheeler on the lower end of I 25, just before he entered the Navy. Lucian refused his share of the estate and insurance pay-out, leaving it all to be split among his five sisters, who had taken their shares and then dispersed to wonderful locations around the country. Lucian didn't need the money. He had his government pension, as well as the generous income from a substantial trust account left to him by his surrogate family, the Morans, shortly after they disappeared. So, Lucian had the financial freedom to consider all of his options on his own time line instead of taking the path of least resistance and signing on with the first aerospace company or airline looking for a pilot with his advanced skillset and military connections. If that weren't enough, this house and property were given to Lucian by his mentor, Whitey Fronsdahl, who, like Lucian, was an adopted member of the Moran Family crew, when Whitey vanished with the others almost twenty years ago. Lucian knew he was blessed. But he was alone.

He stopped by the Moran home shortly after he returned from the service, hoping to reconnect with his childhood friends and confidants, Scarlett, and Savanna McKenzie, who had been left that property at the same time he received his trust. The nice woman who answered the door with an unusual accent explained that they were living in Europe.

He did reach out to his "Moran Family Aunties," Helen and Bobbi, just a week ago when he drove over to Hygiene to visit their restaurant and home at the Oracle. It was wonderful to reconnect with people whose wholehearted hugs made all the pain go away. Their delicious food also reminded him of those wonderful Moran family parties he missed so dearly. As he was leaving that night, Bobbi pulled him aside and told him not to worry, that his parents were doing wonderfully and had been there with him during every tight scrape he had faced during his military service.

Bobbi also told him that she had lots of other extended family information to share, now that he was old enough to understand it all.

Helen promised to host a spectacular welcome home gathering for him and all the remaining members of the Moran crew, including their other gay auntie, Eileen, as soon as the sisters returned home from Europe. Lucian was looking forward to that.

He hit the remote-control button as he entered his long driveway and by the time he reached the garage he was able to cruise right in. He removed and stowed his helmet and gloves and hooked the charging cable to his bike. He didn't notice the large silhouette standing in the entrance way until he went to hit the remote to close the garage door. As Lucian was standing directly beneath the overhead halogen light in the center of the garage, he couldn't make out the washed-out facial features of the visitor. His training as a fighter pilot had honed his fight/flight response reflex to allow him to maintain calm even when events around him reached FUBAR status. Lucian glanced at his old 22 caliber rifle, resting in the recess to his right and waited, patiently, like a coiled rattler.

"What? Too old to hug an old friend?"

CHAPTER TEN
(Lizards Suck)

At first light the next Centauri day, Jimmy rose from his Centauri version of brief meditative sleep and sat with Gina over Jayney's AI prepared breakfast table. Jayney had gone deep within Jimmy's memory to find the proper strength of coffee he desired, the orange juice and an "everything bagel with a schmear" that was lightly toasted and delicious.

As she had done on the first day of every court appearance Jimmy had attended since law school, Gina made sure he looked his best before leaving their living chamber. As was also her ritual before she sent him off to legal battle, Gina kissed her mate and repeated the Spartan phrase, "With it, or on it." Then she winked and added, "No fist fights."

Moments later, Jimmy materialized in his council seat among the nine encircled on the Great Hall Wall. He looked over and saw that Everett was already in place, but the Centaurian hadn't seemed to notice Jimmy's arrival. Jimmy didn't like the worried look on his friend's face, so he reached out telepathically.

01000001 00100000 01110000 01100101 01101110
01101110 01111001 00100000 01100110 01101111
01110010 00100000 01111001 01101111 01110101
01110010 00100000 01110100 01101000 01101111

01110101 01100111 01101000 01110100 01110011
00101110 00100000

A penny for your thoughts.

Everett looked over at his hybrid friend and did his best to smile.

01001001 00100000 01100100 01101111 01101110
00100111 01110100 00100000 01110100 01110010
01110101 01110011 01110100 00100000 01110100
01101000 01101111 01110011 01100101 00100000
01100110 01110101 01100011 01101011 01101001
01101110 01100111 00100000 01101100 01101001
01111010 01100001 01110010 01100100 01110011
00101110

I don't trust those fucking Lizards.

Jimmy had spent the long Centauri night sifting through all the information Petrichor had downloaded about the Reptilian race. As was his way when preparing for any legal confrontation, Jimmy distilled the important bullet points and discarded the rest. First rule of litigation: Know your enemy.

Turned out that Draconians, as expected, come from the constellation Draco, one of the circumpolar star patterns Jimmy studied in the northern Earth night sky as a child. Its tail threaded between the two more memorable bear constellations, Ursa Major, and Ursa Minor. He remembered that the Cat's Eye Nebula could be found in Draco. He recalled studying it through a telescope one summer night with his cousin Apples on the roof of Jimmy's childhood home back in the Bronx. It was a cheap telescope, but they got the "cool" gist of it. Jimmy missed Apples.

The Draconians populated all the small planets throughout their constellation, but their political center of power was an earthlike planet in the Goldilocks zone that orbited its brightest star, Etamin.

According to the voluminous download Petrichor provided, the Reptilians had a long history of interfering with Earth, with contacts as far back as the Sumerians, who referred to them as *Anunnaki*. Hieroglyphs from that period display many humanoid-lizard-like representations. Among the ancient artifacts uncovered in the Tell al'-Ubaid area of modern-day Iraq were similar detailed figurines known as the Ubaid Lizardmen. The Draconians promised early man knowledge, as far back as Eden, but, according to Centauri records, those contacts were solely for purposes of enslaving the early humans and exploiting the natural resources of the blue planet. There were even rumors that the Reptilians may have interbred with some humans, which may explain the Terran's overly aggressive and militant behavior, although the Centaurians have not been able to confirm this independently.

The Reptilians sought to capitalize on utilizing this newer galactic race whose very existence was a result of many centuries of careful Centauri genetic manipulation of other hominoid species evolving naturally on Earth. Unlike the Reptilians, the Centuarians had no ulterior motive beyond the peaceful development and evolution of the human race, with hopes that they would someday be able to engage and embrace the other intelligent species throughout the many galaxies. Jimmy couldn't help but wonder if the fictional Dr. Victor Frankenstein had similar motives as well.

But no matter how you evaluated their collective history, according to Centauri records, Reptilians were the true mercenaries of the universe and direct competitors with the Centuarians for the right to control the future of Earth and its inhabitants.

Jimmy felt comfortable that he now had the lay of the land when it came to the "who" and the "what" of this beef with the Lizards, but he was not sure of the "why" it was coming to a head at this moment.

He set out to get that from his old friend, the resident expert on Earth and its inhabitants.

"Tell me about this complaint by the Draconians." Jimmy said to Everett.

Just download it. Everett replied telepathically. *It's all there.*

Fuck you, Jimmy responded in kind. *I want to hear it from your mouth. I want to feel the passion of your thoughts on the issue.*

Everett looked over at Jimmy from his seat across the wall and stared for a moment, then nodded and smiled. He gestured to the floor of the chamber and disappeared. Jimmy felt a tap on his shoulder and then they were both sitting in two chairs facing each other on the floor.

"Okay," Everett began. "As you know, my primary duty on Earth was to monitor the interrelations of the human race to make sure they weren't destroying themselves and the planet."

"Thank you for that," Jimmy responded with a wink.

"I also was tasked with making sure the humans didn't advance too far into space before they were responsible enough to handle that right of intergalactic intercourse."

"Ah, intercourse," Jimmy said, smiling. "Now you are speaking my language. Go on."

"But another one of my duties was to keep an eye on other visitors to the planet." Everett explained. "The Centaurians didn't want our great experiment to be corrupted by outside influences."

"God forbid," Jimmy mocked him. "You didn't want anyone else tossing in some unknown ingredient into the genetic soup, so to speak."

"Exactly," Everett responded.

"Especially those Draconians." Jimmy continued.

"Damn right." Everett replied. "Fucking Lizards can't stay away."

"But shit happens," Jimmy declared.

"Not on my watch," Everett replied defensively. "What may have happened before my tour is not on me."

"What about Roswell?" Jimmy asked.

"The Greys screwed that one up." Everett responded. "Got a little too comfortable and dropped their guard."

Jimmy knew from his past conversations with Everett and Michelle that the Centaurians used to subcontract their Earth experiments to the Greys from Zeta Reticuli. That race was known for their balls and creativity when it came to abducting, testing, and returning humans in order to measure their evolutionary progress. When it came to all fields of science, the Greys were cutting edge, even among the rest of the galaxies.

"You know the Greys were the first to develop memory suppression." Everett added, almost as an afterthought. "Big selling point in their first landing the Earth gig. Now every advanced race in the universe has it. It's practically over-the-counter."

"But it is not fool proof," Jimmy replied. "The humans started getting around it through hypnotic regression."

"Who saw Freud coming?!" Everett said with a chuckle. "And don't get me started on Budd Hopkins. He's been a nightmare for us."

In that moment, Jimmy's thoughts flashed to a beautiful field, with a pond.

"Do you smell lavender?" Jimmy asked.

"What?" Everett asked, concerned about this sudden change in the conversation. "You having a seizure? Wait, you can't."

Jimmy blocked his mind, so that Everett didn't go snooping, but when he tried to retrieve the image, it was gone.

"So where were we?" Jimmy asked.

"Well, the Greys handled the heavy lifting long before me and for most of my time on Earth, coming and going during the rotating night, in areas where the populace was sleeping. They got careless. Didn't anticipate the range of some of the human weapon systems developed during the 1940s during that world war when we really thought they were about to destroy themselves.

Got too close to where the US Government was developing the captured German V1 Rocket technology out West during the late 40s, and one of their ships went down over Roswell, New Mexico. It was like a Stealth Bomber being brought down by a sling shot."

"Bad luck." Jimmy replied.

"No kidding. That's when the powers that be sent me and Michelle down to keep a watch on things."

Jimmy watched as Everett ran the whole event back through his mind. "I still think those Reptilians gave Hitler that technology."

"Why didn't the Greys just send in a recovery team?" Jimmy asked.

"Everyone got spooked. The Greys don't have the same ability as we do to transport. They would've had to send in another team, and they didn't want to risk it, there was so much publicity on Earth."

"Why didn't we go in?" Jimmy asked.

"The ruler of Centauri at the time, before Petrichor, believed it was a Grey problem. He didn't want to give the humans anything else to draw upon."

He thought a bit more and then added, "And the US government seemed to bury the story almost overnight. So, the powers that be left it alone and sent us down to keep an eye on things."

"And the Greys?" Jimmy asked.

"They continued to do some more research work for us. But they pretty much finished up by the 80s."

"What about the Reptilians?" Jimmy asked.

"As you know, Petrichor limited our contact with Earth after that little shit storm we caused in Oregon. Without our agents in place on the planet, the Lizards probably saw an opportunity to get back into the mix."

"Well, they got what they deserved then." Jimmy said. "Fuck 'em if they can't take a joke."

01010111 01101000 01101001 01100011 01101000
00100000 01101001 01110011 00100000 01110111
01101000 01111001 00100000 01001001 00100000
01110011 01100101 01101110 01110100 00100000
01010011 01110100 01100101 01101100 01101100
01100001 00100000 01100001 01101110 01100100
00100000 01000001 01110000 01101111 01101100
01101100 01101111 00100000 01100010 01100001
01100011 01101011 00100000 01110100 01101111
00100000 01110011 01100101 01100101 00100000
01110111 01101000 01100001 01110100 00100000
01101001 01110011 00100000 01101000 01100001
01110000 01110000 01100101 01101110 01101001
01101110 01100111 00101110

Which is why I sent Stella and Apollo back to see what is happening.

Everett and Jimmy were so focused on their discussion that they did not even feel Petrichor's presence in the chamber. They both perceptively flinched at her telepathic intrusion.

Come on, Petrichor commanded as she appeared before them. *It's time we go interdimensional.*

CHAPTER ELEVEN
(Through The Looking Glass)

"Love the cape." Jimmy said with a wink. "You look like a super hero."

"It's a cloak." Petrichor responded, doing her best not to rise to the bait.

"Tomato . . . potato... a rose by any other name." Jimmy continued. "It really works for you."

"Given the Terran's penchant for violence," Petrichor responded deadpanned, "how has someone with your propensity to annoy, survived this long?"

"Just lucky. Oh, getting zapped by the Hadron Distributor helped."

"A gift that keeps on giving." Everett added.

Petrichor shook her head in frustration.

```
01000100  01101111  00100000  01101110  01101111
01110100  00100000  01100010  01100101  00100000
01110011  01101111  00100000  01100111  01101100
01101001  01100010  00100000  01100010  01100101
01100110  01101111  01110010  01100101  00100000
01110100  01101000  01100101  00100000  01001001
01101110  01110100  01100101  01110010  01100111
01100001  01101100  01100001  01100011  01110100
01101001  01100011  00100000  01000110  01100101
```

01100100 01100101 01110010 01100001 01110100
01101001 01101111 01101110 00100000 01000011
01101111 01110101 01101110 01100011 01101001
01101100 00101110

Do not be so glib before the Intergalactic Federation Council.

"I'm not going if I have to spend my time communicating in binary." Jimmy said. "Soooo fucking sterile."

"I'll request that they communicate in English." Petrichor said. "No guarantee."

"I've never traveled interdimensional." Everett said. "Does it hurt?" He winked at Petrichor.

Jimmy recoiled. "Whoa! Hurt?!"

"Okay, children," Petrichor said patiently. "Get it out of your system."

Jimmy winked, "Hey, none of these folks look like a giant slug, do they?"

"Enough!" Petrichor declared and then, with no perceptible movement, grasped each of their shoulders.

The next moment it was black. Not the color, but the complete absence of light. Jimmy could not see or feel anything. But he wasn't frightened. It felt weirdly familiar.

Jimmy?! It was Everett's thought somewhere in the darkness. Jimmy could sense his friend's tension.

You didn't happen to bring a flashlight?! Jimmy responded telepathically, mustering up some false bravado.

Almost there. Even Petrichor's telepathic thoughts were sultry and soothing.

The sudden light was temporarily blinding. Jimmy reached to his right and tapped someone. They were definitely somewhere physical.

"A grope like that is going to cost you dinner," came Everett's welcoming voice. "And dessert, or I'm telling Gina."

Give it a moment. Petrichor telepathically instructed.

As promised, Jimmy's eyes started to focus and he could see that he was sitting in a large hall, similar to the Great Hall on Centauri. In fact, it was exactly the same as the Great Hall, except there was no wall of circular seats in front of them for the council, just a solid wall of blue, soft light, as if the sky on Earth had become tangible. He felt Petrichor's hand still on his shoulder and could now see Everett standing beside him, just as they were back on Centauri. His friend rubbed his eyes and then gazed around, getting his own bearings.

Same place, same time, different dimension. Everett concluded for Jimmy's benefit.

Could have given me a heads up. Jimmy admonished him.

My first time here. Everett responded. *I stayed clear of politics.*

Jimmy glanced over his shoulder at Petrichor, who stood silently, slightly behind and between her two subjects. Her eyes were fixed forward. For the first time since they met, he detected something different. Anxiety.

Jimmy then sensed that the trio were no longer alone and followed Petrichor's gaze to the front of the hall.

Five figures now stood silently in a semi-circle along the front of the Chamber. They were all androgynous humanoids. All were wearing matching purplish robes that flowed to the floor, covering their bodies.

The one in the center had a human sized head with a bluish complexion. It was smooth skinned and bald. Its almond-shaped eyes were larger than Jimmy's but otherwise human in appearance, its nose and mouth were relatively small.

Andromedin. Everett, following Jimmy's thoughts, coached his friend. *From their namesake galaxy.*

On either side stood two identical forms. They were pinkish pale, with albino white, pin-straight hair, worn in a bowl cut with bangs. Their eyes were large but human in shape and form. Their nose was broad and their lips full and pink. Jimmy could see the tips of their ears poking through their hair on either side of the head. Those tips were narrow, almost pointed.

Tau Cetis, Everett explained. *From Cetis. I agree, Elven looking.*

To the far left of the semi-circle, stood what Jimmy could only describe as what looked like a grey lightbulb rising out the top of the robe. The top of the bald cranium was huge and extended. It had large black oval eyes that curved slightly around the sides of its head. It had no ears to speak of, and its mouth was comparably small, but it had a distinct nose that projected from its face.

That's an Eban, from the Betelgeuse system, Everett projected. *Not to be confused with the smaller Orion Zetas to whom the Centaurians farmed some of our Terran work over the millennium.*

What's that on the far right? Jimmy asked. *Cousins of yours?*

Plejaren. Petrichor responded. *From the Pleiades. Yes, there is a resemblance.*

I thought you guys were tall, Jimmy said, as he mentally compared the similar features of the tall Viking looking form to the far right to his brethren on Proxima b.

01010000   01100101   01110100   01110010   01101001
01100011   01101000   01101111   01110010   00100000
01101111   01100110   00100000   01000011   01100101
01101110   01110100   01100001   01110101   01110010
01101001   00101100   00100000   01111001   01101111
01110101   00100000   01101000   01100001   01110110
01100101   00100000   01100010   01100101   01100101
01101110   00100000   01110011   01110101   01101101
01101101   01101111   01101110   01100101   01100100
00100000   01100010   01100101   01100110   01101111
01110010   01100101   00100000   01110100   01101000
01100101   00100000   01100011   01101111   01110101
01101110   01100011   01101001   01101100   00100000
01110100   01101111   00100000   01100001   01101110
01110011   01110111   01100101   01110010   00100000
01100110   01101111   01110010   00100000   01110100
01101000   01100101   00100000   01110101   01101110
01110000   01110010   01101111   01110110   01101111
01101011   01100101   01100100   00100000   01110100
01110010   01100001   01101110   01110011   01100111
01110010   01100101   01110011   01110011   01101001
01101111   01101110   00100000   01101111   01100110
00100000   01110100   01101000   01100101   00100000
01010100   01100101   01110010   01110010   01100001
01101110   00100000   01110000   01100101   01101111
01110000   01101100   01100101   00100000   01110101
01101110   01100100   01100101   01110010   00100000

01111001 01101111 01110101 01110010 00100000
01110000 01110010 01101111 01110100 01100101
01100011 01110100 01101001 01101111 01101110
00101110

Petrichor of Centauri, you have been summoned before the council to answer for the unprovoked transgression of the Terran people under your protection.

Jimmy wasn't sure who was broadcasting the binary, but the only one with their eyes open was Blue Boy in the center, so he went with it.

If I may speak, your honor. Jimmy projected to the room in telepathic English.

All the creatures at the front of the hall became suddenly agitated.

Shit, shit, shit, Everett let telepathically slip. *They're not used to exchanging words.*

Petrichor stepped forward and addressed the council telepathically.

01010100 01101000 01101001 01110011 00100000
01101001 01110011 00100000 01101101 01111001
00100000 01100011 01101111 01110101 01101110
01110011 01100101 01101100 01101111 01110010
00101100 00100000 01001010 01101001 01101101
01101101 01111001 00100000 01001101 01101111
01110010 01100001 01101110 00101100 00100000
01110111 01101000 01101111 00100000 01101000
01100001 01101001 01101100 01110011 00100000
01100110 01110010 01101111 01101101 00100000
01010100 01100101 01110010 01110010 01100001
01101110 00101110 00100000 01001000 01100101
00100000 01110010 01100101 01110001 II 01110101
01100101 01110011 01110100 01110011 00100000
01110100 01101000 01100001 01110100 00100000
01110111 01100101 00100000 01100011 01101111
01101110 01100100 01110101 01100011 01110100

00100000 01110100 01101000 01100101 00100000
01101000 01100101 01100001 01110010 01101001
01101110 01100111 00100000 01101001 01101110
00100000 01101000 01101001 01110011 00100000
01101110 01100001 01110100 01101001 01110110
01100101 00100000 01110100 01101111 01101110
01100111 01110101 01100101 00101110 00100000
00100000

This is my counselor, Jimmy Moran, who hails from Terran.
He requests that we conduct the hearing in his native tongue.

The council all closed their eyes and their minds, as they silently
conferred with each other. Finally, Blue Boy nodded and opened his eyes.

01010000 01110010 01101111 01100011 01100101
01100101 01100100 00100000 01001010 01101001
01101101 01101101 01111001 00100000 01001101
01101111 01110010 01100001 01101110 00101110
00100000

Proceed Jimmy Moran.

I would like to address the council aurally, Jimmy began.
Blue Boy winced a little, then nodded.
"Thank you," Jimmy responded.
He gazed around the hall. The stands were suddenly filled with creatures, some humanoid, many not. All were focused on Jimmy the ringmaster. There was a contingent of greyish looking humans with wavy black hair, sitting in the first row closest to his right. One, in particular, looked familiar to him.

"Jimmy," Petrichor whispered. "They're waiting."

"Members of the council," Jimmy began, engaging each member of the council with his eyes as he spoke. "Where I come from, the accused is always allowed to confront their accuser."

The council again all shut their eyes and conferred. While he waited, Jimmy turned back to his right, but the grey humanoids were now gone.

Where is this Terran who dares to confront me?

The power of the sudden telepathic intrusion caused Jimmy to spin and search for its source.

There was a new player in the hall.

While the council members were each at least a head taller than Jimmy, this creature, who now stood facing the council, with its back towards Jimmy, was another head taller than all of them. Moreover, its shoulders were a foot broader than anyone else's in the room. Its muscular form was dressed in a fitted, black, militaristic uniform. But the pay-off came when the creature turned to face the Centaurians.

What now stared directly at Jimmy with large black eyes peering over a slightly elongated snout, was the scaled green face of a reptile. Jimmy almost shit himself.

"That would be him," Everett replied proudly, pointing at his friend. "Go get him champ," he whispered to Jimmy.

Petrichor placed her hands back on Jimmy's shoulders. *Maybe I should handle this,* she shared.

"Fuck that," Jimmy whispered to her, recovering. "I got this."

Jimmy transported to a spot directly behind the large creature, reached up and tapped him on the shoulder. "Over here, big guy."

Jimmy was not prepared for the speed at which the creature spun, and before he realized it, he was being lifted from the floor with one hand until he was now face-to-face with his adversary.

The creature studied him carefully.

"I see the Centaurians have taught their monkeys new tricks," the creature hissed. "I should snap your tiny neck for your kind destroying my ship."

Jimmy transported out of the creature's grip and reappeared directly between Blue Boy and the left Tau Ceti.

"Council members." Jimmy continued, "with all due respect, I cannot believe you would even consider the word of Tyranno-Ugly here against that of the leader of the peaceful Centaurians. As you can see, this complainant is totally biased against humans and therefore inherently untrustworthy."

The council members closed their eyes and conferred again. Jimmy smirked at the creature, who smirked right back at him.

The next thing Jimmy knew, the walls of the hall replayed the alleged event.

"Members of the council," Lizard Man began, pointing at the transformed blue wall behind the council members as he mentally projected the event. "I direct your attention to the Draconian reconnaissance ship in question, sitting peacefully above the Earth's satellite belt. It was observing the latest additions to one of the Terran tribes' nuclear weapons systems along its northwestern border."

The council closed their eyes and followed along in their own minds. Jimmy didn't tune in telepathically, his attention rivetted to the wall.

"This image was captured by a sister ship performing similar reconnaissance over another troublesome Terran tribe. As you are aware, these two tribes have been actively competing in their advancement of their respective space programs and their corresponding weaponry."

As Jimmy watched, a small tic-tac shaped drone appeared to rise from the brightness of the Earth's atmosphere and a moment later, fired some form of beam at the sedentary Draconian ship, destroying it in a fireball. The drone then rapidly disappeared back into the Earth's atmosphere.

"If the council recalls," the scaly creature continued, "the Centaurians had committed to this Intergalactic Federation that the Terrans would not develop a viable space program until they first demonstrated their ability to co-exist peacefully on their own planet."

"Members of the Council," Jimmy interjected. "Indeed, Gator-Face is correct, the Terrans are the responsibility of the Centaurians and the Centaurians alone."

"So, you concede my point?" Lizard Man demanded.

"Not a chance. What gave your people the right to be observing Earth in the first place?"

The creature hesitated.

Jimmy pressed. "Earth is a Centauri protectorate."

"Someone has to watch the flying monkeys," the creature finally hissed. "After all, the Centaurians have left them to their own devices for too long."

Jimmy turned and now addressed Petrichor. "Isn't it true that you just recently sent a full contingent of Centauri's best and brightest to resolve this latest aberration in Earth's peaceful transition to a potential future member of this illustrious federation?"

"Yes," Petrichor affirmed with conviction. "I am confident that we have complete control of the Terran situation and that there will be no further issues."

"Members of the Council," Jimmy concluded. "If the Terrans were behind the destruction of the Draconian ship, which we do not concede based on this one unauthenticated depiction, then the Draconians assumed that risk the moment they transgressed upon the exclusive right of the Centaurians to observe and control the future of the humans on that planet. The Draconians provoked the attack."

"Wait," the creature sputtered.

"You were not supposed to be there," the Plejaren agreed.

"Yes, but -" Lizard Man protested.

The council again telepathically conferred.

Blue Boy raised his hand from beneath his robe. It had five long digits and was as azure as his face. "The Council rules in favor of the Centauri."

Jimmy transported to his original spot and high-fived the anticipating Everett. Petrichor left Jimmy hanging on the rebound. Shrugging it off, Jimmy glanced back to the stands. That humanoid grey was back in his seat and staring at Jimmy.

"Wait for it," Petrichor whispered in his closest ear.

"But," Blue Boy continued, "the Council also warns Petrichor of the Centauris that should another similar transgression by the Terrans occur, the offended party will have unrestricted recourse to resolve that matter as it sees fit without further debate or council permission."

Jimmy glanced over at his adversary, who glared back at him, lips pulled back away from its pointed teeth. Jimmy felt like lunch.

He turned to Petrichor, who placed her hands on Everett and his shoulder.

"Time to go!" Jimmy said.

Petrichor nodded and, a moment later, they were again immersed in darkness. But the void wasn't enough to block the telepathic message that followed the trio back between the dimensions.

01010100 01101000 01101001 01110011 00100000
01101001 01110011 00100000 01101110 01101111
01110100 00100000 01101111 01110110 01100101
01110010 00100001 00100000

This is not over!

CHAPTER TWELVE
(A Wolf's Den)

"Love what you've done with the place." Whitey said, stepping slowly into the bright Halogen light of the garage. "Nice crotch rocket. Barely heard you ride up the driveway."

"Where the fuck have you been?" Lucian demanded as he crossed the garage in one stride and locked his friend and benefactor in a huge bear hug. "I thought you were all dead."

"I'll tell you all about it, kid," Whitey said with a faux hoarse whisper, "as long as you don't crack my ribs."

Lucian released his grip and Whitey grabbed him by his broad shoulders and literally lifted him to arms-length. "Jesus! What has Bobbi and Helen been feeding you? You're taller than me!"

Lucian wiped away a rogue tear. He felt like he was ten years old again.

With his pilot's eye for detail, Lucian quickly assessed the man standing before him, who had just lifted his 190-pound frame like it was a bag of feathers. Whitey hadn't aged a moment in twenty years. In fact, he now looked as young as Lucian. And his once wolf brown eyes were now Nordic blue. Lucian remembered those same eyes on the other family members.

He suddenly remembered how much he missed them all.

"Holy shit!" Lucian exclaimed as he put it all together. "You drank the Kool Aid?!"

Whitey laughed long and hard and Lucian could hear semblances of a guttural howl mixed in.

"What about the others?" Lucian asked, excitedly. "Are you all back?"

Whitey placed his arm around Lucian's shoulder and gently began to guide him towards the inner entrance of the house he once called home. "Let's go inside, son. We gotta lot of catching up to do."

CHAPTER THIRTEEN
(Wayward Sisters)

Scarlett McKenzie finished the article about the successful retrospective on 21st Century Celtic Art that just closed at the Jim Kelly Gallery in Atlanta, Georgia that Spring. She then rolled her latest copy of ARTnews and used it to perform an Avifors twirl and tap on the head of her sleeping sister, Savanna Joy.

"*Ádh mór.*"

"Leave me alone, Scary," mumbled the woman from beneath a blanket in the first-class seat beside her. "I'm exhausted."

"We'll be arriving soon," Scarlett said, patiently. "You may want to touch up that pretty face of yours before we land. Don't want to frighten the natives."

The younger McKenzie sister pulled herself up into full sitting position and then slowly opened her eyes. Scarlett handed Savanna a compact mirror retrieved from her sister's classic Bottega Veneta Baguette Bag, and the younger woman studied her features to assess the damage.

The truth was that Savanna did not need a lick of make-up to look beautiful. Even to Scarlett's discerning artist's eye she could see that her sister's alabaster face was practically flawless. Savanna was one of the lucky two percent whose features fell within Da Vinci's Golden Ratio of perfect symmetry. The pin straight, perfectly coiffed, brown hair, thick natural matching brows and eyelashes over steel-grey eyes, perky nose, and full pouty lips were the icing on the cake.

At five foot, ten inches, and an athletic one hundred fifteen pounds, Savanna could have stridden the catwalks of Paris. Instead, she spent her time accumulating financial degrees while increasing and shepherding the family money through financial markets all over the world. The girls had sold the family ranch for twenty million dollars to one of the web-tech billionaires in 2030 and Savanna had tripled it in a diversified portfolio over the past ten years. Her clothing preferences coasted between classic M.M. LaFleur and Tom Ford business suits and Tommy Bahama casual wear. Her dress footwear bordered on the decadent with Stuart Weitzman her designer of choice. Everything about Savanna screamed Master of the Universe.

Her living accommodations followed her high-end taste in clothes, as her two-bedroom flat in The Gessner in Tottenham Hale section of North London would attest.

Scarlett, on the other hand, was a true artist. A bohemian of the first order. She drew her entire wardrobe from thrift stores and her furnishings of her small garret in the 5th Arrondissement from provincial curiosity shops. Scarlett said she loved the "energy" that used items carried into her life. Savanna always said that Scary could make a burlap sack look chic.

Scarlett's beauty arose from her lack of symmetry. She was an inch taller than her sibling. Her full head of strawberry-blonde curls moved like sentient creatures when all else was still and hid a slightly broader forehead that reflected a broader genius. Her skin was fair and freckled, and her eyes were Kylie Minogue blue. But she had a perfect smile that would light up the room and an infectious laugh. Where Savanna was said to move with purpose, Scarlett moved with grace.

Scarlett made an early name for herself when one of her senior high school impressionist-styled watercolors was selected for a student exhibit at the Denver Art Museum. There it was spotted by Denver's notorious art bad boy, Dickie Smeedling. Within a year, every Art Gallery in the

Denver RiNo Art District had at least one "Scary McKenzie" work in its portfolio.

By the time Scarlett returned to Berthoud with her MFA from Rhode Island School of Design, she had works shown in galleries on both coasts. After a few years guiding the aspiring local artists to find their artistic milieu in the Boulder School of Fine Art, a sold-out exhibit in Karma in the East Village in Manhattan put Scarlett on the international map. By the time Scarlett turned thirty, she was an instructor at the École des Beaux-Arts in Paris.

Savanna carried her father's temper. Scarlett carried her mother's love.

Through the years both young women had a series of erratic monogamous relationships and some torrid affairs with men from many countries and all ends of the business, creative, and financial spectrum. None of the suitors could hold the sisters' hearts for any extended period. You see, despite their various accomplishments and CVs, all the men who passed through their lives were pedestrianly human.

The two things the sisters still shared from their childhood was the magic of being part of the Jimmy Moran crew and the Craft, carefully passed down to them both by their "Aunty Bobbi."

* * * * *

Eileen Cotto pulled her Ford 150 Lightning into Denver International's Western Terminal short term parking lot and raced inside to the main mezzanine where the underground train system dumps all arriving passengers en route to their various luggage carousels. She checked the arrival screen for the incoming connecting United flight 1406 from JFK in New York and confirmed that it had landed a few minutes earlier. She chose a spot on the bench on the kidney-shaped center islands with the clearest strategic view of the rising escalators and their disgorging masses. Given the girls' heights, Eileen knew they would be easy enough to spot in even the most tightly packed crowd, and if by chance she missed them, she could catch them at Carousel 12, where their baggage would be dispensed.

Her ass didn't even have time enough to go numb on the hard wooden slots before she saw the strawberry blonde cloud floating above all others, followed immediately by a similarly sized Amazon wearing Burberry sunglasses who looked like she just stepped off the cover of Vogue.

"Bubbles!" Scarlett called out as soon as she saw Eileen.

No one but the two girls ever got to call Eileen by her high school nickname.

* * * * *

Eileen pulled into Casa Claire and gently woke the two young women who were both asleep before Eileen had exited the airport. The house was quiet. Not even the Ericksons' car was in the driveway.

Eileen hopped out of the cab and began removing the two sets of luggage from the truck bed. She knew the matching Gucci ensemble belonged to Savanna while the Salvation Army collection belonged to Scarlett and sorted them accordingly. She watched as the two young women walked over to the Henri the Lion statue to the right of the garage entrance and retrieved the house key. Then she watched and waited while they carefully unlocked the door and slid through its entrance.

A moment later, she heard a raucous, collective shout flying through that same entranceway. "Welcome home!"

CHAPTER FOURTEEN
(Can't Bullshit A Bullshitter)

"I may not be able to solve quadratic equations," Buck said, "but I know how to do simple math. And this doesn't add up."

Mac Corry and Renee Clarke sat across the large desk from their very animated boss. Mac looked anxious. Renee disguised whatever feelings she had behind a poker face which was focused on her iPad's brightly lit screen that her fingers were now tap-dancing across.

"I've just spent this past week going through the last fiscal year's budget, and there is 5 billion dollars unaccounted for. Vanished into thin air," Buck continued. "And what are these allocations to 'Dreamland,' 'Maji,' 'Groundstar,' and a whole lot of names that sound like they come from a Las Vegas Casino?"

"I'll look into that, sir." Mac volunteered.

"Well, good luck with that, Mac," Buck responded. "I have Top Secret security clearance and I have been unable to access those files."

"I may be able to help with that." Renee said, tapping a few more times on her iPad. "I have TS/SCI clearance, which should get me around a few more security firewalls."

Buck studied his Science Officer and wondered why this Lieutenant Colonel's resume warranted Sensitive Compartmental Information clearance by the Director of National Intelligence.

"Strange," Renee said, finally looking up and locking eyes with Buck. "I can't access those files either."

Buck was having a tough time reading those eyes. They were a bit distracting.

Buck had been around the Department of Defense long enough to know that a lot of the tax payers' money falls off the back of Congress' budget omnibus allocation truck in any given year. He had heard rumors around DC card tables and cocktail parties that almost ten trillion dollars from the DOD's budget went to fund unacknowledged "Black Ops" programs. Many of these programs were run by private contractors, which gave the government plausible deniability if the shit ever hit the fan. This smelled like the same shit.

In the past, Buck never really gave a damn about budgets, as long as the soldiers who served under his command were provided for and he had the resources to carry out his missions and objectives. But now Buck was sitting in the top chair and felt his nuts resting on the seat. He was fond of those nuts and didn't want to lose them because someone else had been dipping into his government till.

"This doesn't leave this room," Buck instructed, more for the benefit of his Science Officer than his adjutant, Mac. "But I promise you this. I swear on my grandmother's grave, I'm going to find every fucking penny."

CHAPTER FIFTEEN
(Debussy's Suite Bergamasque)

By the time Eileen followed the McKenzie sisters through the doorway, they had completed multiple rotations through the warm embraces of everyone in the room. Savanna stood off in one corner whispering conspiratorially with a very interested Lucian, while Scarlett was graciously engaging in Bobbi's proud introduction of her oldest protégé to the Ericksons, who, in turn, looked like they had overcome their initial shock, and were beginning to settle into the spontaneous insanity that regularly occurred where the ley lines meet. Eileen was certain that the case of poteen she had left for the party had helped grease the wheels for that transition.

"They really are quite special," came a deep but lyrical voice directly behind her. "For Terrans."

Eileen spun as quickly as her older bones would allow and found Apollo still gazing intently over her shoulder directly at Scarlett, who had just said something enchanting enough to cause Brian Erickson to smile in a way that seemed foreign to him. Eileen had seen that look many times before, when Apollo's father, Jimmy Moran, would stand on the edge of the Beverly Drive crowd and watch this young man's mother, Gina, beguile men, women, and everything in between at one of the misfit gatherings. She missed her mystical patrons and wondered if she would ever see them again, in this life.

Apollo was the taller, younger, perfect mix of the best of his parents' features. His thick burgundy locks were the cherry on his aesthetic sundae. He indeed gave his Olympus namesake a run for his money in beauty and power. He suddenly smiled and when Eileen turned to see its trigger, she saw Scarlett flash him a playful wink before directing her attention to Stella, who had just crossed the room to speak with her. Despite their slight age difference, Stella and Apollo appeared as similar as the closest fraternal twins in size and features. The yin and the yang, Eileen thought to herself.

Eileen could sense the instant connection between the two young women, especially when Scarlett slid past Stella's extended hand and wrapped her guest in a warm, very human embrace. It took just a moment before Stella reciprocated the authenticity of that hug. Love is the ultimate common denominator that connects every creature.

A moment later, Helen and Janice appeared from the kitchen. Helen was carrying a tray of shot glasses containing clear liquid. Eileen's poteen. Janice helped distribute the shots among the guests. Lenny grabbed two of the tiny glasses off Helen's tray.

"Ladies and gentlemen!" Lenny bellowed, to ensure he had the room's attention. "A toast!" He extended both glasses in the air above his head. The rest of the room followed suit.

"To Scarlett and Savanna, the paradigm of the best of humanity in its purest form."

"May I counter that gracious toast with one of my own?" Scarlett responded, raising her glass a little higher.

"Here, here." Eddie waved chivalrously. "The lady has the floor!"

"Get on with it, sis." Savanna called across the room. "Tick-tock. Time is money!"

"And my arm is getting tired and my throat dry." Whitey added.

Scarlett nodded deferentially and gazed at each guest as she did. "Thank you Aunties Bobbi, Helen, and Eileen, for welcoming us back home – for this house will always represent that for Savanna and me.

Welcome, Janice and Brian to the inner sanctum. May you find it as magical as it has proven for us, time and again. Dear Lucian, when did you grow into such a handsome man?" This time Scarlett winked at her sister, whose alabaster skin crimsoned just a tint.

"And finally, welcome back Eddie, Lenny, Whitey, Stella and, last but not least, Apollo. You cannot begin to fathom how much I missed you all." Scarlett met and held Apollo's gaze as she closed.

"To my parents," Stella added. "All three of them."

"And to Claire!" Savanna shouted to make sure her petition made it into the litany before the alcohol was consumed.

Before the crowd could raise their glasses to their lips, a blinding glow appeared at the center of the living room, causing everyone to take a collective step back towards the room's perimeter.

"What the fawk?!" Brian exclaimed as a huge silhouette appearing in its midst continued its evolution to its full holographic form.

"Now *that*, ladies, and gentlemen," came the husky, Lauren Bacall like voice from the arriving creature as the light dissipated and all eyes adjusted, "is how you make an entrance to a party."

CHAPTER SIXTEEN
(Unexpected Ally)

01000001 01110011 00100000 01101101 01110101
01100011 01101000 00100000 01100001 01110011
00100000 01101001 01110100 00100000 01110000
01100001 01101001 01101110 01110011 00100000
01101101 01100101 00100000 01110100 01101111
00100000 01100001 01100111 01110010 01100101
01100101 00101100 00100000 01001010 01101001
01101101 01101101 01111001 00100000 01001101
01101111 01110010 01100001 01101110 00100000
01101001 01110011 00100000 01110010 01101001
01100111 01101000 01110100 00100001

As much as it pains me to agree, Jimmy Moran is right!

"What?!" Jimmy shouted.

Please. Aldor. Petrichor cajoled. *You know Jimmy likes to converse in English.*

"He can continue in Swahili if he likes," Jimmy said excitedly. "I just can't believe he's agreeing with me."

The androgenous Centauri counselor studied his hybrid nemesis sitting across the holographic round table Jimmy had Jayney generate for this meeting. He looked like he was sucking on lemons.

"Petrichor," Aldor continued, "why were you so willing to attack the Earthling military the night we retrieved the hybrids?"

"They were threatening Stella!"

"What am I, chopped liver?" Jimmy countered.

Ignoring Jimmy, Aldor continued. "That's true but, Petrichor, you could have just snatched Stella in a nano-second without anyone knowing you were there and left the rest to sort themselves out."

"Well, they were also threatening our citizens, Everett and Michelle." Petrichor added, gesturing to those now smiling Centaurians also at the table.

"No offense," Everett said, winking at Jimmy, "but rank has its privileges."

We would never have left without you. Michelle shared telepathically with Jimmy.

"Say what you want," Gina interjected. "But you saved us all because you realized that we were Stella's family."

Petrichor thought that over in silence.

"Once you poached Jimmy's tadpoles," Gina continued, with a wink at Dr. Nim, "you lost that scientific objectivity and distance. The Terrans were no longer a grand Centauri experiment. You knew every one of us who was on Earth that night was there to save Stella, because she is our family. So, you cared, like the mother you had become, for her family."

"I was going to say, you gave the livestock names," Aldor addressed Gina directly, "which made them family pets. But that works."

"You really don't like your nose," Gina responded.

"But the Terrans, by their aggressive conduct, have now exposed the Centaurians to criticism and potential liability before the Galactic Federation." Petrichor continued, ignoring the side exchange. "That was the first time in our recorded history where the leader of the Centaurians was summoned before the High Council. It was humiliating. We could have been ostracized, or worse."

"Family is family," Jimmy said, wondering if anyone on Centauri ever saw a real ostrich. "No matter how fucked up they are, no one gets to sort them out but family."

"Which is what you have done by sending Stella and her contingent back to Earth," Everett said.

"And what if the Draconians won't wait for us to 'sort them out'?" Petrichor asked.

"Then we sort out the Draconians." Michelle responded, a hint of bloodlust in her voice.

"Do not underestimate the Draconians," Dr. Nim, who had been sitting silently throughout this meeting, now counseled. "They are a mercenary race and consider all others an existential threat to their survival. Give them a reason to fight and they'll take it."

"The Lizards better not underestimate the Terrans," Everett said. They may once have been monkeys, but I've seen Jimmy and the others in action against their own. They play for keeps."

"Reptiles or not, even Godzilla knows not to fuck with King Kong." Gina added.

"But the Terrans don't have the technology to compete with the Draconians." Aldor said.

"Someone on Earth blew up their spaceship." Everett countered. "We're not talking stones and slingshots."

"So, Jimmy?" Petrichor asked. "What do you suggest?"

"We do what we told the High Council. We let Stella and Apollo straighten things out. And we keep an eye on things. If the Draconians start any mass mobilization -"

"-What mass mobilization?" Aldor cut Jimmy off. "Draconians wouldn't need to send a fleet of their ships. With their weaponry and skills, a small cadre of their warriors, maybe a dozen small ships, is all they would need to evaporate Earth. Anything more would bring great dishonor to them."

"Is that true?" Jimmy asked.

"They have raised your concept of machismo to a whole new level." Dr. Nim said. "They would rather all die in battle than admit they couldn't take a lesser race."

"And we all are considered a lesser race," Everett added.

"What's kept them in check until now?" Gina asked.

"There are over fifty thousand members of the Galactic Federation," Aldor responded. "No one member–no matter how powerful-could withstand the might of the collective whole."

"So, we have enough firepower if they force our hand?" Jimmy asked.

Michelle nodded. "You saw what Petrichor's ship did to the government troops."

"And all of our ships have basic weaponry." Everett added. "Enough to counter minor confrontations in space and any human encounter."

Jimmy remembered the battle at the Beauseigneur Twins' Oregon compound. He recollected how Petrichor effortlessly devastated the powerful United States military air and land weaponry that came for the crew on the tarmac. He envisioned unleashing the "lightning" on the underground bunker to destroy the malevolent AI serving the techno-twins just before they all left Earth twenty years ago.

"How many of those kinds of ships do you keep here on Centauri?" Jimmy asked.

"Thirty exactly," Aldor responded, "for defensive purposes. You saw them encircle Everett's ship the first time you arrived here."

Jimmy thought back to seeing that circle of ships that first time he traveled to Proxima b to defend Everett for reanimating Jimmy after the standoff with the mafia at Casa Claire. He hadn't fully transitioned to the hybrid he now was, so his human body spent a lot of time unconscious every time they moved him from one place to another. It was the only way it survived the stress of dematerializing. Fun times.

"Can you teach us, the hybrids, to handle those weapons?" Jimmy asked.

"Everything works through AI, like the flight controls." Dr. Nim said. "Jayney will do what you ask her to do. Mentally engage, point, click, poof."

"And we can match you with our combat pilots. They've never been in battle, but they have trained for it. Extensive AI simulation," Aldor said. "I completed the program."

"That's nine ships." Gina said. "Counting Stella and Apollo."

"Ten," said Aldor. "I'm not sitting this one out."

"Eleven," Petrichor added. "Someone has to keep an eye on the rest of you. The rest of the ships will remain here. Nim, you'll act as Regent in my absence."

"That's still not enough to beat the Draconians," Everett said.

"We won't have to beat them." Jimmy responded. "We just need to stop them in the first instance."

"Then the Galactic Federation will be forced to step in," Aldor confirmed.

"I'll get Jayney started with the preparations." Dr. Nim said.

"Already on it!" came Jayney's faux-Petrichor imitation.

"We really need to change that voice," Petrichor declared.

Is this going to work? Gina telepathically asked as she glanced at her husband.

Jimmy shook his head left to right almost imperceptibly.

But we are lost without hope. Pray Stella and Apollo keep the humans from doing anything stupid.

CHAPTER SEVENTEEN
(Divine Intervention)

Buck finished reading the headline article in The Catholic News Service on-line edition and picked up his cell phone. The line on the other side rang three times before an out of breath male answered.

"Father Lawlor," the male voice panted.

"Jesus!" Buck barked. "I hope I didn't interrupt your daily devotion to self-flagellation. Whips this time, or is that reserved only for Mother-May-I in the Dominatrix Dungeon?"

"Fuck you, Buck, and don't call me Jesus!" Father Jack snapped back. "Why are you interrupting my morning run? Please tell me you've given us Papists a break and joined the Zoroastrians."

"That will be ten Hail Marys for cursing, with an extra ten for doing so in the same sentence where you used the Lord's name," Buck responded. "And why did I have to read about your appointment to the Curia on CNS?"

"Sorry, didn't Adrienne Stucki call you?" Jack teased, his breath slowing to just slightly labored. "I guess she's been too busy packing for Rome."

"I thought I sensed an air of intimacy with the widow Stucki that went beyond her delicious cake," Buck retorted. "I don't blame you, Jack, she's a fine woman. Just don't be getting any crumbs in the sheets now."

"You've got a very twisted mind, Buck Sheridan!" Jack said. "Mrs. Stucki is coming to Rome for a month just to help get me set up in the new digs. I just cannot do it on my own. I promised I would get her an audience with the Pope."

"You priests got it made. I've never met one that doesn't have three parish women doting over them. You get all the benefits of marriage, including a sexless existence."

"Just say the word, Buck. Once I'm in Rome, I can try to pull some strings and get you into St. Joe's Seminary in Yonkers. You'd like it. It's right next to the Dunwoodie golf course. Help keep your mind off women."

"I'd have to buy my soul back first." Buck said. "And it's never been my mind-on-women that got me into trouble. My issues arise when my thoughts become corporeal. "

"Speaking of weak flesh," Jack said, "any new prospects you need to confess about?"

"You voyeur you!" Buck shouted into his phone. Strange that his thoughts drifted past Dr. Clarke. "Enough about me, go find an internet porn site for your pleasures. I was just calling to congratulate you. Well done on getting one foot in the Holy See. Hope the consecrated water is warm."

"Thanks."

"When are you leaving?"

"Wrapping things up here over the summer, then gone by Labor Day. Will I see you before I go?"

"I have a meeting with some top brass in DC in July. I'll give you a shout as it gets closer. Maybe we can grab dinner."

"Bring Fergus. I know a place that still serves real steak to the clergy, not the Frankenstein lab meat that remains all the rage among the beltway darlings. At least then I'm guaranteed some interesting conversation... from Fergus."

"Fuck you, Father."

"Go with God, my son." The line went dead.

Buck tossed the cell phone on the desk. An annoying tone heralded the screen calendar reminder of his meeting later that morning with Mac and Dr. Clarke to go over his schedule for a tour of the West coast Space Force installations. Buck missed the flip phone he had when he was a teen. Simple, hardy, practically indestructible. And you never had to look at another ugly mug on a zoom call. Basically, an orange juice can with a string out its ass. Now the model he used had more computing power than Skylab 1. But other than that, it really hadn't changed much from the hand sized, thin rectangle he had been using for the past two decades, although the model number had now reached the Roman symbol L.

Buck wasn't a luddite. He actually enjoyed advancements in technology, especially weaponry. But mastering those advancements didn't come naturally to him. He was a slow learner, but once he got it, it was his forever.

Truth be told, Buck was a little disappointed in the relatively small gains being made on the technology front. He really hoped that by 2045, everybody would be traveling in flying cars, like the Jetsons, and communicating telepathically using implanted chips. Sure, there were far more electric vehicles on the road. Buck's gas-powered car was one of the ten percent of combustion engines still in operation on America's roadways. The others had all been forced into the junkyards by high fuel prices and oppressive government restrictions. But the military's weapons still primarily relied on petroleum-based fuel, which Buck had easy access to, so he intended to drive his grandfather's Camaro until they pried those keys out of his cold dead hands.

Buck didn't feel any guilt over his intransigence. Despite massive government support, spending its citizens money, none of the solar, wind or electric energy alternatives had successfully proved viable to consistently supply the needs of the nation's energy grid. Mother nature almost made a game out of regularly destroying wind farms with lightning strikes and solar farms with hail storms having the tenacity of tornados nailing trailer parks. And given the ecological impact that the off shore wind farms had on the birds and sea creatures who found them in their paths, the blind persistence in imposing them along the country's coast lines proved cruel and callous. In the end, none of the green movements of the 2020s had made a substantial difference in the climate or anything else. Many of the other countries with less transparent governments continued to circumvent climate restrictions while steadily increasing their respective gross domestic share of world manufacturing. The air didn't seem any cleaner or warmer.

Still, if scientists ever did build a better energy mousetrap, Buck would be the first to sample the cheese. Until then, he was driving the red monster and he didn't give a rat's ass about the sanctimonious looks he got at stop lights or when he pulled into parking lots. He regularly left the image of the greens clutching their pearls in his rearview mirror. He had more pressing things to worry about. Like where did those billions of dollars of Space Force money disappear to?

But first he had to complete the coordination of his upcoming three-week tour of the western bases with Mac and Clarke. He planned to visit Peterson and Schriever in Colorado during the first week, then a week each at the Los Angeles and Vandenberg bases. There was one other western base Buck wanted to inspect if he could arrange it. It was time for Buck to roll up his sleeves and dig into his new role.

CHAPTER EIGHTEEN
(Collect Call For ET)

Brian Erickson went to step protectively in front of his wife when this large glowing version of a horse-like creature appeared. However, Janice side-stepped him and, like the rest of the guests, converged en mass on the room's center occupant. Thank God, she couldn't slide past these large alien creatures who all had crowded around the animal. The aliens all kept appearing, disappearing, and reappearing in different points on the periphery. Brian couldn't get a fix on any one of them, so he gave up trying.

"Oh my God, Claire, you're back!" cried Scarlett, who threw her arms around the large beast's neck and was kissing her repeatedly on the muzzle.

Savanna grabbed the back end of the creature's flowing mane and with the assistance of Lucian, leapt up upon her back. The young woman leaned forward, hugged Claire's neck, and rested her cheek upon the back of the mule's head, her own tears flowing freely. The other members of the group all reached in as the opportunity arose and patted, stroked, and hugged the creature affectionately, while offering welcoming comments.

Janice stepped back to where her husband had remained rooted by the dining room table.

"Can you believe it?" she whispered without taking her eyes off the spectacle.

"What?!" he whispered back, with his best Southie sarcasm. "That we are looking at a talking horse, surrounded by a crowd of witches and aliens in the center of the living room?!"

"Not a horse, a mule," Janice responded, eyes still glued to the crowd. "No, I can't believe that she's a hologram in solid form." She smiled and shook her head in disbelief, suppressed a giddy shriek, then turned to her husband, grabbed his face with both hands and kissed him hard on the lips.

"This is fucking awesome!" she said as she released him. "I reached in and touched her." She said to no one in particular, and then went back to staring at the spectacle like a child watching a firework display. "Wasn't like anything I ever felt before . . . but the energy she gave off."

Brian stared at his wife, then turned back to the crowd and tried to get a better look at the creature, who had curled her neck around Scarlett's head. That's when Brian realized that the slight luminescence to the animal's form had obscured the fact that there was transparency as well. As he continued to focus, he could see Scarlett's face on the far side of the creature's neck.

Suddenly a shrill whistle came from within the scrum and everyone, including the creature, stopped what they were doing.

"Am I the only one getting this message from Petrichor?" Bobbi shouted. "It's in binary, so it's going to take me a bit to translate it."

Brian thought that Helen, Eileen, and the young people all looked confused, like they weren't in on the joke. The aliens all looked like pagers were simultaneously going off in their heads.

The wonder twins with burgundy hair transported away from the others. Their look of concern needed no translation. Something was wrong. And if they were worried, Brian knew he should be worried as well.

"The shit has hit the intergalactic fan!" Claire declared as she decoded her telepathic transmission. "And what the fuck are Reptilians?"

* * * * *

"Speak English in front of the telepathically challenged," Helen chastised the others, who all had gone silent but, through their physical gestures, were obviously communicating excitedly with one another.

"It's tough enough that our biological clocks keep ticking at a much faster rate than yours obviously does," Eileen added adamantly. "Now you're pulling parlor tricks?! It's not polite to whisper, even telepathically."

The two young women freed themselves from Claire, closed their eyes, cocked their ears, and tilted their faces upwards like they were TV antennas trying to pick up a UHF or VHF analog signal.

"You haven't mastered those tricks just yet, girls," Bobbi consoled them. She placed the palms of her hands on their foreheads and, a moment later, both sets of eyes popped open in shock.

Apollo materialized beside the older sister and took her elbow to support her suddenly shaky legs.

Savanna opened her cell phone and began typing furiously.

"What are you doing, Savanna?" Scarlett demanded.

"Shifting all of our accounts into precious metals!" Savanna replied coolly without looking up from the task at hand. "Nothing else will be worth shit if this goes down."

"You getting any of this?" Helen asked Eileen and Lucian.

"Not a word." Eileen responded.

The young man shook his head then turned to his mentor. "Whitey, what's happening here?"

Before Whitey could respond, Stella stepped up.

"Sorry," Stella said, turning to Lucian, Eileen, and Helen as she gathered her thoughts.

"As I began to explain over dinner, Petrichor sent us back here to convince the powers that control this planet, that they are standing at an existential precipice in their collective future and that they need to dramatically change course. The planet cannot sustain life much longer on its present path."

"Speaking as an average Earthling," Brian interrupted, surprised at his own bravado, "this isn't exactly news to us."

Brian was startled to feel a powerful arm reach across his back and the hand at its end clasp his shoulder tightly. Brian turned in the opposite direction to see Apollo, who a moment before was standing beside Stella across the room, now staring down at him. Apollo held his index finger to his lips, then pointed at his sister, and whispered, "let her finish." Brian nodded. Apollo disappeared and instantly reappeared beside his sibling.

A moment later, Brian felt a sharp pain in his now free shoulder, this time from a hard right fist delivered by Janice. She stared daggers at him and then drew her fingers in a zipping motion across her lips. Brian quickly turned back towards the far less frightening aliens and listened intently.

"As Mr. Erickson correctly pointed out," Stella continued, "most humans understand this. They see everything that is happening around them. But most humans don't get a say in the way this world operates."

"And the rest of us creatures, even less," Claire chimed in.

"The governments don't even have a real say in how this world operates." Apollo added.

"But we have let you all continue along under your own authority hoping that you would finally figure it out," Stella continued.

"Wait a sec -" Brian couldn't stop himself. "Who the fawk are you to 'let us' do anything? We're the United States of America!"

He turned to Janice, expecting another shot to his arm. Instead, she looked on approvingly, and nodded in support.

"We, the people, decide who runs our show," Brian continued. "And fawk anyone who says different."

Now it was Lenny's turn to speak up. "I used to think the very same thing, Brian."

He preened and displayed his new and improved version of his once human self in a way that a young boy would display the new bike he got at Christmas before his friends in the neighborhood.

"Before I was the intergalactic, hybrid stud you see before you, I was an honest, hardworking human citizen who had an insider view of the corridors of power in Washington. I can tell you that from what I saw on a daily basis for over two decades, it wasn't the bureaucrats or even the elected politicians that controlled what happened. It was the people with the money who put those people in place. Their fools, their rules."

He thought about his next words carefully. "Once I realized this, I decided to put a stop to it. At least, in my little part of that world. So rather than allow one more of their protected members to escape justice yet again, who was about to cash in on his get-out-of-jail card, I served it myself one particular night on an infamous pedophile, through the twentieth-floor window of a DC hotel. Whoops!"

"Is Lenny serious?" Lucian whispered to Whitey.

"As cancer." Whitey nodded. The mentor hybrid scanned Lucian's thoughts as he digested what he was listening to. He could sense the conflicting loyalties his protégé was experiencing between the country he had recently served so honorably in its military and the family of misfits who raised him into the man that served that country. Whitey could feel the strength of the love Lucian felt for everyone in the room, especially for the younger McKenzie sister, and knew which group came out on top.

"So, this morning Petrichor informed us that we were out of time." Stella said, stoically. "If the Terrans don't immediately cease all aggressive behavior towards those other races that share the universe right outside the beautiful air of this world's lovely atmosphere, the collective ruling body of the galaxy that this blue marble spins through will allow one of its members to turn off the lights."

"Well, we won't go down without a fight!" Brian declared, honorably but defensively.

"With all due respect, Mr. Erickson," Apollo pointed his finger at the man, and slowly raised him into the air to prove his point while his wife watched in horror.

"Apollo," Claire softly warned him. "Jimmy and Gina would be appalled at your gross display of power."

Apollo met Claire's gaze, then turned to his sister, who nodded. Apollo tightly circled his finger, "Take a good look around you Mr. Erickson."

Apollo slowly spun Brian one clockwise circuit, so he could get a good look around him from his new vantage point before being gently lowered back to his spot where Janice began to fuss over him.

"You won't even see it coming."

CHAPTER NINETEEN
(*Horror vacui*)

```
01000100  01100101  01101100  01110100  01100001
00100000  01110111  01101001  01101100  01101100
00100000  01100001  01100011  01100011  01101111
01101101  01110000  01100001  01101110  01111001
00100000  01101101  01100101  00100000  01110100
01101111  00100000  01010100  01100101  01110010
01110010  01100001  01101110  00100111  01110011
00100000  01101101  01101111  01101111  01101110
00101110  00100000  00100000  01010100  01101000
01100101  00100000  01110010  01100101  01110011
01110100  00100000  01101111  01100110  00100000
01110100  01101000  01100101  00100000  01100011
01101111  01101101  01110000  01100001  01101110
01111001  00100000  01110111  01101001  01101100
01101100  00100000  01110010  01100101  01101101
01100001  01101001  01101110  00100000  01101001
01101110  00100000  01101111  01110010  01100010
01101001  01110100  00100000  01101000  01101001
01100100  01100100  01100101  01101110  00100000
01101000  01100101  01110010  01100101  00100000
```

01100001 01101101 01101111 01101110 01100111
00100000 01110100 01101000 01100101 00100000
01100001 01110011 01110100 01100101 01110010
01101111 01101001 01100100 00100000 01100010
01100101 01101100 01110100 00100000 01100010
01100101 01110100 01110111 01100101 01100101
01101110 00100000 01110100 01101000 01100101
00100000 01110100 01101000 01101001 01110010
01100100 00100000 01100001 01101110 01100100
00100000 01100110 01101111 01110101 01110010
01110100 01101000 00100000 01110000 01101100
01100001 01101110 01100101 01110100 01110011
00101110 00001010

Delta will accompany me to Terran's moon. The rest of the company will remain in orbit hidden here among the asteroid belt between the third and fourth planets.

01001001 00100000 01100001 01101101 00100000
01111001 01101111 01110101 01110010 00100000
01110011 01100101 01100011 01101111 01101110
01100100 00100000 01101001 01101110 00100000
01100011 01101111 01101101 01101101 01100001
01101110 01100100 00101100 00100000 01110011
01101001 01110010 01100101 00101110 00100000
00100000 01001001 00100000 01110011 01101000
01101111 01110101 01101100 01100100 00100000
01100001 01100011 01100011 01101111 01101101
01110000 01100001 01101110 01111001 00100000
01111001 01101111 01110101 00101110 00100000

I am your second in command, sire. I should accompany you.

Alpha waved away the holographic screen displaying the solar system at issue and stared coldly at the nine mirror images of himself staring back with the same cold, black eyes. They were distinguishable only by their long respective histories, across the galaxies, of demonstrated aggressiveness and violence both in battle and in conquest. Alpha had selected these creatures from among the most powerful of his armies for his personal elite cadre of warriors.

Beta was right, he should be the one to accompany Alpha. Beta had proven the utmost loyalty for over a millennium. They had served together during the Draconians' brief reign as the Anunnaki on Earth before the Intergalactic Federation had ordered them off the resource rich planet in favor of the Centaurians, who had a spurious claim to that planet. Beta would protect Alpha with his life. Beta was satisfied in his position as number two.

Delta was far newer in Draconian time than Beta. He had recently ascended from his position as Epsilon, when he vanquished the last Delta in the Coliseums in their Cat's Eye Nebula. Alpha enjoyed the blood lust from competing in warrior games, including slaying all opposition that dare enter the pits against him, but he realized that it was a waste of his best warriors, who should be out conquering other star systems. He hated the Intergalactic Federation for their imposition of restrictions on the Draconian citizens. Any one of its member races were no match for the Draconians, but their collective numbers and technology forced Alpha's warrior race into peaceful subjugation. When the time was right, he would lead the Draconians out from under the Intergalactic Federation's yoke.

But first he needed to conquer Earth. He remembered its vast natural resources from his time as an Anunnaki. If he had had his way, he would have eradicated the Terrans back then and established a permanent base. However, he was not one of the original seven who collectively ruled Draco at the time. Alpha didn't have the power or the following he had now amassed since An, Enlil, Enki, Ninhursag, Nanna, Utu, and Inanna were exposed as the weak leaders who capitulated to the Intergalactic Federation. Ultimately, they were deposed and executed during the Draconian Civil War. Through his innate brutal ruthlessness and natural cunning, Alpha, as he was now known since the Draconian realignment, stepped into that power vacuum, and seized control. He knew there could only be one leader, one Alpha. He had ruled the Draconian people without challenge for the past thousand Draconian anniversaries.

The large reptilian gazed at the nine of his most powerful warlords. He could see that the relatively newer Delta was now flexing his facial musculature subtly. This caused his scales to ripple concentrically down from the top of his skull to his neck in a display of dominance among the others. The extremely competent but less ambitious Gamma, who stood beside Delta, should indeed be worried about his position and his existence. Delta reminded Alpha of itself. But there could only be one Alpha on Draco.

Alpha thought back to his most recent humiliation before the Intergalactic Federation. He should have snapped the neck of that weak Terran-Centauri hybrid whose tongue carved wounds in his psyche in ways none of the nine brutes now standing before Alpha could ever accomplish. Alpha savored his responsive anger. Once his latest plan went into operation, Alpha would make sure that it was his hand that ended the existence of his latest nemesis. And then he would destroy every Terran and Centauri. But first, he needed to make the best use of Delta.

01001101 01100001 01110010 01110100 01111001
01110010 01100100 01101111 01101101 00001010
00001010

Martyrdom.

CHAPTER TWENTY
(Heaven and Earth, Horatio)

Thirty years before, Dr. John Bricker had a promising career ahead of him as the youngest tenured professor in Cal Tech's Physics Department. He could have happily served out his time coddling the feelings and molding the minds of the country's brightest at one of its premier universities, writing research papers, books, and attending cocktail parties with his beautiful wife, Christina. The only promise his future wife extracted from him when she agreed to leave behind her dreams of the pursuit of a principal role with a professional Ballet Company to marry him, was that they enjoy a quiet family life, with a modest home in Pasadena, two kids and a dog. The road to hell is paved with good intentions.

Landing Tina was the luckiest break in John's life. He had come from lower middle-class roots. His father drove buses for LA Metro and his mother was a Librarian with the LA Public Library system. She fell in love with his dad during brief exchanges over the year it took him to consume every copy of the LAPL's Louis L'Amour collection. John's dad, Big Bill Bricker, had grown up wanting to be a cowboy. The closest he ever got to that dream was in the pages of a book.

Young John was also a reader. He spent hours each day as a child, and later, after school, at his mother's library devouring every book he could get his hands on. He tended to follow a series of favored genres until he tired of them but loved fantasy fiction, including everything by Anne McCaffrey. One day during freshman year in high school, John stumbled across an old copy of Michio Kaku's book, *Hyperspace: A Scientific Odyssey Through Parallel Universes, Time Warps, and the 10th Dimension*. It flipped a switch, and he went through everything by Kaku he could find, with the same passion his father showed for Louis L'Amour. But unlike Bill Bricker, John was destined to fulfill his dreams.

Turned out, John had an inquiring mind and an IQ just shy of 200. He blew though AP Physics in his sophomore year and took on-line college level physics in both junior and senior years. He received early admission to Princeton where he was introduced to and mastered Quantum and Particle Physics. To John, quantum physics was as close to real magic as mankind could get. But on a more practical level, he learned that if you worked hard and applied yourself, you could succeed at anything.

By the time John graduated from Princeton, he had already made a name for himself with a paper he published with his mentor and advisor, the renowned Princeton physicist, Michael Abramson, entitled Breakthroughs In the Study of Isotopic Signatures of Celestial Objects. Graduate schools throughout the country were clamoring to admit him into their Ph.D. programs.

During his weekend interview with Cal Tech, the young recruiting professor took John to dinner and an LABC performance of Chopin and Bournenonville's *La Sylphide*. Christina was one of the supporting Sylphs whose performance kept rotating her to the area closest to John's orchestra seat. John was thunderstruck. He told the young professor that if he could get John that dancer's number, Cal Tech could have him. The recruiter had gotten his tickets from his lover, a male ballerino with the company, so one phone call during intermission was all it took.

John's and Tina's lives for the next three years were as magical as the ballet that introduced them. She continued to perform at LABC while he pursued his studies. They shared what little free time they could salvage in each other's company. During John's final year in the Ph.D. program, Tina, who was steadily advancing to stronger roles with LABC, was offered a first soloist dancer's position with the London Ballet. The tearful night after Tina broke the news of the job offer, John countered with his own. He had been offered an adjunct professor position in Cal Tech's Applied Physics Department. He asked Tina to marry him.

John's professional trajectory remained pointed at the stratosphere, literally. After his first term teaching he was approached by an innocuous government wonk at NASA to come work at its Jet Propulsion Laboratory, under the management of Cal Tech. All men love their toys, and the idea of putting his skill and knowledge into the development of spacecraft, rovers, copters, and other extraplanetary exploration vehicles was too attractive to turn down. It meant more prestige and more money, which immediately put John and Tina in a beautiful home in the pricier zip code of San Marino. But it also meant more travel and extended daily hours away from home. After years of unsuccessful attempts to have children, the couple learned that Tina's past sacrifices of a dancer's dietary restrictions, and recurring issues with fibroids, had rendered her unable to conceive. John got her a cat. Tina never complained.

To keep busy during John's recurring extended work-related absences, Tina decided to give back to the greater community. She opened a store front dance studio in the poorer L.A. suburb of Maywood, where she shared her professional knowledge and training with underprivileged youth. Over time, she helped some of her more committed and talented students gain access to some of the local pilot high schools dedicated to the performing arts, like L.A. County High School for the Arts and the Ramón C. Cortines School of Visual and Performing Arts. She shared the unfulfilled maternal love she carried with every child that walked through the dance studio's doorway. And that, for Tina, was enough.

John's star continued to rise, and after five years with the JPL, John was spirited away by the private billionaire Bertram Nicolo, to work with private subcontractors on Special Access Programs. Soon John was working with a company known only as the Advanced Theoretical Physics Group. He split his work weeks shuttling between government sanctioned privately owned laboratories attached to Wright-Patterson Air Force Base and the Air Force Flight Test Center, Detachment 3, at Groom Lake in

Nevada. Along with the prestige and pay came rapid increases in John's national security clearances, and, after a few years, he was finally provided Top Secret clearance by the Defense Intelligence Agency.

By then, John was leading a team working with metallic glass and transparent aluminum. Indeed, it was his team that successfully deconstructed the exotic atoms found in the limited testing materials. This enabled them to reconstruct a slightly modified recombination of the essential molecules to create a simpler working version of those testing materials.

John made it back home to Tina every weekend and tried to make up for his absences with expensive gifts and romantic weekend get aways. Tina was always appreciative of his attentiveness during their limited time together, and never expressed her resentment even when John began catching Sunday night red-eye flights back to Nevada and Ohio in one of Mr. Nicolo's private Citation CJ4s. Tina understood.

Tina kept any misgivings she had over the direction their respective lifestyles had taken, to herself. One Sunday night, after John had returned to work, Tina noticed a blood spot in her panties. She assumed it was just her fibroids acting up again.

Three months after Tina received the oncologist's diagnosis of aggressive, metastatic small cell carcinoma of the ovaries, John Bricker buried the love of his life.

It was at Tina's funeral that John first met Donal O'Cathalain, Bertram Nicolo's head of research and development. Shortly afterwards, John went down the rabbit hole.

CHAPTER TWENTY-ONE
(Drivers Ed)

01001000 01100101 00100111 01110011 00100000
01100001 00100000 01101100 01101111 01110100
00100000 01100010 01100101 01110100 01110100
01100101 01110010 00100000 01100011 01100001
01101110 01100100 01101001 01100100 01100001
01110100 01100101 00100000 01110100 01101000
01100001 01101110 00100000 01100001 01101110
01111001 00100000 01101111 01100110 00100000
01110100 01101000 01100101 00100000 01110010
01100101 01110011 01110100 00100000 01101111
01100110 00100000 01110101 01110011 00101110
00100000 00100000 00100000

He's a lot better candidate than any of the rest of us.

The hybrids all sat in a circle in holographic chairs around the central galley of Stella's spacecraft, which was sitting inside Everett and Michelle's back storage bay. Whitey stood in its center directly addressing Stella and Apollo.

"Can we do this in English?" Lenny barked. "It's taking me forever to do the binary to English conversion. And I miss talking like a human."

"Whitey wants to train Lucian on how to fly this spacecraft." Eddie translated.

"No shit?!" Lenny said. "In that case, I vote yes."

"Has he asked you to train him?" Stella asked.

"No," Whitey responded. "Hasn't mentioned it."

"Then why are we here?" Apollo chimed in.

"We all heard Petrichor's message." Whitey answered. "There's a Lizard shit storm about to happen and we have less than a dozen of us hybrids and a few pure-bloods available to meet that challenge."

"And one of those pure-bloods is Aldor!" Eddie added.

"Exactly!" Lenny exclaimed. "I still don't trust that prick."

"I know this kid." Whitey continued, referring to Lucian. "In fact, we've all known him longer than we've known you two."

"You want to convert him?" Apollo asked.

Whitey thought about that a moment. "Is that really necessary?"

"Everett taught Jimmy before he had fully converted," Lenny replied.

"Yes, but he had already received the dose from the Hadron Distributor," Stella pointed out. "That's what started it all. None of us would be here right now if it wasn't for Jimmy's initial conversion." She touched the small cylinder tucked inside the seamless breast pocket of her uniform.

"Beware the law of unintended consequences." Eddie warned.

"The Centaurians didn't invent that law. Ask any Irish-Catholic parent with a dozen kids." Lenny said, only half-jokingly.

"Shit happens." Eddie shrugged. "When it's all said and done, Lucian is a stand-up guy. He has never said a word about us to anyone."

"How do you know?" Apollo asked. "After all, he just served with the same military that we kicked the shit out of twenty years ago. He could have shared our secret at any time."

"I'm telling you he didn't!" Eddie said emphatically. "I rifled through his memories back at the house."

"I took a peek myself today after we got word from Petrichor," Whitey added, obviously ashamed.

"Trust but verify," Lenny said.

Apollo piped up again. "Well, speaking for myself, I vote yes. Train him up. We've all seen the images about the way that big scaly fucker man-handled my dad in front of the Intergalactic Federation. The more back-up we can bring to the party when they come knocking, the better."

"Yes, from me!" Lenny called out.

"Same," Eddie chimed, raising his hand for good measure.

"You know my vote," Whitey added.

Stella considered everything for a moment more. "Bring him here," she ordered.

* * * * *

Lucian sat across the dining room table, gazing silently at Savanna, who was mesmerizing the human members of the misfit crew with a story about the time she was arrested at The Underground nightclub in Camden, London.

"How was I supposed to know he was one of the Royals?" Savanna declared rhetorically. "And so, what if he was? No one gets to cup my breast without permission!"

"You broke his nose, Savvy!" Scarlett admonished. "And chipped his tooth."

"I'd do it again!" Savanna responded, unbowed.

"You were lucky Aunty Bonnie and Tess were still around to bail you out and quash those charges."

"Not to worry." Bobbi chimed in, "They have been enjoying themselves immensely on the other side. They just came from watching George Michael and Freddy Mercury perform a mash-up concert for Queen Elizabeth."

"Well," Savanna whispered with the perfect flair of gossip, "we all told Bonnie she was going to do herself mischief if she kept driving with those coke-bottle glasses. It was just a matter of time."

"But to slam into a lorry full of holy water bottles destined for Canterbury Cathedral?!" Scarlett exclaimed.

"The irony was not lost on Tess." Bobbi stage whispered. "Said Bonnie's mother was grinning from ear-to-ear when she greeted the two of them in heaven."

Lucian suddenly felt his skin galvanizing.

* * * * *

"Hold on to him." Lucian heard Lenny declare through his haze. "It's pretty disconcerting the first couple of times you transport."

"Jayney, a chair," Whitey called out.

Lucian felt himself being maneuvered into a seat just as his eyes began to clear. He looked around an unfamiliar room with soft pulsating light emanating from the walls, ceiling, and floor. He could recognize the crew of men he called his "Moran family uncles" in chairs around a circle, all facing him. Stella and Apollo sat directly opposite his spot in the circle. He felt a powerful hand on his shoulder and saw a concerned-looking Whitey staring back at him.

"Where the fuck am I?" he whispered; his throat parched.

"You are on Jayney!" Lenny cried.

"Jayney?" Lucian asked as a glass of water materialized in his hand.

"Drink that up, son." Whitey said. "Hydration is key to healthy transportation."

"We call all of our ships Jayney," Eddie clarified.

"Welcome Lucian," Jayney said from the ether in her best Petrichor voice.

"Well, flyboy," Lenny began, "ready to graduate to the big leagues?"

"What are you talking about?" Lucian's head was still spinning.

"I'm not sure this Terran can handle this." Apollo said, as he studied what most of the crew considered his cousin.

Lucian had been around enough adrenaline jockeys in the Navy to recognize shit talking. He gently removed Whitey's hand from his shoulder and downed the glass of water. As he pulled himself up straight in the chair, he held his hand up with the empty glass in his palm.

"Jayney," he said confidently, "would you mind?"

The glass disappeared and Lucian did his best to hide his amazement.

"There hasn't been a machine dreamt of that I can't figure out how to fly." Lucian boasted.

Stella studied Lucian carefully, then rifled through his mind, downloading everything within moments. Lucian felt like butterflies were dancing between his ears.

"If you gentlemen wouldn't mind, Lucian and I need the room," Stella said. The rest of the men looked around at each other. Lenny jerked his chin; Whitey shrugged his shoulders, and Eddie nodded. The three disappeared. Apollo hung around a moment longer.

You sure you don't want a wingman? Apollo asked her telepathically.

I taught you how to fly, remember? Stella responded. *I got this.*

Apollo stared across the circle at Lucian.

"Don't fuck this up." He said out loud with an uncharacteristic seriousness before disappearing.

"Just you and me, kid," Lucian said to Stella, in a terrible Humphrey Bogart impression.

"Better hang onto your seat, Loosh," Stella said with her first smile of the evening. "It's going to get a little bumpy."

Lucian could feel the ship start to slowly move as it exited Everett's storage area.

"Jayney, take us up!" Stella commanded.

CHAPTER TWENTY-TWO
(The Highest Form Of Flattery)

When John Bricker first entered "the Silo," he thought he had stepped into a science fiction movie.

"That's what I was waiting for," Doc said with appreciation, "Your chin literally just dropped."

There, in an underground bunker a thousand feet below the Nicolo facility at Groom Lake, sat three different space crafts.

The two larger vehicles had the archetypal disc shape that sci-fi magazines and questionable internet postings had been sharing with the world for decades. Each of the larger vehicles was over one hundred feet in diameter and about thirty feet in height. Their skins were some forms of metallic alloy, and their outer construction was seamless. The third vehicle was smaller, about the size of a moderate Recreation Vehicle and shaped like a tic tac mint.

Each of the larger vehicles had openings that were obviously carved by plasmatrons and had wheeled stairways leading to those openings. John watched as rotations of individuals dressed in bland scientific coveralls entered and exited the larger spacecrafts like individual bees going in and out of a hive. Off along the left of this area were a series of large labs exposed through floor to ceiling glass. Individuals and groups of similarly dressed workers were busy working with items he recognized to be advanced forms of weaponry, communication, and propulsion systems. Behind one sheet of glass was a room filled with rows and rows of the latest generation of servers that supported a virtual computing cloud that would make Silicon Valley jealous.

There were access stations throughout the area where these worker drones stopped to upload and download information to and from hand-held devices in moments through tapping motions. Any human follow-up would be performed on virtual key boards that appeared and hovered above the stations whenever the drone stood in a certain spot, disappearing once the drone was done.

Doc never said a word, just watched as Bricker's eyes danced around the room.

When Bricker completed his visual circuit, he looked back at the tiny Irishman.

"Where the fuck are we?" John asked.

"Welcome to the heart of Nicolo Aerospace." Doc responded. "We call it Looking Glass."

"Is this real?"

"As real as your testicles," Doc replied. "shot down at different times by Uncle Sam. Recovered by us. Nicolo owns the tow truck routes for ET crashes."

John walked over and peeked into the opening in one of the crafts. Inside was an empty circular gallery. There were no computers or consoles to operate the craft. No obvious weapons systems in sight. There wasn't even a portal to look out of. Bricker felt like he was gazing into the inside of an empty tuna can.

"How do you drive these things?" He asked, still staring around the empty interior.

"Damned if we know." Doc responded. "As you can see, there doesn't seem to be a control system. Some of our think tank nerds believe it might be a holographic system that is tuned to the minds of the pilots. A symbiotic relationship."

Doc rapped on the outside of the ship, but it didn't make a sound. "We haven't been able to reproduce the ship's outer skin either, the alloy is too pure, even when we tried to create it in the weightlessness of space on the Artemis Moon station."

"What about the occupants?"

"Deceased, but we keep them cryogenically preserved at a separate facility in California for research purposes. Little creepy fuckers," Doc said with the nonchalance of a butcher telling you the price of a pound of chicken.

"But we've managed to reverse engineer the older crafts' electromagnetic propulsion system." Doc stated proudly. "Took us eighty years but we got it done. Well, our modified version of it anyway."

Doc crooked his finger and led Bricker down another long hallway and into a second large chamber. There sat a simplified replica of one of the disks John had seen in the first chamber, only he could see seams in the metal skin, where the top part of the craft met its lower chamber. It was made of the same carbon-graphite-titanium composite as on the Airforce's stealth crafts, only formed in a complete disk shape.

"This is our prototype," Doc said. "We have a dozen others sitting in storage in an underground hangar at Vandenberg, all ready to go. We pay top dollar for the retired Top Gun grads that are being trained on them as we speak."

John followed Doc onto the craft's access stairway that lowered from its bottom as the little Mick typed a code into his cellphone. Inside the hull was packed with a control panel, a weapons system, and a large screen sitting before a single captain's chair.

"We inserted our latest navigational systems." Doc said. "Just a tick more advanced than what we have in the FI35s. It's hard wired into our version of their electromagnetic propulsion system."

He pointed at John. "But you're going to figure out how those little Grey Hobbits did it."

"What about fuel?" Bricker asked. "Throwing off that much electromagnetic power needs a large and steady fuel supply."

"Now you've asked the trillion-dollar question." Doc said gleefully. "The one real take away from downing these ET cocksuckers, is this." He walked over to the crafts center console flipped open a cover and pointed to a small rectangular box wedged into its interior, with no wires or buttons or anything.

"That can't be a cold fusion generator?!" Bricker opined.

"You're right," Doc said. "The quantum boys call it an 'over unity' system."

John understood the theory. If you could generate more output energy than it takes to propel the generator, you would have beaten the system. But no one had been able to do it. At least no one he knew.

"We had our best and brightest working twenty-four-seven trying to reverse engineer the electromagnetic propulsion system," Doc continued. "When they came upon what I call the original battery pack in the ET craft, they had no idea what it was. But it gave off over five gigajoules of radiant energy."

"Is that the original?" Bricker asked, gazing at it with the same adoration as if it were the holy grail.

"No. It's our diet version." Doc said. "The boys were able to create a quantum vacuum replica. Don't know the details, as it's beyond my ken. I am told it's the same theory. It taps into the zero-point energy field that is woven throughout the fabric of space and time and pulls the electrons out of the ether. We are now running the entire complex on similar technology."

Bricker now realized that he did not see one wire running throughout the complex. He didn't even notice an outlet. Nikola Tesla would be in awe, and jealous as fuck.

"When are you taking this public?" John asked, then added, "this is a game changer."

John thought about how all the bullshit between the Greens and the Fossil Fuel supporters would be resolved overnight. The environment would be off the political table and who could complain about free energy.

"We're not." Doc said. "Or at least not until the boss figures out how to properly monetize it."

"Nicolo doesn't have enough money?" John asked, incredulously.

The Mick tapped John softly on the cheek.

"Don't you worry about the rest of the world, Dr. Bricker. Mr. Nicolo is going to pay you a lot of money to figure out how those ETs piloted those ships. Leave those larger existential issues to us."

CHAPTER TWENTY-THREE
(Buck The Mushroom)

Buck stared out the window of the USAF C-37B as it hurtled along the 15,000-foot runway at Vandenberg AFB, knowing it would only need 2400 to lift off. Buck hated to fly, but if he needed to take to the air, he trusted this workhorse to get him safely from A to B and back again. Still, he did not release his tight grip on the arm rests until all wheels were up and stowed and the jet had made its turn due east towards Colorado.

Buck's welcome tour had gone just as expected for the first three western bases at Peterson, Schriever, and LA, with the appropriate ass-kissing salutations by the local base commanders and the appropriate pomp and circumstance as he got the sanitized tour of their respective facilities. The only part Buck consistently enjoyed was telling the officers that he would be eating each meal in the enlisted soldiers mess hall. He didn't believe in ivory tower leadership.

Vandenberg was the first place Buck ran into resistance. Major General Terrence Hughes, the leader of the Combined Force Space Component Command, was a crafty prick and was clearly protecting his turf. Word had it that Hughes was on the short list for Buck's job and given his decade of service in the Space Force, he should have gotten the appointment over Buck. Well, shit happens, and the true survivors learn to deal with it.

Buck had been around the military long enough to know when he was being mushroomed. He knew Hughes was feeding him shit and keeping him in the dark about something going on at Vandenberg. Unfortunately, Hughes had the strategic advantage because he knew when Buck was arriving and how long he was going to be on-site, so he was able to get all his ducks lined up and keep Buck distracted with the obvious, the bright shiny objects.

"Mac," Buck called out, just as the jet leveled, "make sure I have a printout of the schematics of Vandenberg when we arrive back at Buckley."

"On it," Mac called back from his spot in the first row of seats. He tapped his cell phone and barked some orders into its screen mic.

Buck looked across the aisle at Renee Clarke, who seemed totally absorbed in something on her iPad's screen. She had an appealing profile. She didn't try to hide her four full decades and wore it well. She was clearly athletic and allowed some grey to mix among the blonde. Confidence makes everyone more attractive.

"How long until we reach home Dr. Clarke?" Buck asked.

"Three and half hours," Renee responded without looking up, "depending on the head winds."

"Does our route take us anywhere near Groom Lake?" Buck followed up.

"About fifty miles south," Renee responded, this time looking over at Buck. "Why?"

"Mac," Buck called out. "Tell the pilot we are making a pit stop. Homey Airport."

"General." Clearly disturbed, Renee crossed the aisle and sat in the open seat facing Buck. She leaned in and almost whispered. "We can't just drop in on Groom Lake."

"Mac," Buck called out again. "Does Groom Lake fall under Space Force jurisdiction?"

"Technically, yes, Sir." Mac replied.

"And who runs Space Force, Mac?" Buck continued, never breaking gaze with Dr. Clarke. He couldn't help but smile.

"You do, Sir."

"You better have a good reason to land there." Dr. Clarke warned.

"I flew out of Vandenberg with too much shit in my system," Buck replied. "I'm completely full of shit. Some of it's got to go. Now."

Renee turned and pointed towards the jet toilet.

"Oh no." Buck said, following her point. "I can do a lot of things in the air, but shitting's not one of them. And I ain't carrying any more shit with me back to Buckley."

Just then, Mac arrived next to Buck, leaned in, and whispered. "The pilot says their control tower won't authorize us to land at Homey Airport, Sir."

Buck's smile disappeared. He stood up, pushed past Mac, and headed for the front of the plane. Mac and Clarke followed behind. Buck opened the cockpit doorway and addressed the two junior officers piloting the jet.

"Major Bell," Buck said to the woman pilot presently at the controls. "Who told you we could not land our plane at Homey Airport."

"The staff sergeant supervisor at its control tower, Sir."

"Get that asshole on the radio." He barked. The co-pilot tapped the console screen.

A moment later, a voice was heard on the speaker.

"This is Staff Sergeant Davis."

"Sergeant Davis." Buck said in his most commanding voice. "This is General Sheridan, Chief of Space Operations of Space Force."

He let it sink in a moment.

"Sir?!" Sergeant Davis responded.

"Major Bell," Buck said. "How long until we reach Homey Airport?"

"Twenty minutes, sir." She replied.

"Sergeant Davis," Buck said, "you have twenty minutes to clear my jet for landing."

"But . . . Sir?!" The voice trailed off.

"Twenty minutes, Sergeant," Buck repeated. "In twenty minutes, I'm going to be on the ground taking a shit. And depending on what you do next, it's either going to be on an overpriced, government-issued latrine or it's going to be down your throat. And I promise, that's the last meal you'll have on the government dime. Do we understand each other, Sergeant?"

The line remained quiet for a few pregnant moments.

"You're cleared to land," Sergeant Davis finally replied. "Runway 3, South."

Buck winked at the pilot. "Take us in, Major."

* * * * *

By the time Buck's jet had come to a stop, the stairs deployed, and the door opened, a line of HMMWVs were parked along the side of the airstrip. All but one was military green. That odd man out was powder black.

A nervous-looking Colonel was standing at the foot of the stairs waiting to meet Buck as he disembarked. There was a trail of subordinate officers standing in a welcoming line behind him. Buck returned his salute but was already looking past him at the civilians standing by the black vehicle on the side of the tarmac. One looked familiar. After a moment, Buck recognized Bertram Nicolo from a recent Forbes article Buck had glanced at while having coffee at the LA base. The man looked amazing for someone in his late seventies. But money will do that for you. Buck didn't recognize the man standing with him, but he looked as Irish as Patty's pig.

A third man stood a few feet away from Nicolo and his Mick. He looked more like an intellectual, a professor or scientist, not a business man. He also looked uncomfortable and turned away the moment Buck made eye contact.

"Sorry about the mix-up, General," the Colonel offered. "It's just that this is a restricted area, so we don't allow unscheduled visits."

"I'm not visiting," Buck responded, "Colonel –?"

"Smith. Colonel Smith."

"And last time I checked," Buck continued, "a General outranks a Colonel, so you don't get to tell me where I'm allowed to go."

By now, Clarke and Mac had joined Buck on the tarmac.

"Of course, General." Smith replied. "You have free access to every inch of the military base here on Groom Lake."

"Why that's very generous of you Colonel," Buck said with as much condescension as he could muster.

"But the actual military base is just one square mile over in the Southern quadrant of the Groom Lake facility. The rest is leased by privately owned companies." Colonel Smith said with a sweep of his arm.

The arm sweep area covered eighty percent of the entire base. Buck looked at Clarke.

"Is this true?"

She checked her screen and then nodded affirmatively.

"We will gladly provide you with a tour of the base, General," Colonel Smith offered.

The Colonel gestured towards the rest of the base. "You don't have the necessary security clearance to access the private section," the Colonel added, "assuming it was even possible for you to obtain permission to go there from Mr. Nicolo."

Buck looked back at Clarke, who confirmed it again with a nod.

Buck stared over at Nicolo and his tiny Irishman, who opened the rear car door for his boss, and then slid into the front passenger seat. The science geek ran over to their vehicle and slid into the other back door. Then the vehicle sped off along the tarmac and through a gate into the restricted area.

"That won't be necessary at this time, Colonel." Buck responded. "But I shan't forget your hospitality."

"Mac," Buck called over his shoulder. "Tell Major Bell we'll be leaving for Buckley immediately." Mac turned and raced up the jet stairs.

"I'll be in touch to schedule that inspection." Colonel Smith added.

"Don't bother," Buck said as he turned and headed back up the jet stairs, ignoring Smith's salute. "Tell Mr. Nicolo that next time I come, I won't be alone, and I won't be asking for anyone's permission."

"You may want to start thinking about your next posting, Colonel." Clarke added. "Somewhere cold, I imagine." She glanced up the stairs after Buck, smiled, and then took the stairs two at a time until she passed through the jet's portal.

CHAPTER TWENTY-FOUR
(One Small Step)

Dr. Michael J. McBride rolled out of his bunk and pulled on the light-weight thermal coveralls that were the standard issue to the inhabitants of the Artemis Base Camp on the South Pole of the Moon.

One more day. Michael thought to himself. After two years, he was looking forward to retiring to his quiet home in the bucolic dale of Tarrytown, New York back on Earth. Dr. McBride, as the esteemed Ph.D. in Earth, Environmental, and Planetary Sciences from Brown University was referred to by his colleagues at the Goddard Space Flight Center, was completing his tour as Chief Lunar Geologist at the jewel in the United States' space exploration program. Under his supervision, the members of this base camp had successfully mined the lunar landscape to extract both oxygen and water from the ice in its nearby Cabeus crater.

Recent scientific breakthroughs in unlimited energy production were a game changer. Described one time to Michael only as a Quantum Vacuum Energy Extractor that produced Zero Point Energy from the ether in the dark matter that made up over eighty percent of the universe. The concept was beyond the scope of even his prodigious intellect. Details of its creation were limited to those with a need-to-know, special access program, security clearance.

Michael didn't need to know. The system's proof was in the pudding. When Michael turned the switch or pressed a button, the electricity flowed.

But this shoe box sized power source now powered every structure and vehicle at the Artemis camp, including the Biodome where the settlement grew its food. The unlimited energy had allowed Michael to design and implement exotic methods of extraction of air and water needed for the successful establishment of the base. Given the costs of energy, using traditional petrochemical, coal, or nuclear resources, Michael's extraction methods would have proven too expensive to implement back on Earth.

Michael was able to use the post-extraction soil residue that otherwise would have been considered a waste product, to design construction materials using the advanced 3-D printers at the Artemis Camp. That allowed the original four-person mission crew to expand from living and working out of their Lunar Landing Module into the five newly constructed, permanent outer structures. The building now housed a group of a dozen men and women, who were stationed in staggered, overlapping tours to allow for continuity in the work being performed.

Michael was proud of his accomplishments. But he was ready to go home. He would have loved to continue teaching and sharing the amazing things he had seen on Artemis at one of the Ivy League bastions of education in the Northeast upon his return. However, as part of his retirement package, Michael signed a Non-Disclosure Agreement that threatened ten years in a federal penitentiary should he disclose anything about the Artemis Base Camp after his return to Earth. But the severance package was extremely generous, and the fish on Earth weren't going to catch themselves, so Michael was happy to take the money and run.

He poured the one coffee a day he rationed himself and gazed out through one of the thick tempered portals at the eternal dusk like view of the surrounding lunar landscape.

He stared at the now redundant solar farm system, that was mostly buried beneath the gathering moon dust and recalled how the earliest Artemis settlers were forced to ration their limited power grid. Even the most advanced solar storage batteries couldn't withstand constant exposure to negative 400 F. The QVEE system rendered those worries a thing of the past.

Michael's attention was drawn to the Lunar Terrain Vehicle that exited the Security Barracks on the southernmost tip of the camp. It was heading towards the landing zone just over the lip of a smaller crater that contained most of the dispersing dust kicked up from launches and landings and kept it from spreading out towards the settlement. He knew that the driver in the space suit must be Mike Kojak, head of the Artemis security team, going out on patrol. The sight always invoked that image of the spaceman in the red Tesla Roadster that Elon Musk launched decades before. If it wasn't for that South African visionary, Michael wouldn't be sitting there.

He looked forward to making that same trip the next day and taking that last view of the Artemis camp as the Lunar Module spirited him back home.

Gulping down the last of his coffee and licking the remnants off his very bushy grey moustache, he thought to himself, *Fuck it. It's my last day. I'm having a refill.*

CHAPTER TWENTY-FIVE
(Gleaming The Cube)

01001010 01100001 01111001 01101110 01100101
01111001 00101100 00100000 01110011 01101000
01101111 01110111 00100000 01101101 01100101
00100000 01110100 01101000 01100101 00100000
01101110 01101001 01100111 01101000 01110100
00100000 01110011 01101011 01111001 00101110
00100000

Jayney, show me the night sky. Stella instructed telepathically.

Lucian grabbed onto his chair to keep from falling when the ship's outer skin seemed to disappear, leaving the young man and Stella firmly suspended in the air in Everett and Michelle's back yard. Neither party shifted, as the ship remained as it had been, only its outer skin was transparent.

"Better grab him, Jayney," Stella called out as she manifested a holographic control panel. "Hang on, Terran!"

Lucian was suddenly encased and immobilized in an invisible cocoon of solid warmth. Stella wiggled her fingers on both hands in a controlled blur over the hand-shaped controls and Jayney began to rise through the sky in a direct vertical climb accelerating at a speed Lucian had never approached in his years as a top flight Naval pilot. In less than two heartbeats the ship had surpassed the Kármán line and the crystal blue of Earth's atmosphere conceded its reach to the initial darkness of outer space. Lucian's only sensation of the steep climb was visual, as he never felt the shift away from a feeling of being horizontal. Nor did he feel the g-forces that would certainly have caused him to pass out in an earth-made vehicle.

Stella scanned his thoughts. No fear, just wonder.

She eavesdropped on a replayed memory of when Lucian had taken an SR-71 on a training flight to 94,000 feet, and she shared his feeling in that moment that he wanted to continue to climb if he could have.

"You going to let me out of this?" Lucian asked. "Since I've come this far, I'd really like to take a good look around while I'm here."

Another telepathic signal from his host and Lucian was free and on his feet. A flick of Stella's finger and he was now standing right beside her. While she didn't seem to respond to their close physical proximity, Lucian was suddenly very aware that, despite their different genetic codes, Stella was all woman. Suddenly the outer skin of the ship was visible. A large holographic screen appeared before the console, focusing all eyes on what was in front of the space craft.

"Left hand controls speed, the right, direction." Stella said without looking up. A moment later, Lucian was standing where Stella had stood, with his hands now in the same templates of the holographic control panel.

"Don't have to tell me twice," Lucian said, this time as he rifled his left-hand fingers, pinky to thumb and Jayney moved forward like a thoroughbred out of the gate.

"Incoming," Jayney chimed.

Lucian spotted a string of stargate satellites looming on the screen before him.

"Pressing all five fingers simultaneously of the right hand raises the ship over the obstacle," Stella coached. "The heel of the palm drops below it."

"That kind of avoidance is for pussies," Lucian said without taking his eyes off the screen. With the heightened dexterity of a fighter pilot, Lucian nimbly maneuvered his right thumb and pinky to weave in and out between the oncoming line of hurtling satellites. He didn't even reduce his speed.

Are you seeing this, Jayney? Stella asked telepathically.

He's better than the hybrids, Jayney responded.

"Fucking A!" Lucian shouted as he dodged the caboose in the satellite chain. He held his right pinky down which forced the ship into a tight barrel roll.

"Take *that* Maverick." Lucian whispered as he reduced speed, righted the ship, and then stepped back from the panel. He turned to Stella, his eyes displaying the adrenaline rush that his thoughts were broadcasting.

Incoming. Jayney shared with Stella as the ship almost pirouetted in place. An energy bolt flew past the front of the ship.

"What the fuck?!" Lucian shouted as grabbed onto the console and went to insert his hands back into the templates. But Stella was suddenly in his place, raising the ship just as another energy bolt passed beneath it. Lucian had been returned to the safety of Jayney's energy cocoon.

Where is it coming from? Stella demanded telepathically.

Earth, Jayney responded.

"Who is shooting at us?" Lucian demanded, as Stella sent the ship hurtling into deep space.

"Jayney?!" Stella demanded so Lucian could hear. "Whose got that kind of plasma weaponry?"

"The United States." Jayney responded. "Those blasts were fired from 37° 16' 36.03" N 115° 47' 56.17" W".

"We really are out of time." Stella lamented. "Take us back, Jayney."

And if anyone comes to greet us, Jayney, take them out. And I don't care where they're from.

CHAPTER TWENTY-SIX
(Don't Touch My Lucky Charms)

"Colonel Smith is here, Buck," Renee announced as she intercepted the General in the hallway outside his office. "And he's brought back-up."

Buck looked down at his pup, Fergus at his heel. "So did I."

Buck marched into his office and didn't acknowledge the four people sitting in the two chairs and on the settee along the wall until he got behind his desk, where he turned to them and roared.

"Who the fuck fired those missiles from Groom Lake?!"

Colonel Smith leapt from one of the chairs in front of the desk to his feet and weakly chattered. "It wasn't us, Sir."

"Who else was it then?" Buck shouted back at him. "It came from your base!"

"That would be us," came the soft southern Irish brogue from the Mick in the chair beside him. This well-dressed man didn't make any attempt to stand. "But they weren't missiles."

Fergus started to growl softly from his basket on Buck's side of the desk.

"And just who the fuck are you, Mr. Leprechaun?" Buck seethed, his anger now laser focused on his wet-back Celtic cousin lounging comfortably in the leather chair before him. Buck wanted to grab this tiny

Mick by the scruff of his neck and toss him out the doorway. But not before he made the imp give up his gold.

"Donal O'Cathalain, from County Kerry," the Mick said, finally standing and extending a soft hand. "But my friends call me Doc."

Buck ignored the two men standing before him and focused on the older, silver-haired, well-turned-out man sitting on the settee against the back wall of the office. He glanced at the nervous looking intellectual sitting beside him but immediately reengaged the man he knew was calling all the shots.

"I don't give a fuck how wealthy and powerful you are Mr. Nicolo," Buck said to him. "That was my base and Space Force weapons you were playing with -"

"Technically," the Mick interrupted, "That was Mr. Nicolo's weapon. He hasn't sold it to the government, just yet."

Buck looked at Colonel Smith, who avoided his eyes, then over at Renee Clarke, who was reading something off her iPad.

"It was some form of plasma cannon," Renee responded.

"That's a fair enough description," the Mick said. "Simplistic, but fair enough."

"Lieutenant-Colonel," Buck said, "tell Mac, I want him in here now, and to bring MP's."

"That won't be necessary, General," Mr. Nicolo said, standing up and crossing to the front of the desk. He glanced at Colonel Smith, who hopped up to vacate the chair. Nicolo made himself comfortable and then extended his hand in a gesture for Buck to do the same. Buck remained standing.

Fergus growled in support.

"Look, General," Nicolo said in a tone that was surprisingly condescending. "You called this meeting."

"I *ordered* Colonel Smith to appear in my office." Buck corrected him. "You can take *Finn Bheara* and get the fuck out of here."

"Let me ask you a question, General," Nicolo ignored the insult. "It's been twenty-four hours since the event. Has anyone in the Pentagon, or the White House for that matter, responded to any of your many inquiries?"

Buck glanced over at Renee. She shook her head almost imperceptibly.

"Anything in the media?" Nicolo asked rhetorically.

Again, Renee shook her head.

"A return phone call, perhaps?" Nicolo needled.

Buck just stared at him, seething.

"So, nothing happened." Nicolo stood up and faced Buck, who for the first time realized they were close in height. Buck stared directly into Nicolo's eyes. They were as dead as a shark's.

"Last night was a defense of the country you have taken an oath to protect." Nicolo said, now turning his back on the General as he adjusted his jacket. "From enemies you cannot begin to comprehend." The older man now gestured for the others to prepare to leave. "Take the win, *Buck*."

Buck glanced down at the Mick, who smiled back at Buck in a way that should have cost him a couple of teeth. The Mick rose and stood beside his boss, this time he didn't offer Buck his hand.

"It's a need-to-know basis, and you just don't need to know." The Mick quipped.

"Time to go," Nicolo called as he headed towards the office door. The intellectual opened the door for his boss and waited for everyone, including Colonel Smith, to follow him out before turning to Renee and awkwardly reaching out and shaking her hand. He then hurried out the door after the rest.

"What the fuck just happened?" Buck asked.

"I'm not sure," Renee said, then handed Buck a small microchip that the intellectual had pressed into her palm as he exited.

CHAPTER TWENTY-SEVEN
(War Consigliere)

Jimmy rolled his craft one final time and then headed back to Centauri. He was disheartened but kept his mind locked, so that none of the others would pick up on it. He removed his hands from the console templates and manifested a captain's chair. He was mentally fatigued.

Jayney, take me home.

Jayney had been putting the crew through virtual reality drills over the past two Centauri weeks. Over the past four exercises, despite their best efforts, and their mastering of their warships' weaponry, the virtual Draconians beat them. It wasn't a massacre, but when the exercises were completed, the Draconians always had some chess pieces left on the board. The Centaurians were wiped clean. Jimmy hated losing.

Even Jayney's most advanced AI renditions of battle never left Jimmy actually feeling pain or spitting blood. He never felt the immediacy of death in a virtual world. The Centauri pilots were treating these battles like video games to be reset once the screen went dark.

As his own crew quickly mastered the warships, Jimmy jettisoned the Centauri pilots that had never been battle-tested, believing in the back of his mind that they just didn't have enough of a natural killer instinct. Defensively, they didn't anticipate the unimaginable from their opponent. Offensively, they didn't understand the concept that there were times you dropped all of your guard and just went balls in on the attack. It was not something you can teach. It's either in you or it's not.

And you had to be able to take that unexpected hit and still keep moving forward towards your opponent. Jimmy used to size up his legal opposition by assessing whether or not, at any time in their life, they had ever been punched in the face. It's easy to trash-talk someone, especially polysyllabically, if you haven't taken that physical shot to the eye or mouth. To feel the pain, the release of adrenaline, the labored breath, the fear, the flushed skin, and that fight-or-flight response kicking in, creates that survivor instinct.

Jimmy's legal opponents all knew he had taken real shots in his life. A lot of those shots came from his siblings, and others from strangers in bars or the ring.

Jimmy was the human embodiment of a badger because he never went into a fight believing he could win. But he knew he would always voice his opposition in an unforgettable fashion. In nature, even the biggest grizzly won't fight a badger because they know that even if they win, the permanent damage the badger will cause them will render the victory pyrrhic. The bear will never fully recover from it. Jimmy's opponents growing up all knew that same thing about Jimmy. If they started with him, he was in it to the end. His legal opponents sensed the same thing. It was always better to work out a compromise rather than lose a professional eye, tooth, or limb to the lawyer then known as Jimmy McCarthy.

Jimmy's hybrid warriors all had that same killer instinct and had proven that on Earth. But they didn't have the technical skill that could turn their warships into extensions of their bodies. There was always that half-second count for the lethal synapses to fire. Gina was always the quickest and most adept hybrid in her mastering of warship technology and the most brutal in her attacks, but she often left herself exposed by coming to Jimmy's aid in the simulations. Jimmy's counterpunching style always placed him deep in the shit during battle.

The pure-blood Centaurians on this team understood and mastered the warship technology and were surprisingly effective in battle, especially

Michelle and Petrichor. Michelle knew death, up close and personal from the crew's battles on Earth. She had demonstrated her blood lust, and usually was the last ship to go down in the simulations. Petrichor had no problem engaging in the battle, as she also demonstrated that last night on Earth. She liked to lead from the front. The ultimate bad-ass beauty. For her, she was the mother lioness, and everyone was her cub to be protected. She deserved to be the Queen Poobah of Proxima b, and her and Jimmy's daughter, Stella, had gotten the best of her mother's genes.

But in the AI simulations, the Draconians always went after the leader first. Cut off the head and the body will fall. Petrichor always took a few with her, but she always went down.

Everett was a journeyman warrior. He was a slow boil in the battle but once the steam rose, he gave it his all. He usually took out the first Draconian ship he encountered, but never survived the confrontation. Always a wash.

The biggest surprise of this crew was Aldor. He was smart and effective, and just a bit sneaky in his approach to battle. He often followed another Centauri into the dogfight and once his comrade went down, came in blazing out of the wreckage and took out the assassin. And as Jimmy well knew, Aldor had taken his punches in the face. And he still stepped up. Respect.

But Aldor's cunning never lasted far beyond his first engagement. And the Draconians didn't like surprises.

Those tiny failings were all it took to lose. They were playing catch-up against a race that was born with a warship and weapons coming out their asses and who loved the very idea of battle. To die at war was a glorious thing. But if human history had taught Jimmy one thing, it was that there is nothing glorious in war.

Jimmy's thoughts went back to the two tech twin assholes, the mercenaries, and the military drones his crew faced off with their last night on Earth, and he wondered if his home planet was worth saving. Then he remembered his human and mystical friends, and his sister, who had stayed behind that night. Over the years, Bonnie and Tessa ultimately crossed the veil, but the others and his siblings' families all remained. His crew had all stepped up when he needed them most. He couldn't let them down.

He knew they could not win but he was going to take as many limbs off these fucking Lizards as he could.

Jimmy didn't realize he had company until he felt something nuzzle the back of his shoulder. Before he could turn around, he heard that familiar Lauren Bacall whisper.

"Practice is over, Jimmy. Game time!"

CHAPTER TWENTY-EIGHT
(War Council)

"In my humble opinion," Brian called out from the kitchen, where he had put the kettle on, "our POTUS has been a puppet of the boys at the WEF since the 2020s."

"Nothing but eunuchs in the harem since 46!" Janice added, as she placed the Belleek cups on a tray and dropped a dozen Irish Wild Berry tea bags into a beautiful matching shamrock-themed teapot.

Stella listened carefully to her human counterparts. She had learned from her father that if you want to know what the leaders are doing, ask their citizens, who had to live with the leader's choices. She also knew she was only going to get one big move to make her case to the Terrans, so she didn't want to waste it.

She eaves-dropped on the Ericksons' minds to get some context for their opinions and was disappointed in what she learned. While Centaurians functioned seamlessly as one collective people and planet, it seemed that any attempt for the citizens of Earth to do so was corrupted by the selfish self-interests of the powerful economic elite who controlled information, technology, pharmaceuticals, food and most importantly, energy. Through artificial rationing they maintained control of the masses by always presenting the possibility of scarcity, which kept the citizens worried and afraid. This made the citizens selfish and divided, as they each concentrated on protecting their respective access to this limited supply.

Religion remained the wild card. Convince the masses that there was an angry, selfish, jealous, judgmental, omnipotent being waiting to punish them in the afterlife if they didn't comply with the dictates of self-proclaimed prophets here on this energy plane, and you could pretty much get them to do whatever you told them. Fear was humanity's greatest flaw.

Centaurians understood that this reality is just one stop in a series of endless possibilities, and that while there was a sentient entity behind the creation of all, it had one and only one driving characteristic. Love. The rest was up to us.

Scarcity in any form had not been an issue on Proxima b for eons, once Centaurians converted to individualized zero-point energy generators which drew unlimited power from the dark matter in the universe. They powered their cities and their space ships. Zero-point energy was the skeleton key that opened all portals to unlimited potential. There was no machine that could not be built, no idea that could not be brought to fruition. Water and any other resource could be siphoned from the ether and converted into a holographic form that was real in every known concept of the word. With zero-point energy, the Centaurians were free to create their perfect and peaceful world.

Centauri's best and brightest advanced their society based on this unlimited energy source. They contributed their now freed up collective intellect and selflessness to the preservation and increasing of resources and the ending of disease. Finally, the Centaurians created a benevolent Artificial Intelligence, a god-light entity that for the last century had been dubbed "Jayney," by her uncle Everett. Jayney looked after the needs of every Centaurian. Jayney was the genie in every Centaurians' lamp, and she drew her sustenance from the same zero-point energy field.

Petrichor had explained to Stella that the one flaw of the Centaurians was that over time they had lost the ability to recognize the baser elements of other races, or among their own. When their ancestors discovered Earth, with all of its natural resources, and the creatures that inhabited it, some of their more arrogant scientists decided that they could replicate the origin of a new species. Through genetic manipulation, they kept advancing the brain capacities in different species of hominids and then observed them over time to see how they evolved. Unfortunately, the more successful hominids had an aggressive gene that provided for their survival in a potentially dangerous environment. As their minds developed and advanced, those dominant hominids continued to ensure that survival by applying that aggressive gene and reducing the competition.

At some point, the Centaurians decided that they would stop actively intervening in the development of the human species. They limited their connection to this human experiment to observation alone. But by then, human intelligence had reached the point where, like any properly constructed artificial intelligence, it could advance on its own. The result wasn't always pretty.

Stella understood better than the pure-blood Centaurians that you cannot control everything. And the mixing of her father's altered human genetic structure had introduced variances that had provided her with abilities that no other Centaurians before her shared. Similarly, the breeding of genetically altered hybrids had created her half-brother Apollo, whose own powers seemed to increase every day.

Centaurians planned and the Universe laughed.

But Stella also knew that her and her brother's genetic constructs and familial history had brought them both to this moment where the existence of their blended races were now under threat by another race that made the most aggressive humans look passive in comparison. Stella knew that she would need to call upon all of her genetic gifts, including her human aggressiveness, if she was going to save them.

"Well, I say that when you are at war, deal only with the warriors," Lenny stated, bringing Stella back to the moment. "Politicians may give the orders but it's the soldiers that carry them out."

"Yeah, but it was the soldiers from this country who were shooting at us," Lucian responded.

"I don't know why you just don't let me take care of them," Apollo chimed in.

01000100 01101111 01101110 00100111 01110100
00100000 01110011 01110100 01100001 01110010
01110100 00101100 00100000 01100010 01110010
01101111 01110100 01101000 01100101 01110010
00101110 00100000 00100000

Don't start, brother. Stella cut him off.

"What about Space Force?" Scarlett asked. "That's what we're talking about, right?"

"That's right, dear," Bobbi responded, in a proud, maternal fashion. She looked lovingly at Helen and winked. "The coven is in capable hands."

"Out of the mouth of babes!" Apollo responded, with maybe a little too much enthusiasm.

Stella wondered if Scarlett was blushing.

"Not a bad idea – let's deal with the warriors. Fuck the politicians," Lenny interjected. "We are talking war. The politicians would just be looking out for their own interests, anyway."

"That would be General Peter Sheridan, then." Lucian volunteered. "His appointment was a bit of a surprise among the troops, really. Known for his propensity to do his fighting on *terra firma*. But well respected by all that serve under him."

"Good luck trying to speak with him." Eddie added. "All soldiers know that even the best of generals remains tucked away from exposure."

"Space Force website says General Sheridan moved his command to Buckley AFB, right here in Colorado!" Savanna said, glancing up from her iPhone.

"Guess it's time that the mountains go pay Mohammed a visit." Lenny mused.

CHAPTER TWENTY-NINE
(The Last Detail)

The last of Centaurian warships, piloted by Aldor, rose from its access portal in Proxima b and joined the formation now hovering over their home planet. Petrichor's solo ship assumed lead point, and Aldor could count ten vessels. Jimmy, Gina, Everett, Michelle, and Aldor piloted their own warships, and each ferried a tandem vessel for use by Lenny, Whitey, Eddie, Apollo, and Stella once the team arrived on Earth. Jayney would control the ghost ships until then. Aldor watched as Everett dropped out of the formation and did a final circumference of their planet before returning and assuming the spot he had vacated.

Once the formation was again intact, Petrichor telepathically shared a download.

```
01000100   01100101   01110011   01110000   01101001
01110100   01100101   00100000   01101111   01110101
01110010   00100000   01110010   01100101   01110011
01110000   01100101   01100011   01110100   01101001
01110110   01100101   00100000   01101111   01110010
01101001   01100111   01101001   01101110   01110011
00101100   00100000   01110111   01100101   00100000
01100001   01110010   01100101   00100000   01100001
01101100   01101100   00100000   01000011   01100101
01101110   01110100   01100001   01110101   01110010
```

```
01101001  01100001  01101110  01110011  00100000
01110100  01101111  01100100  01100001  01111001
00101110  00100000  00100000  01001001  00100000
01100001  01101101  00100000  01101000  01101111
01101110  01101111  01110010  01100101  01100100
00100000  01110100  01101111  00100000  01101100
01100101  01100001  01100100  00100000  01110100
01101000  01101001  01110011  00100000  01100111
01110010  01101111  01110101  01110000  00100000
01100001  01101110  01100100  00100000  01101001
01100110  00100000  01110100  01101000  01101001
01110011  00100000  01101001  01110011  00100000
01110100  01101000  01100101  00100000  01100110
01101001  01101110  01100001  01101100  00100000
01110100  01101001  01101101  01100101  00100000
01110111  01100101  00100000  01100001  01101100
01101100  00100000  01100111  01100001  01111010
01100101  00100000  01110101  01110000  01101111
01101110  00100000  01101111  01110101  01110010
00100000  01110000  01101100  01100001  01101110
01100101  01110100  00101100  00100000  01110100
01101000  01100101  01101110  00100000  01001001
00100000  01101011  01101110  01101111  01110111
00100000  01110111  01100101  00100000  01110011
01101000  01100001  01101100  01101100  00100000
01101101  01100101  01100101  01110100  00100000
01100001  01100111  01100001  01101001  01101110
00100000  01101111  01101110  00100000  01100001
01101110  01101111  01110100  01101000  01100101
01110010  00100000  01100101  01101110  01100101
01110010  01100111  01111001  00100000  01110000
01101100  01100001  01101001  01101110  00101110
00100000 00100000 00100000
```

Despite our respective origins, we are all Centaurians today. I am honored to lead this group and if this is the final time we all gaze upon our planet, then I know we shall meet again on another energy plane.

I take it back, Jimmy chimed into the collective mind meld, *those digits were as passionate as any words that have ever passed a Terran's lips.*

Fuck you Jimmy, Petrichor snapped, *from this point on we all switch to English. I want us all to remember why we're here. Terrans. And I want to be able to curse at Jimmy in a way he fully appreciates. He's right, when it comes to passion, numbers do not cut it.*

Atta girl, Gina retorted. *Now let's go skin some Lizards. Momma needs a new purse.*

We cannot traverse the regular wormhole route through the galaxy, Petrichor shared. *Earth is running out of their concept of time.*

Holy shit, we're hopping dimensions! Michelle spouted. *Hang on, hybrids.*

Jayney, assume control of all the ships. Petrichor commanded.

Yes, Petrichor. Navigation systems all unified under your command.

Even your thoughts sound alike! Jimmy chimed in. *Though Jayney's is a little sweeter.*

Try to keep up with me, Jimmy, Petrichor chided.

And try not to pass out. Aldor added.

Is someone with a fist going to punch Shecky Green, or am I going to have to materialize and show him some equine love?

01000011 01101100 01100001 01101001 01110010
01100101 00100001 00100000

Claire! Responded five minds in unison.

I'll be seeing you soon, Aldor. Claire intoned. *Jimmy, mind if I hitch a ride with you?*

Fine, but I'm driving.

Okay everyone, take a deep breath. Petrichor advised.

By the time the interdimensional gateway completely tore through the fabric of space and time directly above Proxima b, all eleven ships were exiting its mirror portal in the Kuiper belt.

CHAPTER THIRTY
(Misbegotten Moon)

Mike Kojak piloted the LTV toward the lip of the crater at its top speed and whooped with joy as the vehicle flew thirty feet through the thin lunar atmosphere before landing with a soft spongey G-out as the vehicle's sensitive suspension fully compressed.

"Never gets old!" Mike shouted into his helmet, followed immediately by, "What the fuck!?"

There, next to the Artemis landing module, was another, much cooler looking, spaceship. A tall figure encased in some form of transparent covering was examining the US craft. The figure had its back to Mike's approach and didn't seem to take any mind of him, even when Mike pulled up before the alien spacecraft, grabbed his laser rifle from the seat beside him and slid out of the LTV.

Mike kept the laser rifle pointed towards the lunar surface as he walked towards the distracted figure, who was now examining the portal to the Landing Module. Mike had heard rumors that the Chinese had established their own settlement on the opposite pole, but this figure was taller than any Asian that ever graced the NBA, even Yao Ming. When the figure finally turned to face Mike, the security officer almost lost his shit. There, staring back at Mike, was a face that would make Godzilla proud. Mike drew his weapon but before he could release the laser, a flash of light came from behind Mike and evaporated the Lizard man. As Mike spun to confront its source, he spotted another Lizard creature. But before Mike could fire he was consumed by the same plasmatic blast from this creature's weapon.

The creature then fired on the Lunar module, which glowed for a moment before it silently disappeared, imploding.

* * * * *

What the fuck was that flash? Dr. McBride thought as he stared through the portal towards the landing crater.

"Holy shit!" He exclaimed as he saw the alien ship lift over the horizon. The coffee cup he dropped never even hit the floor before the plasmatic light that leapt from the front of the ship consumed the entire Artemis settlement. There were not even smoldering ruins left in its wake.

CHAPTER THIRTY-ONE
(Pandora's Box)

"Again. In English this time. What the fuck am I looking at here?"

Buck Sheridan had never felt so overwhelmed in his life. Renee Clarke had just taken him through an hour tour of everything on the microchip Nicolo's tech wizard had slipped her at the end of their meeting. While she seemed completely comfortable with what they were viewing, Buck felt like his mind was about to shear. Spaceships, aliens, plasma weaponry, worm holes, multiverses. The shit he just viewed made the most advanced weaponry the United States military had to offer look like pea shooters. If this was true, why the fuck hadn't ET conquered us a long time ago?

"From the beginning?" Dr. Clarke asked.

"No, some of that shit I'm never going to get. Especially the zero-point energy field magic. I want to see how those cocksuckers used my money to go into business for themselves. Take me back through how Nicolo has reverse engineered his own squadron of saucers."

Just then, Mac threw open the door and raced into Buck's office, completely out of breath.

"Buck," Mac shouted before the General or Lieutenant Colonel had acclimated to his presence. "We've lost Artemis!"

Mac took control of the large holographic screen and replaced the schematics with a grainy video of the moonscape.

"This was the last transmission from the security cameras along the perimeter," Mac said, still breathless.

The three of them watched as an alien space ship rose up over the edge of the Shackleton crater.

"Tell me that's not the Chinese, Mac," Buck whispered. Mac shook his head without taking his eyes off the screen. A moment later, a wide plasma blast from the ship enveloped the camera shot, and a moment after that, blackness.

"Jesus!" Renee whispered, her eyes starting to tear. It was the first time Buck ever saw her lose her shit.

Suddenly, a commotion was heard in the parking lot directly outside Buck's office quarters. Trucks and vehicles arrived and were braking en masse, muffled orders were barked, and soldiers leapt from the vehicles, weapons drawn, and were forming a perimeter around a small group of people who were huddled in its center. There stood five tall beings, all dressed in the same body form unitards. Three of the males looked to be in their forties. Two younger beings with matching shoulder-length, burgundy hair were circling the older ones, looking around like they were searching the perimeter for something.

When the soldiers all raised and pointed their weapons at this group, the burgundy male swept his arm which sent all the perimeter soldiers flying in backward tumbles as if they were caught in a tornado wind shear. Before the soldiers could recover, one of the older men grabbed the younger man's arm with an unnatural speed before the young man could continue.

"They're soldiers," said the older man. "Don't hurt them."

"Eddie's right." One of the other men shouted clearly for the soldiers' benefit. "They're not going to fire unless provoked."

The burgundy female then turned and faced the window where Buck, Renee and Mac now stood mesmerized. She pointed in their direction, locked hands with the others, and they all vanished.

"What the fuck is happening?!" Buck whispered.

"I assume you are General Peter Sheridan," came the emotionless female voice from behind them.

CHAPTER THIRTY-TWO
(Lounge of Lizards)

Alpha Draco gazed out through his ship's portal at the eight other replica warships now all resting in the Aitken Basin most recently occupied by the Chinese-Russian International Lunar Research Center on the dark side of the moon. The only thing remaining after Alpha's attack, was the dust covered Chang'e-4 module rotting off in the distance.

Images appeared on the ship's interior screen showing the last moments of Delta Draco apparently suffering an unprovoked attack at the hands of an aggressive humanoid that approached him in a terrain-based vehicle. A Terran. The remaining members of its company, Beta through Kappa Draco, stood studying the image on the screen.

```
01001001  00011001  01110110  01100101  00100000
01110100  01110010  01100001  01101110  01110011
01101101  01101001  01110100  01110100  01100101
01100100  00100000  01110100  01101000  01100101
00100000  01101001  01101101  01100001  01100111
01100101  01110011  00100000  01110100  01101111
00100000  01110100  01101000  01100101  00100000
01001001  01101110  01110100  01100101  01110010
01100111  01100001  01101100  01100001  01100011
```

01110100 01101001 01100011 00100000 01000110
01100101 01100100 01100101 01110010 01100001
01110100 01101001 01101111 01101110 00101110
00001010 00001010

I've transmitted the images to the Intergalactic Federation. Beta shared.

Some of the Draconians responded with a crocodilian-like hiss.

We shall only communicate in English among ourselves and with the enemy from this point until our mission is completed. Alpha telepathically commanded. *There is only one group among this miserable race of Terrans that poses even the slightest threat. They have shot down our observation ship, and now have terminated Delta. From this moment on, we will communicate in their language, so they fully comprehend who destroyed their leadership and subjugated their survivors. The messages they receive must be as instantly terrifying as the carnage that will be visited upon them. I want them to understand in their last moments, who is killing them.*

The subordinates collectively responded with a series of ecstatic grunts.

A three-dimensional image of the Earth appeared in the center of the chamber. Alpha provided each of his minions their responsibilities over the land masses that could offer any military resistance, reserving what Alpha referred to as Terra Prime, the North American landmass, for the top three Draconian ships, Alpha taking lead. The others were to join them there as soon as they crippled all other potential threats.

We advance on the planet's next rotation when Terra Prime is first touched by solar light. Do not destroy their satellites until they all have gotten a good look at what's coming. Destroy any threat that rises from their land masses and any bases that launch them. No exceptions. Then attack all of their largest collectives, the cities the Terrans so graciously gather in to allow us to vanquish the vermin without destroying the resources of the planet.

Where will we strike? Beta asked.

Alpha allowed the three-dimensional image to rotate slowly until the North American east coast appeared directly before them. Alpha then moved his fingers and a separate 3-d version of Washington DC, the

Capitol building at its center, rose out of the Terra hologram and began to rotate slowly before the group.

This is the Terran's nucleus of power. Their collective leadership, for what it's worth. This dies first.

CHAPTER THIRTY-THREE
(Soul Searching)

"Now I see what all the fuss is about." The husky female voice appeared out of the ether before the glow that followed gave form to the large holographic figure.

Jimmy spun around in his captain's chair and faced the center of his ship's chamber, just as his best friend materialized directly before him.

"This is pretty cool," Claire said as she glanced around, before leaning forward and nuzzling Jimmy's chest, just above his heart.

He reached around her jowls and began to scratch her ears. She closed her eyes and rested her chin on his shoulder.

"Ooohhhh, that's it," she whispered. "Right there."

Jimmy still could not understand how Claire could manifest this holographic version of herself. It wasn't the body she had when she was living. It was slightly more transparent and seemed to change hues depending on her mood. But then again, Jimmy never quite understood all the holographic manifestations, from clothing to furniture to chambers to food, that had become part of his daily life on Proxima b. Jayney just made it all appear whenever any Centaurian needed something.

"Jayney," Jimmy said, "take over and stay in formation. You know how easy it is for me to get lost out here."

Jayney laughed. Jimmy almost fell out of his chair, but Claire managed to steady him. In the twenty-plus years Jimmy had interacted with this ubiquitous entity, he had never heard the AI laugh telepathically or aurally. Even with his A game, Jimmy was lucky if he could get the Centaurians to smile.

The hybrids all carried this human proclivity with them into their new form. There were times when Jimmy wasn't sure whether the boisterous sounds of Lenny's laughing he had heard since their arrival on Centauri was in his head or in his ears. It was usually followed immediately by some murmuring half-hearted chastisement by Petrichor, but those never seemed to curb his friend's propensity to laugh. Everett and Michelle had developed their own version of laughter from their years on Earth, and the more they hung around with Lenny, the better they got at it. But those pure-bloods that hadn't spent much time on Earth never quite acclimated to the experience. Not one guffaw. They didn't know what they were missing.

"Do you still get to laugh in heaven?" Jimmy asked the ecstatic Claire as he sped up his scratching along the length of her ears.

"Oh yeah," Claire responded. "The creator has a hell of a sense of humor. And the Ginger is a pisser. Your poor mother is worried he's going to get himself kicked out because of his antics. He's raised the practical joke to a new art form."

Jimmy tried to view Claire's thoughts from the other side of the veil but couldn't pick anything up.

"Jimmy, what happens in heaven stays in heaven," Claire said as she lifted her head off his shoulder and looked away, avoiding his glance.

"Now that's mule shit if I ever heard it. I shared everything with you when Everett brought me back," Jimmy said defensively.

"You never made it to heaven Jimmy," Claire responded with a hint of condescension. "That wasn't even the lobby. Everett pulled you back before you crossed the turnstile."

"But my brothers were there!" Jimmy exclaimed.

"They were sent to meet you because the creator knew they were the only ones who could send you back across without an argument, although

I was told your brother Eddie offered to give you one final beating if you really needed convincing."

"Shouldn't you be up there racing Sea Biscuit, or watching the Ginger's stand-up routine, or eating unlimited carrots, or something?" Jimmy asked.

"I am doing all those things right now as we speak," Claire shared, without turning back. "There is no linear time on the other side of the veil. Everything is occurring at once."

"What about Mr. Rogers?" Jimmy asked. "I used to always see you together when you first passed, whenever you appeared on this side."

"Mr. Roger's was sent back to make my transition easier. I needed him to show me how to cross back and forth, so I could be with you. They don't give you a user's manual after the crossing. Your loved ones show you the ropes."

"You mean they all made it? There were quite a few I didn't think would pass inspection."

"Everybody makes it Jimmy." Claire said. "Life here, on this energy plane, isn't a test. It's a journey."

Jimmy took Claire's face in his hands and brought it close to his own.

"So, why are you here with me now? To make my transition easier?"

Claire pulled back a moment and studied him carefully. Jimmy thought he saw pain in her eyes but the deeper he looked he realized it was love.

"I'm here to help you on this next part of your journey." She said. "I will share with you what I think you need to know, when you need to know it."

Claire leaned in and kissed him on the forehead. "But don't worry about heaven, Jimmy. You still have your work to do over here."

Petrichor is instructing the team to land on Mars to allow a chance for some final reconnaissance with Stella and the advance party. Jayney shared.

Can't she just upload it from them? Jimmy asked.

"I think she wants to communicate with her daughter in English." Claire whispered. "One last time before the shit hits the fan."

CHAPTER THIRTY-FOUR
(Voilà)

"Pardon my French, but who the fuck are you?" Buck demanded in an attempt to regain control of a world that was rapidly spinning out of his wheelhouse.

"Do you kiss that pretty young lady with that foul mouth of yours?" Lenny asked Buck, while gesturing towards Renee. Without looking, he snatched the cell phone out of Mac's hand before it had moved from his pocket to his ear. Lenny held the phone's speaker to his own ear just as a voice answered, "Security."

"Make sure General Sheridan is not disturbed for the next half-hour," Lenny commanded, then killed the screen with a tap of his finger and tossed Mac his broken phone. "Whoops."

Fergus growled and went to leap out of his basket, but Apollo pointed a finger, froze him in mid-air and gently returned him to the soft pillow he had been resting on.

"What did you do to Fergus?" Buck shouted.

"He's fine, General Sheridan." Stella answered calmly. "And as long as everyone stays calm, you'll have no problems with us."

Eddie leaned his back against the office door.

Whitey peeked out the window at the various groups of soldiers racing around the perimeter, checking inside buildings, and inside and under vehicles while astonished looking officers did their best to maintain their composure after witnessing the impossible.

A fireteam of soldiers headed up the walkway towards Buck's office.

"Incoming!" Whitey called to the others.

Stella waited until the last of the soldiers had entered the building and then waved her hands. Everyone but the crew froze mid movement, including Buck and Renee. Whitey looked back out the window. Even the sentry at the door was frozen at attention, and none of the squads patrolling the streets even noticed.

Stella scanned Buck's mind and then touched his forehead, reanimating him.

"What the hell?!" Buck shouted, holding his forehead like he was trying to keep his brains from leaking out. He stepped back from Stella, just as Apollo appeared behind him and forced him into his chair like the large man was a three-year-old. "Is Nicolo behind this?"

Buck spotted Renee and Mac still standing like mannequins. "If you hurt either one of them -"

"Relax, General." Lenny said, cutting him off. "We come in peace!" He looked at the other hybrids and grinned. "Damn, I've always wanted to say that!" Then he turned back towards the general and in a more serious voice continued. "But sir, we need to talk. Now!"

Stella mentally scanned Renee then touched her forehead. The Lieutenant Colonel looked around like she had just woken from a deep sleep. She appeared a bit unsteady.

"Jesus Christ!" Renee said as she tried to recover her bearings. "Who are you?"

Stella gently ushered Renee around the desk and sat her in one of the chairs. Renee focused on the still frozen Mac. "Is he okay?"

"It's okay, Renee," Buck said, trying to calm her. "These folks are not here to harm us." He looked to Lenny for confirmation. Lenny nodded. Buck then looked up at Apollo, who, scanning his mind, also nodded.

"Not sure what 'drawn and quartered' is General," Apollo added with a smile, "but if I was here to hurt any of you, you would already be dead."

Stella began. "Given what you just learned from those files, General, which you have now involuntarily shared with me, you know the Earth is punching above its weight class." She then animated the holographic screen and rapidly replayed the computer files. She slowed to focus on some of the included reports and videos regarding downed extraterrestrial aircraft. One in particular caught her eye. It was a nighttime thermal image taken by a helicopter gun ship at night. It showed a missile striking a space craft hovering by a grounded chopper. It also picked up the thermal signatures of a group of people huddled by the chopper. Two of those images were obviously children. One was pointing at a heated shell which hung frozen in the air and then exploded, taking out a nearby chopper. The other small figure pointed a hand directly at the filming chopper and, a moment later, that chopper was forced to the ground where the video went dead.

Stella and Apollo locked eyes in recognition.

"We were just kids," Apollo said to Buck, barely restraining his anger.

"The General had nothing to do with that!" Renee said defensively.

"But some general did!" Eddie countered. "Someone gave that order to fire on kids."

Stella studied the female officer. She was clearly the smartest human in the room, at least when it came to the infinite potential of science, but Stella sensed that there was something more than military esprit de corps driving this woman's loyalty to her superior officer. Stella thought she had picked up a reciprocal vibe when she was scanning Buck.

"What about the other night?" Whitey demanded. "Someone was firing plasma weapons at one of our ships."

Buck shook his head as he realized the connection. "That wasn't us either. Mr. Nicolo is a private contractor who has been running off-book operations. He is non-military and apparently answers to no one. My people don't even have an Earth-fired weapon capable of reaching a craft until it is well within our atmosphere."

Apollo rifled Buck's thoughts concerning the incident and, satisfied that the general was telling the truth, said. "I'll be sure to give my regards to Mr. Nicolo when this is over."

I'm going to kill that bastard. Apollo shared with the others.

Not if I get to him first, Whitey responded, recalling how close it had come to taking out Lucian and Stella.

"Look," Buck interrupted. "I don't know who you are, or where you're from, but trust me, after reviewing those files and seeing some of what you can do, speaking for the Space Force, we have no beef with you or your people."

"Well," Lenny responded, "we appreciate that clarification. And knowing first-hand how your government works, I accept your sincerity. But it's not my friends you've got to worry about." Lenny continued as he replayed the grainy video clip that Mac had cued up for Buck and Renee. Lenny froze it on a split screen just as the Draconian ship lit up the Artemis Moon Base. Then Lenny scanned back through the computer file until he located a document referencing Nicolo company's recent destruction of a Draconian space craft just above the satellite belt using a plasma cannon and left it opened in a separate screen. Renee read it.

"Shit, shit, shit!" she cried. "Was that one of the Lizards ships?"

"Bingo!" Eddie responded. "And now it looks like they're coming for you."

"Unless we can stop them." Stella added.

"How much time do we have?" Buck asked. "We need to mobilize. Jets in the air."

"Jets are just knives at a gun fight." Lenny said. "Won't stand a chance against that ship," he added, and then pointed towards the sky. "And trust me, as tough as they may be, no one up there comes this far to a fight alone."

"If they are on the moon, given how fast our own ship travels," Whitey offered, "they are already within striking distance. You are now operating on their schedule."

"I'll transport back to Casa Claire and take our ship up." Apollo offered. "Run interference. If it is only one, I can hold them off a bit. Maybe take it out."

"I'm going with you." Whitey added.

"Wait!" Stella commanded. She closed her eyes as she accepted the incoming message from her mother. The numbers never came. This was in English.

Stella, the Draconians intend to take Terran. Petrichor shared her memory of their hearing before the Intergalactic Federation. *We are coming to stop them.*

Stella responded by sharing her memory of the Artemis moon video with Petrichor. *Hurry, they are already here.*

Leave Terran now! Petrichor commanded.

Stella stared at Buck and Renee and thought about the rest of the human Moran crew waiting back at Casa Claire.

Stella replayed Petrichor her childhood memory from their last night on Earth, of hugging Apollo and refusing to leave Terran without everyone she loved.

Both Centaurian minds went silent for a moment.

Do whatever it takes to protect the family until our arrival. Petrichor finally responded. The image of the child Stella hugging Petrichor's legs that same night flashed, and then her mother's voice concluded. *I love you.*

Stella turned to Buck. "You need to shut down Mr. Nicolo!"

CHAPTER THIRTY-FIVE
(*Mare Imbrium*)

Bobbi sat on the chaise lounge between her two similarly reclined acolytes, Scarlett, and Savanna. Helen exited the second floor of Casa Claire with a full tray of drinks onto the back deck and served the three women equal-stemmed measures of a reserved Cabernet Sauvignon. She then retreated with her tray to the opposite end of the deck where she placed two frosted rock glasses, filled with Metaxa Ouzo, neat, on the small table between herself and Lucian. She placed the bottle down on the center of the table for good measure.

"*Yassou!*" Helen shouted, taking a long pull from her glass, and sighing in approval. "That will put hair on your chest!"

Lucian watched his favorite Moran Aunty finish her first sip before trying his own.

"Fuck," he said. "That's got a kick to it."

"I can water it down for you, if it's too strong?" Helen said with a daring smile that highlighted her challenging his machismo.

Lucian smiled right back at her and then tossed down the remainder of his glass.

"*Yamas!*" he shouted as he slammed the empty glass back on the table.

"Look at that! You have been paying attention. We'll make a Spartan out of you yet!" Helen said approvingly.

"Speaking of Spartans," Lucian replied as he caught his breath. "How do you think the others are doing at Buckley AFB?"

"Hold on a second," Helen said, "Bobbi, have you gotten anything from the hybrids?"

Bobbi closed her eyes and opened her thoughts. After a few moments she reopened her eyes and called back, "Nothing, sweetie. No news is good news."

"Good news?!", called Eileen Cotto's voice from inside Casa Claire. "Somebody please give me good news to drink to!"

"Out here on the deck, Auntie Bubbles," Scarlett called out.

"I told you not to call me Bubbles, Scary!" Eileen countered as she blew through the doorway and out onto the deck carrying a large jar of poteen. She made her rounds to all the seated family exchanging air kisses with the speed and intensity of a whirling dervish before throwing herself into the last available seat on the deck. She unscrewed the top off the jar and took a long pull of the clear liquid nitroglycerin.

"Ahhh," Eileen sighed then smacked her lips. "That's pure gold."

"Tough day, Auntie Bubbles?" Savanna cackled.

"Poor young bull got caught in some barbwire up in Ft. Collins," Eileen responded, shooting Savanna the stink eye. "Decided to bull his way out of it. What is it with the males of every species?!" She took another pull from the jar. "Had a hell of a time stitching those legs back together. . . which is what I'm going to do to the lips of the next young lady who calls me Bubbles!"

"Have you eaten?" Helen asked. "Janice dropped off a wonderful lasagna on their way out. Said Brian made it for us before they left. It's in the fridge."

"Sounds heavenly," Eileen whispered. She took another long pull from the jar. "It will help soak up some of this Celtic white lightning before I stumble back across the way."

"Speaking of Celts, is Brian taking Janice on another trip back to Boston?" Scarlett asked.

"This time was Janice's call." Bobbi responded. "Going to visit her family in Toronto. They'll be back in September before you two head off to Europe."

"They're good people." Scarlett said. "Although Brian's accent is even worse than Jimmy's."

"Took me a while to understand Jimmy too, when we first met him." Savanna laughed.

"That's because the Southies and Bronx Irish are kissing cousins," Bobbi explained. "Two different branches off the same Celtic tree. Both can torture a vowel."

"I miss Jimmy and Gina." Scarlett said. "And Claire."

"He was funny, even silly at times. But I always felt safe in his presence." Savanna added. "And both Gina and Claire were bad asses."

"Think we'll ever see them again, Bobbi?" Scarlett asked.

Bobbi closed her eyes for a moment and put the question out to the Universe.

"Spirit says 'yes'!" She said with a smile, holding up her drink towards the heavens. The three witches clinked their wine glasses together and sipped. The two sisters then leaned over and gave Bobbi a hug.

On the opposite side of the deck, Helen refilled the two glasses on her table, handed one to Lucian and then stood and held hers up towards the full August supermoon illuminating the night. "*Μια πρόποση για τον άνθρωπο στο φεγγάρι!* Which to those less cultured among the Western World means – *to the Man in the Moon!*"

Everyone repeated the English translation in unison and then sipped from their glasses.

When Helen looked back at Lucian, she saw that he was staring over at Savanna. He blushed when he glanced back at Helen and realized she had caught him.

"Doesn't take a psychic to read those signals." Helen whispered. "Why don't you just ask her out?"

Lucian waved her off. "Nah," he whispered back. "She'll always think of me as a little brother."

She took another sip from her drink. "After the age of thirty, age differences don't matter."

Helen gave him the once over and shook her head. "And there ain't nothin' little about you."

"Actually," Bobbi called to her lover. "The Moon is feminine. A goddess! The Egyptians called her Isis."

"We called her Selene." Helen confirmed. "The man is actually that ugly dark circle where all the meteors like to strike. Go figure."

Lucian laughed.

"I understand how to incorporate the moon into our practices, but why is it so important to witches?" Savanna asked.

"Well," Bobbi began, savoring her times to mentor these two young women. "The obvious answer is that humans for centuries have associated the moon goddess with fertility. They have witnessed its impact on the cycles of nature, the seasons, and the tides. It is constantly transforming. As it waxes, witches use its energy to manifest their desires, and when it wanes, we release what is no longer useful to make room for something new in our lives. I've shown you both how to draw and direct moon energy in your crystals.

"I never go anywhere without my moonstone pendant." Scarlett confirmed, lifting the silver chain around her neck to display the translucent blue stone on its end. "My studios are filled with labradorite, opal and blue topaz. I love to paint during the full moon cycle."

"I channel my moon energy into how I handle our investment portfolio." Savanna added. "You can track my purchases and sales activities to the waxing and waning of the moon goddess. Hasn't failed me yet."

"Well," Bobbi whispered, gazing up towards the heavens. "I wonder what this Sturgeon Moon has in store for us?" She sat up in the chaise lounge and tried to focus her eyes as she detected a string of tiny dark specs floating like a snake across the face of the moon.

Bobbi, Stella's telepathic voice responded out of the ether. *Gather everyone and meet Whitey over at Everett and Michelle's-I mean Eileen's house. Back by the craft. And make sure Lucian is with you.*

CHAPTER THIRTY-SIX
(The Cub)

"Stella said she wants you to fly it." Whitey pointed to Lucian as they both stood outside Stella's spacecraft. "I'm just coming along for the ride to make sure you find your way to Buckley without any issues."

"Atta boy, Loosh!" Savanna shouted a bit more exuberantly than expected.

The others couldn't tell whether Lucian's Cheshire Cat grin was from the promotion to fly boy or the cat call.

Scarlett glanced at her younger sister and winked. Then she went over and gave Lucian a hug. "We'll see you when you get back, Loosh."

"But you're all to come with us," Whitey said. "Stella's orders."

"I can't go looking like this!" Savanna said.

"You look beautiful!" Lucian blurted. Then he looked around at the others sheepishly. "I mean you look just fine."

"Finally," Scarlett whispered. "We'll get to see the stars up close."

"But I don't do spontaneous!" Savanna whined.

"First time for everything," Whitey said. "Don't worry, you won't be alone."

"Better than a broomstick," Bobbi added. "Come on, honey," she said taking Helen's hand. "Let's do this."

"Are you kidding?!" Helen said. "I've been dying to take this ride since Jimmy and the others went to war with the psycho twins. I'm in!"

"Me too," Eileen chirped, then ran toward her house. "But first I need to pee!"

* * * * *

Whitey watched proudly as his protégé worked the holographic controls like he was born with them attached. They had risen just above the satellite belt to avoid any unwanted attention. Whitey had Jayney convert into translucent mode, so everyone sat in their holographic chairs while being carried through space in this invisible vehicle. The only other thing visible in their midst was the glowing holographic control panel where Lucian stood confidently piloting the craft.

"I wish I had this when I was in the Navy." Lucian said. "Makes what we have look like paper airplanes."

"This feels like a Universal Studios ride!" Eileen cooed.

"Stella was right," Whitey commented. "You're a natural. It took me years on Proxima b to reach your level of proficiency."

"Can I give it a try?" Savanna called from her seat a few feet from Lucian.

"What happened to you not doing 'spontaneity'?" Scarlett asked. "I do want to arrive in one piece."

"I'm not sure that's a smart move." Whitey warned Lucian. "Stella said you fly it. Her ship. She's calling the shots."

"I promise I won't let Savvy dent Stella's car," Lucian said. He gestured for Savanna to come stand between him and the control panel. She glanced at Scarlett and stuck her tongue out, then stepped up to the plate.

"Slip your hands on top of mine," Lucian whispered as he reached his arms around from behind her and flexed his fingers in the templates, "and then just follow the movement of my fingers with your own."

Savanna smiled and did as instructed. Lucian then took the ship through some soft maneuvers, as her smaller and slender fingers shadowed his own. After a few minutes her fingers began to anticipate the movements of Lucian's fingers, and they moved in synchronicity. The others all breathlessly cooed in excitement with the way the two danced this ship through space, while Whitey looked on worriedly feeling every bit vulnerable because he knew it was his nuts on the line.

Suddenly, Lucian spotted a Tesla string of satellites approaching the ship over the horizon.

"Watch this," he whispered from slightly behind Savanna's ear. She shuddered imperceptibly at the feeling of his warm and pleasant breath on the back of her neck.

"Get a room!" Scarlett cat-called, while she and Eileen laughed.

Lucian then effortlessly wove the ship through the line of satellites like a gold medal skier in the slalom event.

The dilation of Savanna's pupils, racing heart and her bated breath were the only things the young woman could not mask as she tried to take in everything she was experiencing. She slid her fingers between Lucian's and gripped them tightly during his agile execution of the maneuver.

The whole time Whitey's eyes anxiously followed the trajectory of each of the satellites as Lucian deftly avoided the objects like Cayetano Ordóñez dodged the horns in his prime.

"You haven't told us why we're going to Buckley," Helen called out, trying to distract Whitey from his misery.

"Holy shit!" Bobbi shrieked after rifling through Whitey's thoughts.

"Damnit." Whitey shouted, turning away from Lucian. "I forgot you could do that."

"Spill," Helen demanded.

"Shit is hitting the fan and Stella wants us all where she can protect us!" Bobbi delivered.

"Don't be telling anyone you got that from me." Whitey begged.

Just as Lucian was approaching the final two satellites, Jayney blasted "Incoming," just a moment before the caboose in the series of large metallic rectangles vaporized. Lucian reflexively pressed hard with his right pinky while pressing equally hard with his left palm on the templates, sending the ship hurtling downward at a hard right angle in a way a jet could never do, just as the satellites before and behind him disappeared.

The rest of the passengers collectively closed their eyes, shrieked, and prepared themselves for a whiplash and explosion that never came. They didn't even feel the g-force from the tortuous shifts the ship was executing and in a moment found themselves a thousand miles away. Lucian was amazed that he never even felt his body sway throughout the maneuver. He didn't move at all until he and Savanna were physically shoved out of the way by Whitey as the older man assumed the controls. Jayney caught them both in their own chairs, and Scarlett immediately reached over and grabbed her sister's hand.

Jayney, what the fuck was that? Whitey demanded as he turned the ship sharply towards the Kármán line above Earth. *Did that come from below?*

No. It came from just outside the moon's orbit.

Fuck. Put the word out to the rest of the crew, we're coming in hot. And we may not be alone. So, if the shooting starts, I don't want to be dodging any friendly fire from the military.

"What the fuck is happening?" Eileen whispered nervously to Bobbi and Helen.

"Damned if I know," responded Helen.

"Shit, shit, shit!" Bobbi whispered back through clenched teeth, with her eyes still closed. "Spirit says, whatever we do, don't look up or down, and hang on!"

Plasma shields up, Jayney, Whitey instructed, *this is going to be a bumpy ride.*

CHAPTER THIRTY-SEVEN
(Strangest Bedfellows)

"General Dowling at Luke AFB." Mac called out as he clicked off his cell. "They've picked up an anomaly coming this way over Canada, and she scrambled the F35s at Luke AFB."

Better get down here quick, Whitey. Apollo shared.

Doing my best, Apollo.

"Scramble the F16s for cover!" Buck commanded. "Surround their craft as it hits airspace and walk them through the door."

"Not enough time to intercept them." Renee counseled.

"I better warn Dowling." Buck said.

"What, that ET is coming in for a landing?" Renee asked. "She'll think you are nuts."

"What's the call, Buck?" Mac asked. Buck could see that his aid was still feeling the stress from his suspended animation.

"We can't let them fire on my family," Stella warned him.

"Send the F16s up," Buck ordered Mac. "At least it will give Whitey a crowded sky to hide in. And the F35s won't fire on their own."

Whitey don't fire on the jets. Eddie shared. *Unless you have no choice.*

I'm more worried about what's coming behind me. Whitey responded.

* * * * *

"Got company." Jayney announced aurally. "Seven Hundred Earth-miles ahead and closing fast."

"How far to Buckley, Jayney?" Whitey called out.

"Two hundred," Lucian answered, now up on his feet and standing beside his mentor.

"Can I get a visual, Jayney?" Lucian asked. The screen split and five F35s appeared in clear blue sky rapidly approaching in a wedge formation.

"Take us down," Lucian shouted.

Whitey looked at him like he was crazy. "It's tough enough handling this in open space."

"If we don't get low they're going to fire on us," Lucian counseled. "They have ASRAAMs – fucking infrared missiles – the only way we can keep them from unloading on us is if we skim the treetops and swing into Colorado from the northeast. Otherwise, we have to deal with the Rockies."

Whitey stared at Lucian for a second, uncertain.

Incoming. Jayney telepathically shared. A moment later, a plasma bolt flew past the ship, just missing it.

"Shit!" Whitey shouted. "They're firing on us."

"Motherfuckers!" Helen shouted.

"That's not the F35s," Lucian said. "But I've seen that before."

Jayney offered. "37° 16' 36.03" N 115° 47' 56.17" W"."

"Groom Lake." Lucian interpreted. "We need to get low, now."

The ship dipped under Jayney's control just as another plasma bolt flew above it.

Whitey stepped away from the controls. "Take us in," he told Lucian. "But don't dent the car."

Someone's shooting at us from below. Whitey broadcasted to the others at Buckley. *Better shut it down or we're toast.*

CHAPTER THIRTY-EIGHT
(The Piper Arrives)

The Draconians brought their entire squad to a standstill, hovering silently and completely still in a line formation a few hundred feet above the Atlantic Ocean, directly over the Atlantic Ridge. The sun was just crossing the sky above them. Alpha, Beta and Gamma were pointed west. They brought the East Coast of the North American land mass onto their holographic ship screens, and focused their visuals on the area that appeared on Earth's navigation system as 38° 54' 25.892" N 77° 2' 12.735" W.

Alpha understood from centuries of reconnaissance the full reach and timing of this crude world's weaponry. He realized that his ships had alerted all the Terran's satellite warning systems, and that the citizens of the entire world were now scrambling to mobilize against a threat they were told did not exist, that they never fully believed could present itself, and were now ill prepared to defend against. The truth was that the Draconians' technology could have destroyed the planet from space. But there's no glory in that.

Alpha was satisfied that this full-on assault would completely terrorize the Terrans, and that through surgical strikes, he could minimize the damage to the precious resources the Draconians desired to exploit, while salvaging a sufficient pool of slaves from the populace. What were the Centaurians thinking when they created humankind?

They have launched their land-based weapons. Beta confirmed.

Wait until they have left their coastline and then destroy them all. They are all fuel based. There's plenty of time. Alpha ordered.

Their aircraft are now also en route. Gamma shared.

Do not let one of them reach the water. Alpha commanded, satisfied that each member of his team was acclimating to his order to communicate in the language of the soon-to-be-vanquished. It would be good practice for when they approached the survivors once the assault was complete and useful for controlling them afterwards.

And those ships already on and beneath the water? Beta asked.

Destroy them all, now! Alpha ordered.

The eight other Draconian ships around Alpha's all began to move out of formation in different directions as they engaged to carry out his orders.

Alpha focused back on his intended landmass on his screen. If his thickly scaled facial muscles would have allowed for it, he would have smiled.

CHAPTER THIRTY-NINE
(The Sun Also Rises)

Father Jack Lawlor closed the last quarter mile of his three-mile work-out with a sprint. His heaving lungs burned just enough to show him this daily attempt to stave off death was worth it. The priest continued to jog slowly back towards the entrance bridge to Teddy Roosevelt Island and back to where his red Tesla roadster sat waiting. At the middle of the entrance bridge, Jack leaned on the railing and stretched his legs and back for a few minutes. The glow of the sun was just beginning to peak over the eastern horizon as he completed his first lunge.

"Thank you, Lord, for yet another glorious day," he whispered, as he watched a young woman power her scull out from beneath the bridge eastward towards the Potomac proper. She reminded Jack of a water strider skimming along the top of the tiny tributary. He wondered what she was listening to on her ear pods.

Jack liked to get his daily constitutional in early each morning, so that there was plenty of time to shower, shave, eat and glance through the Washington Examiner before administering his first mass of the week day. During the summer months, Jack liked to complete his work out during the blue hour, just before dawn, before the Washington humidity began to rise with the sun. Those early starts also ensured that Jack had the tiny public island to himself. Privacy was a valuable commodity within the beltway.

Over this past week, Jack switched up his post work-out routine to grab a coffee and bagel to go from Bourbon Coffee on his way back to the rectory. He couldn't wait for Adrienne Stucki to return from her summer holiday, with her family in Idaho. He missed her home-cooked meals. Jack missed her fussing over him. He looked forward to exploring Rome with her in the fall.

Jack extended his calf stretch a little longer to work out a kink in his right leg that had been annoying him. He grasped the rail for balance to allow for a deeper stretch. As his eyes dipped to the level of the top rail, he watched as the thin uniform glow of the rim of dawn's sunlight seemed to gather and rise in a concentrated ball towards the center of the horizon, like a mini version of the sun that didn't share its light with the rest of the sky.

The next moment, this light coalesced into a beam that rushed forward from the Atlantic and consumed everything to Jack's right. There was no sound or heat, no blast impact, but the light was so bright Jack was forced to turn away towards the park as the light seemed to spread like a piss puddle over the DC land mass. It was over in a second. When Jack was finally able to look back, everything as far as the eye could see was gone and a massive, smooth, cauterized crater now rested where his nation's capital once sat. It looked like a large black glass bowl.

As the real sun now began to rise over the horizon Jack could make out a large dark object silently approaching from the east, flying just a few thousand feet over the Atlantic. A moment later, the deathlike quiet was broken by the sonic boom of a squadron of jets flying over head towards this object. That sound disappeared when a thinner beam flew from the front of the approaching craft and a ball of light consumed the entire formation of jets. They all vanished without any flame, sound, or wreckage. They were erased.

The absolute silence that followed was terrifying.

"Mother of God!" Jack gasped as he dropped to both knees and began to pray.

CHAPTER FORTY
(Out Of The Pan)

Lucian took Stella's craft to 100 feet just as the Northern Colorado night sky became filled with a swarm of F16s and F35s above him. At first it looked like the more numerous older jets were running interference against the faster and more powerful stealth fighters. But no sooner had he passed beneath their cloud of maneuvering lights than all the jets appeared to drop off pursuit and head due east toward the approaching dawn. Lucian didn't give them any more thought once he brought the craft over highway I-25 and followed it south until he reached Aurora and Buckley AFB in what seemed like moments. The few trucks he passed at that hour would have at best felt him passing overhead, but he would have been gone before they could have looked up to see him. Once clearing the base's security perimeter, Lucian lowered the ship in a soft vertical landing onto the first open tarmac he came to, the way he had dropped the F35Bs onto moving ocean carriers so many times during his career with the Navy.

"Stay here," Whitey ordered, once the vehicle was down. "If I'm not back in 5 minutes, take off fast, straight up, and stay out of harm's way until Stella reaches out to you. Jayney, do not open that portal for any human."

Whitey dematerialized and a moment later, Bobbi fainted.

* * * * *

As Whitey materialized on the tarmac, he was surrounded by an enclosure of dozens of soldiers on foot and in armed vehicles, with weapons drawn.

"Get on the ground, you alien piece of shit!" Ordered a surprisingly young staff sergeant from his position standing on the back of a Willy CJ behind a thirty-caliber pedestal machine gun.

Before Whitey could react, another jeep raced down the tarmac in his direction, breaking into the line of fire between the sergeant and Whitey.

"Stand down, Sergeant!" shouted Renee Clarke as she rose above the windshield so the others could see her Oak Leaves. She slowly turned to address the others, "and the same goes for the rest of you."

"But he could be one of the scumbags who took out DC!" The obviously agitated sergeant remonstrated, keeping his hands tightly on the safe end of his weapon, finger on the trigger.

"I ordered you to stand down, Sergeant." Renee repeated. She looked at Whitey. "Where are the others?"

He hooked his thumb over his shoulder towards the craft.

"Sergeant." Renee barked, looking back over the antsy soldiers on the perimeter. "No one gets within 10 yards of that craft. No one."

She turned back to Whitey. "Get in."

Whitey scanned her mind as he materialized beside her in the shotgun seat.

"Fuck me, the Lizards have landed," he shouted, as the two raced back towards the general's office on the far side of the compound.

* * * * *

"Sweetie, are you all right?" Helen asked. She was alternating between stroking Bobbi's right hand and cheek while her mate slowly recovered consciousness in the chair Jayney had expanded to a recliner.

Eileen held Bobbi's left wrist for a minute while studying her watch before declaring, "Okay, her pulse is back below 70, and she's coming to."

"This is really bad," Bobbi mumbled as her eyes opened.

"What's bad, honey?" Helen asked, anxiously.

"Everything that's about to happen." Bobbi whispered, tears welling up in both eyes.

The two sisters joined hands and began to repeat softly, "Great Goddess of day and night, protect us all with all of your might."

CHAPTER FORTY-ONE
(The Light Brigade)

"I have Major-General Hughes, at Vandenberg, on the satellite phone, sir." Mac called out. "The Joint Chiefs are gone, everyone's gone. DC's a crater. We're on our own!"

"Was it a nuke?" Buck demanded. "Was it China?"

"No, sir," Mac responded. "They've got their own problems. Beijing is toast."

"Not the Russians?" Buck asked, incredulously.

"Deep in the same shit, sir," Mac responded.

Buck struggled to get his head around what he was hearing. "What are we facing?"

"Reports of only three crafts hovering just off the east coast, sir," Mac replied.

"We can't stop three crafts?" Buck shouted, shaking his head.

"It's worse than that, Buck. NORAD is gone. Everything that they threw at them. Vaporized."

Mac gazed suspiciously at Stella and the crew as he delivered this last line.

"How dare you!" Apollo shouted, scanning Mac's mind. A moment later, he was standing beneath a flailing Mac, holding him airborne by his shirt collar. "We are risking everything to stop them."

Buck started to reach for something in his desk drawer, but Eddie materialized beside him holding the Desert Eagle Buck had hoped to recover. Eddie dissembled the weapon in a blur and tossed its parts across the room. Lenny placed his hand firmly on Buck's shoulder to prevent it from getting further out of hand.

"That's not us, General!" Stella shouted angrily as she plucked the accusatory thoughts from Buck's mind. She turned to her brother. *Apollo, put him down.*

Apollo hurled Mac across the room and onto the couch.

"We should leave them like crickets to the Lizards." Apollo seethed.

At that moment, Renee came through the door with Whitey.

"It's bad out there. We need to get control of this."

"Fucking shitstorm," Whitey added. "Natives are restless."

Buck looked up at Lenny, who scanned his mind and then reluctantly removed his hand, before the general stood and faced Stella.

"Mac!" Buck shouted. "Get out there and get those soldiers in line."

Mac got to his feet and stormed out the door, never taking his eyes off Apollo.

"You better have something huge in your ET bags of tricks young lady," Buck said to Stella with a frightening calm in his voice. "Because this country is not going down to anyone. Not today. Not on my watch."

Stella closed her eyes and reached out telepathically. *Mother?*

01000101011110000110000101100011011101000010000
00110110001101111011000110110000101110100011010
0101101111011011100011111110010000

Exact location? Petrichor demanded.

Stella opened her eyes and uploaded every memory from the moment she landed at Buckley, plus what she had gleaned from her latest scans of her military hosts. She walked over to the window and gazed around the base just as dawn was approaching its eastern perimeter.

A moment later, Michelle materialized beside Stella.

"Jesus!" Renee shouted, trying to maintain her composure. "A little heads-up today would go a long way."

Michelle gave Renee the once over. "I like her. Ballsy."

She looked around and greeted the others telepathically. *We okay here?*

They all responded affirmatively, in kind.

"Time to go, momma's waiting for us." Michelle said audibly.

"Has she been asking for me?" Lenny chimed in. Michelle smiled and winked. "Always."

"Clear the air space over head, General." Stella said. "We'll be back with reinforcements."

"The cavalry has arrived." Lenny added, just as their entire crew disappeared into the ether.

CHAPTER FORTY-TWO
(Going Live)

We don't have time for any further training on the battle cruisers for those that just joined us, so Jayney has downloaded the best of our collective knowledge to you all and you will just have to rely on your prior flight experience on your other ships. Petrichor shared. *From this point on, everyone remains open to telepathic communication, no exceptions.*

Each of the Earthbound team members that had arrived on Petrichor's vessel were immediately transported to their respective ships. They, along with the others, now telepathically shared their acknowledgement of Petrichor's communication. Their collective eleven ships were now all hovering just outside the Earth's ionosphere about four hundred miles above the planet, where the neutral atmospheric gases are in constant circulation with the ionic plasma of space, making it harder for any known Earthbound systems to get a clear read on them.

Stella and Apollo watch out for one another until this shit is over, Gina added.

Yes mom, both shared simultaneously.

Apollo, Petrichor continued. *Are we clear to descend?*

I scanned General Sheridan and Lieutenant-Colonel Clarke just before we left, Apollo responded. *He cleared us to enter their airspace. Not sure he could stop us now if he wanted to.*

While I don't necessarily have one-hundred percent confidence in that big bastard Buck, Whitey chimed in, *Clarke stepped up for me down there. She confirmed our clearance, so I trust her.*

Buck's okay, Lenny added. *Prick's in a difficult situation. Duty, honor and all that bullshit. We're the unknown feces in the middle of a shit storm.*

I'm sending Claire down to keep an eye on the rest of the crew, just in case. Jimmy shared.

No, Jimmy, Claire responded. *I'm staying with you.*

I'll be fine, Jimmy shared. *Your girls down there need you more than I do.*

They're with Lucian and the others on Stella's ship, westernmost tarmac, Whitey shared. *Can't leave them down there alone.*

I've got 'em. Claire responded, then added. *You never make it easy for me, Jimmy. See you on the other side.*

So, where are the Lizards? Petrichor asked.

Three ships are now slowly moving west across the landmass evaporating everything the United States military is throwing at them. Their northernmost ship destroyed the country's nuclear arsenal before it could be launched. Gone. Then it destroyed New York. Michelle responded.

Their six other ships are having a much easier time against the other military powers around the rest of the planet, including the oceans. Everett added. *I don't get it. With their weapons, the Draconians could have taken care of it all from lower space without ever risking a lucky shot by the Terrans.*

It's like they are playing with their food. Gina shared.

They need to terrorize the conquered. Eddie added. *Fear alone assures continued dominance over the subjugated.*

That ends now. Once we hit the atmosphere, Petrichor continued, *me, Jimmy, Gina, Everett, and Michelle, will head east —*

All due respect, P, Lenny cut her off. *I'm sticking with you.*

Fine. The six of us will press our numerical advantage against the three Lizards over this landmass. Come in high from space and sweep in behind them with the sun at our backs. They won't expect any threat to arise from their ashes.

Aldor, drop in over this central area and protect our Earthbound family. Petrichor continued. *If we fail, you snatch them up and take them to Proxima b.*

Just what Centaurians need. Aldor responded. *More Terrans.*

We won't fail, Whitey chimed in. *Hybrid vigor, Aldor!*

The rest of you head towards the western end of the continent and don't let any of the other Draconian ships that may arrive get close enough to do any further damage. Petrichor continued. *No negotiations. Fire first. Them, or us.*

Watch out for their continuous plasma beams. Stella warned. *They've taken out entire cities from thousands of Earth-miles away.*

Sounds like some form of cosmic napalm. Lenny interpreted. *Eradicates anything it touches and sticks to its target like glue.*

Stay as physically far apart as possible and keep moving – no hovering, Eddie warned. *Their aim doesn't have to be perfect when they are firing a plasma shotgun.*

Hear that Lenny? Jimmy asked. *Don't stay too close to Petrichor.*

Just worry about your own ass, Jimmy, Lenny responded. *Let me worry about P's ass.*

I'm not going to tell you again, Lenny, Petrichor warned.

Sorry dear, Lenny responded. *But you do have a nice ass. And I do worry -*

Right! Petrichor cut him off. *Time we terminated some reptiles.*

No close formations. Michelle reminded everyone. *But stay in touch.*

Hooah, Eddie shared. *Rangers, lead the way!*

CHAPTER FORTY-THREE
(Friendly Fire)

"Major Hughes has launched the RES from Vandenberg," Mac shouted, flipping the satellite phone to Buck.

"RES?" Buck asked Renee, with his hand over the receiver.

"Reverse Engineered Spacecraft."

"Terry," Buck barked into the satphone. "What the fuck are you doing and on whose orders are you doing it?"

"All due respect, General," Major Terry Hughes replied. "I'm doing what I think is best for what's left of this country. I'm not taking orders."

"Those are my Space Force pilots!" Buck shouted back.

"No sir." Major Hughes responded. "They are all ex-military. Independent contractors."

"Nicolo?" Buck demanded.

"Yes sir." Major Hughes responded. "Only ones trained to fly RES."

"I have special assets in the air, Major." Buck barked.

"Well, they better stay clear of the West Coast, that's my Maginot Line." Major Hughes responded and hung up.

"I don't suppose you have the wonder-twins number?" Buck asked Renee.

* * * * *

"We have company," Jayney informed Lucian, and a holographic screen appeared showing a female officer arriving in a jeep just outside Stella's craft. "She's unarmed."

Bobbi closed her eyes and focused her thoughts. "Spirit says she's okay."

Dr. Clarke turned to the Master Sergeant and instructed him to have the soldiers hold their positions. Then she knocked on the skin of the space ship.

"We need to talk." Renee shouted in a firm but respectful voice.

"Jayney, can you bring her in?" Lucian asked.

A moment later, Renee Clarke felt a tingling sensation before finally succumbing to the darkness. Lucian and the others watched the screen as the officer dematerialized, a look of shock on her face.

"Holy shit!" Eileen shouted. "Is that what we looked like coming in?"

A slight glow in the center of their chamber soon developed into Dr. Clarke, who Jayney wrapped in a transparent energy cocoon to keep her unconscious body upright.

Eileen reached in and placed two fingers on the carotid artery of Renee's neck.

"She's okay," Eileen confirmed. "Give her a moment."

"What the fuck?" Renee mumbled a few seconds before her eyes slid open. She gazed from face to face at the six humans staring back at her.

"Spirit says she's fine," Bobbi added.

"Shall I release her?" Jayney asked, causing Renee to suddenly shake her head as she fought to regain full consciousness.

Lucian nodded.

"Who's in charge here?" Renee finally said as she recovered her voice.

"Nobody." Helen responded, then gestured to Lucian. "But he flies the ship."

"Can you get a message to the others?" Renee asked.

"Bobbi?" Scarlett asked.

"Not sure," Bobbi said, "but I can try."

"I am in contact with each ship." Jayney interjected. "I am each ship."

"Then you must warn them that there are now a dozen U.S. saucers, we call them RES, along our west coast," Renee pleaded. "And they are not friendly."

* * * * *

Aldor listened simultaneously with the other members of the Centauri squad as Jayney repeated Renee's message about the saucers to all the ships.

You got that Stella and Apollo? Gina asked.

Got it mom. Apollo replied.

Jayney has their positions, and we soon will have visuals. Stella chimed in.

These are not friendly. Jayney repeated.

Fuck 'em then. Eddie replied.

The RES has got bigger problems than you. Jayney interjected. *Those other Draconian ships have finished their chores around the rest of the planet and are cruising towards the North American land mass.*

Classic pincer movement. Eddie shared.

Space hop over the Lizards. Jimmy instructed. *Come in behind them and follow them into the RES line and then give those Lizards a taste of their own medicine.*

Aldor, Petrichor shared. *How goes our humans?*

Just entered Terran's atmosphere, Aldor responded. *It's actually a pretty planet when you see it in the right light.*

Wait! Aldor added. *What's that?*

CHAPTER FORTY-FOUR
(Casualties of War)

Aldor is gone, Jayney reported. Jimmy thought he could discern regret from the AI.

I tried to avoid the energy bolts —to get clear-but there were too many too quickly. Jayney reported. *Aldor tried to steer the ship in the opposite direction, and he flew right into the path of the next bolt.*

What about the plasma shield? Petrichor asked.

It took the first two hits. Jayney responded. *The third one vaporized him.*

Didn't you battle test these things? Eddie interrupted.

Centauri has never been at war, Petrichor responded.

It's not your fault, Lenny consoled her.

Where was the Lizard? Apollo demanded.

It wasn't a Lizard. Jayney replied. *It came from Earth.*

Nicolo! Stella blurted.

Stay focused folks, Whitey counseled. *The Lizards are going to make Nicolo look like an amateur.*

Jayney, Jimmy shared. *Get word to Lucian that Nicolo is in play. He is not to go airborne in Stella's ship.*

Jimmy was surprised at how much pain he was feeling. Aldor was annoying as fuck, but Jimmy respected his intelligence and skills in a courtroom. He could also take a punch, and stepped up to come with them to Earth when he could have sat on the side-lines until the smoke cleared. And that mattered.

"See you on the other side, Aldor." Jimmy whispered to himself. "Claire, take him home."

Don't mention Aldor to the others, Jayney, Michelle added, picking up on Jimmy's feelings. *Don't want to frighten them any more than they are now. We need to keep their hope alive.*

All right, everyone, Petrichor shared. *We will deal with Nicolo when we're finished with the Lizards. Stick with the plan. Get back safe.*

CHAPTER FORTY-FIVE
(The Berthoud Militia)

"Petrichor instructs you to remain grounded," Jayney repeated for good measure. "You all will remain safe if you stay in the ship."

"What's happening out there?" Renee asked the ether, not really sure where she should look when speaking with Jayney.

"Everything is going as to plan," Jayney responded.

"Oh no!" Bobbi cried out.

"What's the matter?" Helen asked, placing her arm around Bobbi's shoulders.

"It's starting." Bobbi whimpered.

"What's starting?" Eileen demanded.

"Death!" Bobbi sobbed. "Aldor is dead."

"Which one is Aldor?" Lucian asked.

"One of the pure bloods," Bobbi answered.

"No relation to us?" Savanna asked.

"He is now," Helen said solemnly.

"Claire, carry his energy beyond the veil." Scarlett prayed.

"Was it the Lizards?" Lucian demanded.

"No," Jayney responded.

"Groom Lake?!"

"I cannot lie to you." Jayney replied. "Yes."

"Does this ship have weapons?" Lucian asked.

"Yes. But it is not a warship."

"Can you help me operate the weapons?" Lucian continued.

"Yes." Jayney responded.

Lucian turned to the others. "I need to drop you somewhere safe."

"Back at Buck's office?" Renee offered.

"Jayney," Lucian commanded. "Can you –"

* * * * *

"Where the hell is she?" Buck whispered to the ether as he stared out the window of his office. Buck didn't like the fact that Lieutenant Colonel Clarke had been gone for close to an hour on the worst day of his life. He felt her absence more than he wanted to admit, and he realized his feelings were not just professional. He was now bordering on worried.

"Mac," Buck said. "Can you get anyone else on the satellite?"

"No, sir. Dead air."

Just then, a glow appeared in the center of Buck's office and seven figures materialized in a circle, all leaning on each other for support. Renee Clarke was one of them.

"What the fuck?!" Mac shouted.

"Wow, that was amazing!" Scarlett said as she recovered her land legs. Eileen and Helen assisted Bobbi to the settee on the far wall, while Lucian held onto Savanna for a half-click longer than she needed to recover. The younger sister gently freed herself from his grasp, strolled across the room and threw herself in Buck's chair and put her feet up on his desk.

"So," Savanna said. "Which one of you two calls the shots around here?"

Buck ignored Savanna and used the second Renee took to recover and collect her thoughts to cross the room and place his arm protectively around her shoulder. "Are you all right?" He asked her, tenderly.

She looked up at his face as she continued to acclimate.

Were his eyes always that green? She thought to herself.

"Renee," Buck continued. "Are you all right?"

Renee's head finally cleared, and she blurted out. "Nicolo shot down one of Stella's team's crafts. Somebody named Aldor."

"Mac, do we have any more jets?" Buck asked.

"No sir." Mac replied. "They all went east."

"Ground based missiles?" Buck asked.

"The Sentinels and Gryphons were all launched when DC went down." Mac responded. "We have SM-6 mobile typhons and tomahawks."

"Buck, you can't fire on one of our own bases," Renee counseled.

"General," Lucian said, raising his hand in salute. "Lieutenant Commander John Lucian Benson, VFA-125 Argonauts, retired."

"Where the fuck did you come from?" Mac asked.

"Long story, sir," Lucian answered. "But I have a better way to take care of Nicolo. And he'll never see us coming."

"Better move quick, General." Bobbi called from the settee. "Shit's hitting the fan."

CHAPTER FORTY-SIX
(Doc's House Call)

"You just make sure these techs don't shoot down any of those RES!" Doc shouted at John Bricker as he pointed at the team of nerds working the three stations controlling what looked like a cross between Chile's ELT and a rail gun. "Everything else airborne gets lit up. Friend or foe."

"I'm not shooting anything!" John shouted back at him. "I never signed on for this shit."

"You cashed Nicolo's checks," Doc barked. "Now, you carry his water."

"I want to talk to Nicolo!" John said, trying to regain control.

"As soon as we get back," Doc responded. "Right now, I'm taking him somewhere safe in the Prime RES."

The little Mick headed for the passage that led to the Prime RES John first saw on his first day at Groom Lake.

"Don't wait up," Doc called over his shoulder as he exited through the hissing sliding doors.

"Fuck you-you Irish prick!" John shouted after him.

John looked around at the swarm of jump suit zombie geniuses that continued milling around their stations, carrying out their duties to their billionaire overlord and his Celtic Renfield, completely oblivious to the fact that the world outside had gone to shit.

The Doc was right. John had become a millionaire working for Nicolo. He had sold his soul to Mammon. And as with every deal with the devil, John was the latest soul to get fucked. That money was now worthless in this post-apocalyptic scenario.

"You were right, Tina, this can't be all there is," He whispered to himself.

CHAPTER FORTY-SEVEN
(Petrichor)

Pair off. Michelle and Everette take out the Lizard in the South. Gina and Jimmy go after the Lizard in the north. Lenny, follow me.

On it, Michelle responded. *Ev, let's do this!*

Lead the way, sweetie!

Hell yeah! Gina chimed in. *This one's for the Bronx!*

See you all on the other side! Jimmy shared.

Got your six, babe. Lenny responded.

The leader of Centauri guided her team in low over the Atlantic towards the center edge of the Eastern sea-board of the North American land mass like a phalanx. She watched on her screen as Jayney noted the other sets of ships flaring off in the respective directions of their assigned targets.

Petrichor locked her mind as she approached the location of the city that had always been identified to her from an early age as the central authority of the most powerful Terrans on this planet, the ones that identified as Americans. She gasped audibly for the first time in her centuries of existence as she cruised over the now seventy square human miles of a rapidly rising bay that was replacing the vacuum left by the reptilian assault. Along its perimeter, frantic Terrans coalesced like assaulted ants, as they tried to recover from the terminal blow by a technology they could not begin to fathom. Petrichor wondered if this was, indeed, the end of this fine Centauri experiment.

Then Petrichor began to think of those Terrans she had grown to love and respect. Gina, who was like a sister to her since she arrived on Proxima b, embodied everything good, including her ability to love and trust those around her with abandon. It was no surprise that Jimmy Moran chose her as his mate, even when Petrichor offered herself to him.

Whitey, the mercurial wolfen changeling, who never lost his pack-like devotion to the Terrans they left behind that night, which changed the future for both planets. Then there was Eddie, the quiet warrior whom Dr. Nim had grown so fond of.

Petrichor smiled when she thought about Lenny, her paramour, her protector. Over his decades on Centauri, he had won her heart through his devotion and his humor. She wished she could have shown her appreciation through that Terran expression of laughter. It came so easily to the hybrids, and even to her subjects, Michelle, and Everett, who after all those Earth-years living among the Terrans could engage in what they called laughter-light.

Lenny seemed completely satisfied by just the smiles he could regularly elicit from her, as their minds shared the joy he had brought her, while their bodies shared the pleasure she had never experienced before. And while she never aurally expressed it, Lenny knew that she loved him.

This crew of hybrids, whose junk DNA gave them evolving powers never before witnessed on Proxima-b, had infected the hearts and souls of the pure-blood Centaurians like a powerful virus. Claire, that magical creature so devoted to Jimmy Moran, had once described that virus as hybrid-vigor.

That virus had manifested most dominantly in the children. Stella, her beautiful daughter, had just enough Terran DNA to lift her abilities above all others. On top of all of her physical and mental gifts, she had the ability to heal, without the technological machinations of the Hadron Distributor. She also shared many of the positive personality traits of her father, Jimmy Moran, including the insufferable stubborn streak that could sometimes lead her into mischief. Stella was also a leader by default.

The others, even the elder pure-blood Centaurians, sought her counsel. Petrichor's daughter was the jewel in her crown and was destined to rule Centauri when the time was right.

Stella's half-brother, Apollo, was a Centauri-Terran by a miracle birth to the hybrids Jimmy and Gina. Over time, Petrichor had grown to love him through the eyes and heart of her daughter. Apollo had the innate charisma of both parents, his father's wit, and his mother's feistiness. Apollo could prove to be the greatest warrior ever to have arisen from either planet, his physical gifts unmatched by even the Greek god he was named after. He was totally devoted to his sister and the two were inseparable. Petrichor hoped that their closeness would be their salvation, and that of their two planets.

Finally, there was Jimmy Moran, the catalyst of change both of these planets needed so badly. He had a unique way of seeing the magic in the world around him, and the ability to teach others how to see it too. He wasn't a warrior by nature, but he was fearless, and loyal to a fault. He had proven that he would fight to the death to protect those he loved. And she knew he loved everyone in his family, blood or chosen. That is what drew all others to him—including Petrichor.

That night, human-decades ago, when Petrichor last brought the destructive power of her ship and its weapons to bear on the worst of the Terrans, was engendered by Petrichor's love and innate instinct to protect her daughter, and those Terrans Stella had chosen as her family. Today, Petrichor came to protect the race that was spawned by the genetic experiments of her elders, but was there, not out of some misguided *noblesse oblige*, but because that race had given life to all of those she now loved above all others.

Fuck, Lenny shared. *Those Lizards know how to trash a hotel room.*

Well, it's time they paid the bill. Petrichor replied. *Let's do this.*

Darling, I'll follow you into hell.

Lenny . . . Petrichor started to share.

I love you too, P.

CHAPTER FORTY-EIGHT
(Nicolo)

Sitting alone in the Prime RES, waiting for Doc, the silver-haired polymath made the most of his time doing what he did best, visualizing. Nicolo had created immeasurable wealth and accumulated unbridled power in a world which he and his other Davos brethren had subjugated without its citizens even realizing it. Nicolo saw this tragedy unfolding around him as an opportunity. Aliens had now played their cards and were asserting a technological dominance that even Nicolo was unprepared for. Not even the hives of geniuses he had fostered could reverse engineer their way out of this. The only option was to negotiate the best surrender possible. To salvage his resources and sacrifice everyone else. Historically, Marshal Philippe Pétain didn't share Nicolo's genius or his survival instincts. Nicolo would pull it off.

Nicolo knew that his reverse-engineered squadron of RES was a caricature of the originals. He ordered them up out of Vandenberg to buy time. Figure out his negotiation strategy. Maybe impress the conquerors.

His world's technology couldn't reproduce the purity of the isotropic ratios of the metamaterials going into the alloys that covered the spacecraft, and despite the recent inroads of his newest genius, Bricker, they had not managed to crack the holographic-mind control systems for their crafts. They were forced to jerry-rig the latest navigational hardware cobbled together from the U.S. Stealth program and from technology stolen from the Israelis, who led even the U.S. in aerospace advancements. If the Chosen weren't so busy diverting their resources trying to keep from being destroyed by their theologically hostile geographic neighbors and their petrochemically reliant foreign overlords, they could have figured it out.

But it wasn't a total loss. Nicolo's brain trust had figured out how to reengineer, to a similarly lesser degree, the zero-point energy generators that propelled these downed UAP crafts, and the electromagnetic pulse engines that lifted them airborne and into at least lower space. Theoretically, they posited that these generators pull unlimited energy from the planet's magnetic flux fields and from the dark matter that makes up about eighty-five percent of the universe. This powered the torus that generated the electromagnetic fields that allowed the craft to fly without any obvious propulsion system. Even Nicolo's Mensa-tested intellect couldn't fully comprehend how it worked, but it did.

Those zero-point generators were the game-changer and would have made Nikola Tesla weep. His geniuses managed to get them operational, indeed, they powered most of Nicolo's aerospace technology and his labs all over the world. They also powered Nicolo's photon cannon and the smaller versions operating in his RES.

And these same zero-point generators could have radically changed this world for the better. They could be individually scaled to power everything from cell phones to cities. Unlimited power could be brought to everyone on the planet and would create cheap unlimited resources of all kinds. But the one thing Nicolo loved more than technological advancements was the money they generated. And these zero-point energy generators were perpetual motion machines. Once operational they never needed replacement. That is why they would never see the light of day.

The true failure of Nicolo's scientists lay in their inability to recreate the originals' seamless alloy shells that could easily withstand the extended pressure of outer space, or to develop a comparable plasma shield that would allow the vehicles to circumvent the destructive G-forces that limited true mastery of the crafts. Maybe these attacking Aliens could help Nicolo get over that hurdle.

These Aliens may have done Nicolo a major favor. He and his Davos cronies wanted to impose a New World Order. These future over-lords were doing Nicolo's work for him. To capitalize on their sweat equity, all Nicolo had to do was survive. That was his strong suit.

But he had to show the Aliens that he was a team player and wanted to play for their team. This had to be a grand gesture that could not be misconstrued. He instantly realized what his next move had to be.

* * * * *

Doc entered the Prime RES, slid into the pilot's seat, and began checking the monitors while powering up the navigational system. He looked over at his boss, who appeared to be lost in his own thoughts.

"Better strap yourself in there Mr. Nicolo," Doc said in his soft Irish brogue. "Next stop, the Karman Line, and then we'll hide among the satellites until this all sorts itself out."

Nicolo suddenly animated and focused his squalus eyes on his main minion.

"First, we need to pay a visit to Buckley AFB," he whispered.

CHAPTER FORTY-NINE
(The Minx)

The Terran world has really gone to shit, but I've never felt more alive.

Michelle kept her mind locked as she thought back to that first moment she and Everett pulled up beside Jimmy Moran, in his old human form, looking every moment of his over six human decades of existence, bald and with a paunch, desperately trying to hack down the tall Colorado grass in his front yard with his scythe. Michelle was sure he was about to have a heart attack. The present Centauri hybrid Jimmy was a definite upgrade, although he still would only be a seven out of ten on the Centauri scale.

She shuddered when she remembered the old human forms she and Everett had to maintain back then. It was necessary to ensure their own cover amongst the Terrans for all of those decades they were observers. Never again. She gave herself a once over and was quite pleased with how she looked in all of her Centauri glory.

During his decades as a faux human, Everett had gone native, and his friendship over the last of years of that time with Jimmy Moran had accelerated his feral transition. She palmed her perfect breasts and smiled as she remembered Everett's last comment to her as they were preparing to leave their personal space on Centauri.

"Da girls look good!" Ev had aurally cat-called in his perfect rendition of a Bronx accent.

God how I love that man!

Didn't start out that way. When the Centauri elite packed them both off to babysit the planet's longest running science experiment, they were just colleagues out of the academy. At first, they managed to maintain their purely platonic and professional relationship. But as years turned into decades of close proximity, their shared secret evolved into something more.

They would observe the Terrans' spontaneous public displays of affection, and Michelle especially enjoyed coming to learn and appreciate Terran terms like "puppy love" and "honeymoon sex." The Terrans' greatest, innate trait, the one that set them apart from any other race in the cosmos, was the unbridled passion they brought to love and war, and everything in between. And it was infectious.

Michelle thought back to that first night of intimacy with Everett on Earth. June 1960. They were attending an outdoor Concert in Brickle Park, which was the town square in Berthoud Colorado. It was a warm summer evening, and the featured ensemble was performing selections of the works of Claude Debussy. The Brickle family had their Salon Grand Steinway moved to the park for the Berthoud Day occasion.

The young couple on the blanket next to theirs graciously offered to share goblets of the wine they were drinking. That was Michelle's first-time sampling Terran alcohol. Turned out that it truly was the nectar of the gods.

During the rendition of *Clair de lune*, Michelle felt the pinky of Ev's right hand overlap the pinky of her left. Since they had never shared any intimacy during the two Earth-decades cohabitating, that simple touch was arousing. It remained there for the rest of the performance.

As the concert progressed, she and Ev shared a few more goblets of their neighbors' wonderful Chardonnay. Once the stars made their appearance overhead and the only light came from the small stage at the park's center, Michelle had stolen a few glances at the young couple's equally stolen kisses, whose duration appeared to extend and deepen with the darkness. On her home planet, that would have been considered pornography, if they even had a Centauri word for porn.

By the time the last note was played, Michelle grasped Ev's right hand with her left and lifted him to his feet. Not even stopping to pick up their blanket, she led Ev around the far side of the largest oak on the park's perimeter, pushed him up against its trunk and pinned his mouth with her own just as the young couple beside them had shown her. It was electrifying.

What was even more electrifying was how Ev had instantly transported the two of them back to their house and literally torn her nice summer dress from her, sending the buttons like shrapnel bouncing off the four walls of their bedroom. In the moments it took to render themselves naked, they had reverted to their pure Centaurian forms. The sex they then shared was fumbling, explosive and instantly addictive. They literally demolished the bed they had never before slept in. It was the first time Michelle had experienced sweat on her Centaurian skin.

It turned out that in the late fifties, Ev had secretly began exploring Terran sexuality through devouring Dr. Alfred Kinsey's treatises on the sexual behaviors of human males and females, and after downloading his findings to Michelle in that moment, they went at it like Terran rabbits. They never looked back.

And while Michelle never raised this with record keepers on Centauri, Michelle was quite sure she was the first female of their race to experience an orgasm. The hybrids, Jimmy and Gina gave her and Ev a run for their money on Proxima b, with their residual human abandon. Michelle once thought she caught a comparable telepathic reverberation escaping on Petrichor's mental channel during that first night she and Lenny shared some intimacy after she brought them all back from Earth, after Oregon. Always the control freak, restricted by the decorum Petrichor believed she needed to maintain as the leader of Centauri, her liege had gone radio silent since then. But, like Michelle before her, Petrichor never saw that first one coming. Michelle also happily suspected that the hybrid Eddie might be exploring those same possibilities with Dr. Nim.

The French were right about one thing, it was indeed *la petite mort*. And over the human century since Michelle's first little death, there were not enough stars in the sky to match the number of those that followed. How Michelle loved her man. And she didn't care who knew.

Funny how the present idea of facing death in that moment operated for Michelle as an aphrodisiac.

Hey Ev, Michelle reached out to her mate.

Yes, dear?

When this is all over. I'm going to fuck your brains out.

Yes, please! See every bit of you on the other side.

CHAPTER FIFTY
(*Pteromerhanophobia*)

"So, the only way to attack without tipping Nicolo off is to tickle our belly with the treetops," Lucian explained with surprising nonchalance.

"You realize that every AR-15 between here and Nevada is going to unload on that belly." Mac responded.

"By the time they are sighting those weapons, I'll be gone." Lucian countered. "Anyway, that ammo would never pierce the plasma shield."

"But Nicolo is firing a whole different ammo." Bobbi cautioned.

"You can't do this alone," Savanna added. "You've always had someone with you on the space ship."

"I'll have Jayney."

"And you'll have me," Buck added, brooking no argument.

Mac tried anyway. "Sir, generals don't engage in combat."

"Old rules for old soldiers, Mac," Buck responded. "I'm not even sure there is a military left to enforce the rules."

"But Buck," Renee interrupted, her personal alarm transparent. "You hate to fly!"

"I hate eating vegetables, too," Buck replied, with a softness to his voice. "But every once in a while the good Lord forces my hand."

"Can you show me how to work the weapons?" Buck asked Lucian. "If I'm going to shit myself, I want to make it worth my effort."

"Whitey tells me that there's only one on this craft, but it's a motherfucker, Sir." Lucian answered. "He said he saw it take out that compound in Oregon back in the 2020s. And Jayney does most of the work. You sight the target visually and give the command. Jayney does the rest."

Buck recalled the whispers back then among the top military brass, that something equal to the destructive power of a US MOAB left a major crater in the woods of Baker Oregon. Of course, there were no official confirmations of the event from the Pentagon elite, and the government-controlled media never reported it. Since it didn't impact the soldiers under his command, Buck just didn't give enough of a shit to follow up even unofficially on hallway gossip. But Buck now wanted in his very soul to believe that it was true, just so he could drill another huge hole in Area 51 and vaporize Nicolo and his henchman in the process.

"Well, Lieutenant Commander John Lucian Benson," Buck said. "Can you get us close enough to take out that rat bastard Nicolo and his minions?"

"Sir, with this craft, I can get you standing behind Nicolo at a urinal in an empty bathroom before he hears you fart."

"Mac," Buck shouted. "You have command."

The General pointed at Bobbi. "Ma'am, I understand you have a direct mental line with the Centaurians. I'm counting on you to sort out the white hats from the black ones for Mac here, should there be any confusion."

"Mac," Buck continued. "Nothing happens to these civilians while you are still breathing. Understood?"

Yes, Sir." Mac responded. When he looked over at the five women gathered around Bobbi at the settee, he could have sworn he saw Scarlett wink at him.

"Anything sketchy comes within ten miles of this base Mac, unleash the typhons and tomahawks. I want every able-bodied soldier manning our perimeter until this shit is settled. Repel all boarders."

"C'mon Fergus," Buck called to his best friend as he headed toward the door. "You can ride along with the good Lt. Colonel and see us off."

Fergus was up and across the room before Buck's back leg had exited his office.

Renee glanced over at Bobbi before she followed Lucian out the office door.

Bobbi nodded at her supportively, mouthing. "He's going to be okay."

Renee returned the nod. "Thanks," she mouthed back, then hurried out of the exit.

"What about Lucian?" Savanna demanded of her mentor.

"Lucian's in for a bumpy ride," Bobbi answered, taking her youngest acolyte by the hand in her best soothing fashion. Scarlett placed a comforting arm around her sister's shoulder.

"Don't worry about Lucian," Helen added. "Kid has cojónes!"

"And while I've never seen the attraction in cojónes on bulls or men, Savvy" Eileen added with a wink, "I'm sure Lucian will make the best use of his until you can both figure out a more palatable alternative use for those damn things."

Savanna blushed; her fear replaced with something else.

"And besides," Eileen continued. "Your Auntie Bobbi has got everyone working overtime on both sides of the veil."

"Speaking of which," Bobbi said. "Helen, and you too, Mac, I need you to shift these chairs into the middle of this office."

She reached into her large shoulder satchel, removed a canvas sack, and handed it to Scarlett.

"Scarry, I need you to create a salt protection circle large enough to allow us all to converge inside its perimeter."

She removed a large blue candle and placed it on Buck's desk, then a twin purple candle and set it beside the first.

"Do you have a match, Mac?" She asked just as he finished shifting the last of the chairs within the now completed salt circle.

"You can't have an open flame in government buildings." Mac responded.

Ignoring Mac, Bobbi instructed, "Girls, Do the honors."

Savvy and Scarry approached the candles, the older sister standing before the purple and the younger before the blue.

"Hestia," Scarry began, "provide me with the purging fire to protect us from all enemies who seek us harm."

"Holy shit!" Eileen shouted as a purple flame appeared above Scarry's right index fingertip.

"Hestia," Savvy continued, "provide me with your impenetrable flame to protect our loved ones from those who desire their destruction."

A comparable blue flame appeared above Savvy's left index finger tip.

The two sisters looked to Bobbi, who nodded in the direction of the candles. The girls reached forward, and the flames leapt from fingertips to wicks, where they flared with a distinct and crackling roar.

Bobbi slid between her two acolytes and stood before the two candles, arms extended before her, allowing herself to feel their heat on her palms. She then reached back and grasped one each of the sisters' hands with the two of her own. All three women closed their eyes and began to chant in unison.

"Moon Goddess, who watches over us all, please consider our request. Protect this room from all that is dark. Protect all who take shelter here too. Protect the places that we call home, all whom we love and those that are true. Protect us all with your ever enchanting light and the magical fire from which it rises. So, mote it be."

This time the flames on the candles leapt high towards the ceiling, curled with each other, and then extinguished themselves, leaving the spectators with a temporary flash blindness.

"Now what do we do?" Mac asked.

"We sit together in the center of this protective circle." Bobbi responded, taking her seat on the settee. "We visualize a protective aura around each member of our family who is out there risking it all. And then we wait."

* * * * *

The perimeter of jeeps blocking the runway approaching Stella's craft shifted to allow Renee's jeep to pass, then sealed behind it. The Master Sergeant leapt to his feet and saluted when he saw Buck sitting in shotgun beside the Lt. Colonel. Lucian hopped out of the jeep's back seat and approached Stella's craft. As he went to knock on its skin, he dematerialized. Renee could hear the soldiers close by, whispering their astonishment and fear.

"Come here, buddy" Buck called to Fergus, who leapt onto his lap and began to lick the burly man's face frantically while Buck did his best to keep his shit together. Finally, Buck gained control of the pooch, lifted him into the air and held him at eye level. Buck's eyes were brimming.

"Fergus, as much as I would love to take you on this mission, I need you to stay here and protect the Lt. Colonel in my place." He maneuvered Fergus so the pup was now face-to-face with Renee who did her best to smile. Buck turned his tiny friend back and kissed him softly on his nose, while Fergus let out a soft but submissive whine. Buck gently reached between the two seats and set Fergus on the back seat of the jeep, where the dog spun in circles and curled into a protective ball, refusing to look at his companion.

Buck looked over at Renee and whispered. "Please take care of him. He's all I got."

"You're wrong, Buck," Renee whispered in response. "We'll both be waiting when you get back."

She leaned over, grabbed the lapel of his uniform, and pulled him into a soft but delightful kiss.

"Now go out there and help save the fucking world," she said, smiling coyly, while wiping away the trace of her lip balm from the corner of his lips with her thumb. Before he could utter a word in response through his shit-eating grin, Buck dematerialized.

CHAPTER FIFTY-ONE
(Gina)

The first time I saw Jimmy McCarthy, he was dead to the world. Gina recalled and laughed audibly. *It wasn't the last time I saw him like that. But that first time he just looked dead. The last time they played together, Jimmy cheated Death. It's been my job to make sure Death doesn't even the score. Yet here they all were again, bellying back up at the poker table. This was a no limit game and Jimmy was all in.*

Gina needed a few moments with her own thoughts before all hell broke loose, and, with all due respect to the promise to her Centaurian sister and ruler, Gina didn't take orders, but she would occasionally accommodate suggestions when she thought they had merit.

* * * * *

It was the first morning of summer session at college. Gina Buccola was entering a rigorous nursing program in the fall, one of the best in the state, and wanted to get some of the core science courses out of the way. Gina was a planner, and when she arrived that Monday morning in June 1976, she was perturbed because she had no idea which of the many dorms located on this sprawling bucolic, riverside campus was going to be her home for the next six weeks. Gina would have arrived the day before, but she wanted to draw one more day's pay from the part-time job as a grocery store bookkeeper she was leaving behind. Now she was on to better things.

Gina knew the building she was looking for was hidden somewhere on the steep hill that led down to the Hudson River, but she didn't want to overshoot the mark, and be forced to challenge her classic Ford Falcon's extremely mercurial tranny with hillside roadwork if she could avoid it. She also didn't want to waste any time trying to figure out her dorm's location on the shitty mimeograph map the college had included in its acceptance package. How did the world survive before the iPhone?

Gina loved the smell of mimeographs.

When she arrived in her car at the southern gate at the entrance to the still deserted summertime campus, she spotted a pair of worn black shoes peeking above the plexiglass window on the upper half of the otherwise industrial metal guard booth. It resembled an oversized telephone box that you would find on every street corner in New York City.

"I feel safer already." Gina said to herself as she threw the car in park and fished one of the forms with her name and schedule on it out of the pocket of the notebook that lay on the cloth bench seat beside her. When she arrived at the booth, she peeked through the glass. There, just below the window, lay the sleeping guard, slumped down in his chair with an open book across his chest, feet up on the small desk at the front of the booth.

Gina studied the sleeping form for a moment to see if he would psychically sense that someone was staring at him and awake on his own. He was young, about Gina's age, and while not a pretty boy, had a certain *je ne sais quoi*, as Gina's mother, a Francophile, liked to say. She was surprised and just a little impressed to see that the worn book on his chest was Homer's The Odyssey. But after thirty seconds, more time than she normally wasted waiting on anything, Gina's patience wore thin, and she started to rap on the window.

"Hello," she called, just loud enough to wake the dead while she continued to tap her index knuckle on the window. The guard didn't move. Maybe he was dead. Pleasantries having missed their mark, Gina kicked it up a notch.

"Hey, asshole!" She shouted in her sonorous, nasal voice, while adding the rest of her knuckles to the plexiglass percussion. "Are you going to sleep all fucking day?"

At that, the sleeping sheepdog slowly opened his eyes and stared up at Gina. He had the most innocent look she had ever seen on a male face, an almost childlike wonder about it. And those baby blue eyes, a novelty in Gina's Italian American neighborhood, almost took her breath away.

Recovering, Gina went back on the offensive. She had a nine-a.m. class and a car full of boxes she needed to move into her dorm room beforehand.

"Oh good. You're alive. Now get off your cute little ass and show me which one of these fucking dorms is mine."

They were never meant to be together. Gina wasn't in college to find herself a husband, or even a boyfriend. She was there to master a respected profession that would give her financial security and allow her to save some money and someday travel the world. She was going to prove to everyone in the old neighborhood that she could make it on her own.

Jimmy was just one dream shy of Walter Mitty with no real direction in life and nothing but inconceivable stories that no one in their right mind would ever believe. But he had an authentic charm about him. And he made her laugh.

Jimmy's family was crazy, but she never felt safer than when she was in their presence. Gina fell in love with Jimmy's grandfather, Spaghetti, the night he taught her how to tie a four-in-hand knot, despite never once wearing a tie in her presence. Two years later, Jimmy and Gina were married, and she never looked back.

Turned out that Jimmy provided Gina with a life as unexpected and uncanny as the stories he used to tell her when they first met. Jimmy literally dreamed his bullshit into reality. *Who fucking knew?*

Well, at least I got to travel, Gina thought to herself. Again, she audibly laughed.

* * * * *

Sweetie?! Jimmy telepathically intruded on Gina's reverie. *A favor?*

Ask and you shall receive. Assuming I think it's a good idea.

No, really. I'm serious. Jimmy responded.

Okay, who are you and what have you done with my husband? Serious isn't even in Jimmy's dictionary, human, Centaurian or binary.

Jimmy now appeared on the holographic monitor on the ship before her.

"Someday, you are going to not make me beg for something." Jimmy said. He wore his still charming smile, but she could see a worried look in his eyes. He blocked her attempt to peek into his mind.

"Hi ya Gina!" Claire called over his shoulder in her husky female voice, before sliding her face into the screenshot.

"Keep an eye on that asshole." Gina said, and then laughed. "You know how he gets into trouble when he's left to his own devices."

Gina fought off the memory of Jimmy dying on Gnome Hill at Casa Claire.

"Don't worry honey," Claire responded. "I'm not going to let anything happen to our boy."

"Gina, listen to me." Jimmy interrupted. "When we get to the target, you have to let me take the lead."

"Jimmy, be fair, I can fly rings around you."

"Yeah, I know that. But that's why I need you to hang back. Let me engage the scaly fucker. Draw him out. If I get in a jam, you can save my ass like you always do."

Gina studied her husband, frustrated that she couldn't drill down on what he was really thinking.

"Look, we're almost at the target." Jimmy continued. "Just hang back in the beginning until we see what the Lizard's got in his bag of tricks. If you see a shot, take it. I promise I won't do anything stupid."

Gina thought about it a few seconds more.

"Jayney," Gina said, loud enough for the AI to hear in both ships. "You keep Jimmy alive."

"Yes, Gina." Jayney responded in both ships simultaneously. "I promise."

"Okay then Jimmy. I promise to let you take the lead. You promise not to play the hero."

"Deal!" Jimmy said. "Love ya, honey."

"I'm not kidding , Jimmy." Gina said, trying to mask the slight tremble in her voice. "Do not die on me."

"See you on the other side, lover." Jimmy whispered and his screen went blank.

At that moment, Jayney scrutinized both pilots from a 360-degree vantage point at the same moment and wished she possessed two fingers to cross as well.

CHAPTER FIFTY-TWO
(Alpha)

The prime Draconian watched his monitors tracking the six ships that were closing rapidly from behind on his, Beta's and Gamma's vessels. The major Terran cities from the east coast through the first third of the land mass were erased. All major munition opposition from air, ground and water had been eradicated with the exception of isolated barrages of land-based shells and missiles that not only could not penetrate the Draconian ships' defense systems but also exposed the source of the opposition to instant surgical obliteration. Draw your pleasure but salvage the resources.

Alpha could have performed all of this destruction alone from a safe and anonymous position in space just as easily, but he knew he needed to display this demonstration of superiority and power in order to terrify the Terrans. As a Draconian, he had no comparable emotional experience to Terran fear. But over the eons, the Draconians warriors had witnessed its display in every race they conquered throughout the universe. The more palpable the fear they evoked during battle, the more glory, and indeed, the more pleasure it brought to his warriors. It was their aphrodisiac.

Alpha considered this oncoming assault by the approaching Centaurians an unexpected gift. He would be able to destroy this last opposition in full view of the conquered. Out with the old gods, in with the new.

But now that the Terran opposition had been sufficiently quelled, Alpha wanted to display a battle that the Terrans would never forget. The one take away Alpha had gleaned from his own studies of these weak creatures is that from the earliest time they were taught to read and write by their gentle Centaurian messengers, they meticulously maintained their chronicles of war. The vermin seemed fascinated by the suffering they imposed upon each other. Alpha was determined to generate the contents of their final volume. There would be plenty of suffering to go around.

And today Alpha would have his chance to even the score with the upstart Centaurian who dared to humiliate Alpha before the Intergalactic Federation. He bridled at the memory of the sound of the hybrid's voice. With any luck, Alpha would kill that puny being himself.

Turn off your automated defense systems, Alpha ordered his troops. *Any of you that cannot defeat the Centaurians on your own skill alone does not deserve to serve with me.*

And just to ensure that the weakest of his own did not succumb to a primal desire for self-preservation, Alpha nullified the automatic systems on all nine of the Draconian ships with a quick sweep of his fist over the holographic panel before him.

01010111   01100001   01110010   01110010   01101001
01101111   01110010   01110011   00100000   01010100
01101111   00100000   01010100   01101000   01100101
00100000   01000100   01100101   01100001   01110100
01101000

Warriors To The Death. Beta replied.

Now, kill them slowly but kill them all. Alpha commanded.

CHAPTER FIFTY-THREE
(Apollo)

Stella's was the first face I saw with my eyes. Apollo thought, as his craft joined those of the other Centaurians hovering in lower space orbit over the Northern Mariana Islands, in the Pacific Ocean. *Hers were the first arms to hold me after she reached in with those mystical hands and lifted me from my mother's womb. An act that saved both Gina and me during my delivery. Since the moment I drew my first breath, she has protected me. I will do everything I must to protect her to my last.*

The six Draconian ships have just crossed the Hawaiian islands. Jayney collectively shared with the four Centaurians. *They have destroyed the last of the United States military resistance at Joint Base Pearl Harbor–Hickam and the nearby communications station. The Island of Oahu is gone.*

Apollo tried to scan his sister's mind, but it was locked.

The Lizards are advancing as a wedge towards a dozen unidentified craft waiting in a linear holding pattern just off the West Coast.

Eddie and Whitey, swing in from the southwest. Stella broke the hybrids' telepathic silence. *Apollo and I will approach from the northeast. Skim the water. Wait until the Draconian phalanx engages the resistance. Then attack the rear wingtips of their formation and work our way towards the front. Hit and run. Double team, our two, to their one. No one stands still or goes toe to toe with the opposition. After each kill, withdraw and regroup.*

What about the other twelve bogies? Eddie asked.

Initially, the enemy of our enemy is our friend. Stella replied. *But if they fire on you, take 'em out. No apologies accepted. No second chances.*

Jayney, Whitey ordered, *shields up, lock and load.*

With Stella in the lead, the four Centaurian crafts dropped through the Karman line like synchronized swimmers entering an Olympic pool; Eddie, Whitey and Apollo following their leader. A moment later, their crafts glowing forms were making a linear low pass over the Marianas in the last remnants of pre-dawn darkness.

Only live heroes today, gentlemen, Stella commanded.

Hooah! Eddie shared; the excitement palpable in his thoughts. *If I knew how much fun the sky-jockeys were having, I would have joined the Air Force.*

I'll take running down my enemy with four paws, on terra firma, anytime! Whitey shared as he peeled off from the formation and headed south east. His craft was so low it left a wake on the ocean which Eddie traced directly behind him. Apollo thought he heard a wolf howl.

Okay brother, Stella shared as she dropped her craft just over the whitecaps and headed north east. *Playtime is over. Time we sat at the adult table.*

Apollo responded, hesitantly. *Sis, no matter what else happens today. Survive!*

I will never leave you. Stella replied after a moment. *Follow my lead. We got this.*

Apollo shared his memory of their first postnatal embrace.

Stella returned the favor with her memory of the two siblings hugging each other for dear life on the Oregon tarmac the night Petrichor came to save them.

"Okay Jayney," Apollo said as he refocused on the mission before him, flashing for a moment on the image of locking eyes with Scarlett, while she was standing in the dining room of Casa Claire. "Let's go skin some Lizards."

CHAPTER FIFTY-FOUR
(Lucian)

As Buck materialized in the cabin, Lucian could see the general did not have his sea legs.

"Jayney," Lucian shouted. "Wrap him up tight until he's safe enough to stand."

"Got him." Jayney replied.

Buck shook his head to get his bearings and began to struggle when he realized he was incapacitated by something soft and invisible.

"Easy, General," Lucian called out as the holographic control panel and front screen appeared before him and he slid his hands into the waiting templates.

"Jayney, drop Buck into a captain's chair beside me so he can get a good look at what's going on."

Lucian glanced back over his shoulder to make sure Buck had heard him. When the large man calmed a bit more, Jayney did as instructed. Buck arrived beside the younger man with his face betraying his astonishment.

"Okay, Jayney, free him up."

Lucian glanced over at Buck and smiled like the kid who just won the spelling bee.

"Not too shabby," Lucian bragged as he gestured towards the control panel. "Wait until you see what this baby can do."

Lucian's fingers on both hands began to dance on their templates and the ship was suddenly hovering a thousand feet in the air. Buck never felt the G-force and didn't even realize they had left the ground until Lucian instructed Jayney to go translucent.

"Jesus Christ!" Buck pulled his knees up towards his chest in the chair, as he suddenly found what appeared to be the two of them floating in the morning sky. He looked down at the troops gathering below all pointing upward in astonishment and prayed none of them were trigger-happy. He could see the jeep with Renee and Fergus in the distance heading back toward his office building.

Lucian didn't notice the silver speck hovering miles in the distant sky until Jayney called out, "Incoming!" A moment later, a plasma bolt burned a thirty-foot circle in the center of the soldiers, while the survivors spilled backwards from the crater that suddenly appeared in the tarmac. A second bolt took out another patch of humanity just as Jayney shifted upwards to avoid the third passing directly below them.

"Motherfucker!" Buck cried out as what appeared to be a blinding dayglow telephone pole flew within yards of Buck's dangling feet.

"Lizards?" Lucian demanded.

"No." Jayney responded. "That's a Terran ship."

A fourth plasma bolt appeared to strike the General's quarters in the distance just as Renee and Fergus cleared its doorway.

"Please God, no!" Buck shouted, as Lucian recovered his reflexes and touched a separate panel that suddenly appeared on his right just below Buck's eye level. A brilliant flash of light flew out of the front of their craft, as if ejected from the ether. Before he could blink, Buck saw the bolt's light glint off the approaching saucer as the craft barely dodged the counterstrike. Buck glanced back down towards his office and was surprised to see a large moat-like circle of destruction around the circumference of the building, destroying the road out front and the jeep that was parked there. The building appeared completely unscathed.

Buck reflexively blessed himself, then pointed at the disk before them.

"Recycle that scumbag." Buck barked at Lucian.

"Ever play chicken, General?" Lucian responded as the craft leapt forward firing in rapid succession at the disk. It dodged and weaved in a way that defied Terran physics to avoid taking the hit. At a half mile it again fired its own plasma bolts. Lucian suddenly had the craft turning at a right angle and heading skyward.

"What are you doing?' Buck demanded, now on his feet.

"Leading them away from the base," Lucian responded, never taking his eyes off the screen.

"Jayney," Lucian commanded. "I never flew combat naked. Wrap us in a condom and give me a screen." Jayney complied just as Lucian leveled off and headed west.

"Incoming!" Jayney reported just as Lucian rolled his way left and a plasma bolt flew past his right.

"Jayney," Buck said tentatively. "Could you show me where they are?"

Another screen appeared before Buck showing the heat signature of a ship rapidly approaching the center of the screen.

"Can't you go faster?" Buck begged.

"I don't want to lose them." Lucian responded, glancing down at Buck's screen. They had just entered into the eastern desert region of Nevada. Lucian's fingers danced again, and the ship dipped just as another plasma bolt flew overhead.

"Where are you taking us?" Buck demanded.

"Area 51," Lucian responded with the calmness of a Top Gun. "I'm going to burn that motherfucker in his hometown."

Lucian lowered his craft into the Pahranagat Valley, scanning his screen as the craft passed over the ghost town of Crystal Springs.

"There it is!" Lucian shouted as his fingers moved like Michael Flatley shoe tips.

"What?" Buck responded, trying to make sense of the blurs passing below them.

"Nevada State Route 375," Jayney answered.

"Extraterrestrial Highway," Lucian confirmed. "We're taking these fuckers right through the front gate at the end of Groom Road."

Lucian shifted his hands almost imperceptibly and the large metal aircraft hangar just off the highway with its giant ET statue out front disappeared in a fireball at the lower right of the screen.

"Speed the fuck up, Lieutenant Commander!" Buck barked. "That's an order!"

"I'm retired, General." Lucian replied, eyes glued to his screen but his grin wide enough for Buck to see.

"Well then," Buck responded. "Speed the fuck up or I'm going to whip your ass when this is over, citizen." This time Buck was grinning, but only for a moment, as the truck passing below them evaporated upon contact with the latest plasma bolt meant for them.

A final bolt took out the Little Ale'Inn sign as they passed over the tourist town of Rachel, Nevada, but Lucian, unperturbed, continued to stare directly ahead.

"I'll give you this," Buck said, barely able to mask his own anxiety. "You gotta a cool hand, Luc—"

"There it is!" Lucian shouted, cutting Buck off. "Groom Fucking Road!"

The Terran munitions of all calibers that were immediately launched en mass from the military base in their direction had Buck ducking for cover until he realized that their ship's plasma energy shield was absorbing everything the Terran military threw at them. Even the typhoons and tornadoes appeared to explode a few yards off their mark.

"I gotta get me one of these." Buck whispered.

"You already have 'em." Lucian responded. "That's what's chasing us."

Buck checked his screen and could see that the referenced disk had closed to half the prior distance. Ahead, on Lucian's screen, he could see the front gate to the base, lined with every form of ground armored vehicle, all with guns discharging at will in their direction.

"Let's hope Nicolo hasn't figured out how these energy shields work." Lucian shouted as his allegro along the templates took their ship straight up at a ninety-degree climb.

Buck never heard the explosion behind him but the blast waves that slammed into the rear of their ship drove it into an upward tumble, like a tossed coin.

"Jayney, a little help!" Lucian cried out as he fought to recover control.

"Hang on," Jayney shouted, just as a second, more focused impact clipped the rotating back end of the craft, sending it into a new spasm of revolutions, as their passing screen captured the metallic dust cloud that used to be the pursuing disk before Nicolo's own plasma cannon had struck it dead center.

Lucian's fingers now danced like Rachmaninoff's as he fought to right their spacecraft while Buck fought to keep from hurling. Intuitively, Lucian accelerated the ship in the direction of the spin which allowed him to regain its control and level it into a straight advance.

"Was that last one from the ground?" Lucian asked after he caught his breath.

"No," Jayney replied. "Lucky shot from the disk just as it got taken out. Blast waves masked its approach. Couldn't avoid it."

"Who took them out?" Lucian continued.

"Friendly fire." Jayney responded. "Nicolo's plasma cannon missed its mark."

"Who let you retire?" Buck gasped as he placed his hand on the younger man's shoulder to lift himself out of his chair. "I'm court marshaling that cocksucker."

"Are you kidding?" Lucian responded. "Prick did me a favor. I would have been in one of the first waves of F35s the Lizards took out. I'm going to name all five of my future sons and daughters after the officer that processed my papers. Captain Steve Morley."

"Put your pecker away, Lucian. First things first." Buck said. "Jayney," he continued in his softest and most polite voice as he sidled up to Lucian's weapon screen. "Do your thunderbolts still fire?"

"Yes, Buck." Jayney replied in her most seductive imitation of Petrichor. "I'm all yours. But be gentle."

"Take us down, Lucian. Groom Lake." Buck commanded. "I'm tired of dancing. Time they pay the piper!"

CHAPTER FIFTY-FIVE
(Another Brick In The Wall)

"What the fuck were you thinking?" John Bricker shouted at the lead tech at the control panel of the Plasma Cannon.

"Following orders," the Tech responded. "Nicolo gave explicit instructions to shoot down any UAP within range."

"Well," John countered, pointing at the screen as a speeding hot blip emerged from the exploding cloud of heat signature. "You only nailed one. If that was Nicolo and Doc, there goes your bonus. And it looks like the other one's pissed."

"What should we do?"

"Me?!" John replied. "I'm getting the fuck outta Dodge."

He stared back down at the screen and shook his head.

"You?" Bricker added, pointing at the approaching blip, and patting the Tech hard on his shoulder. "You may want to bend over, tuck your head between your legs, and kiss your ass goodbye."

Bricker knew he only had a few minutes to get as far away from the Plasma Cannon as he could before the ET space ship heading their way unleashed its "fuck you" technology that Bricker was only beginning to understand. The thought of it made Bricker's sphincter pucker mid-stride as he picked up his pace and exited through the hissing portal. This led into the hallway that continued to the fortified storage facility where the most precious of the non-lethal, alien technology Bricker had been working on was sequestered, while Nicolo tried to figure out how to monetize it. Bricker knew Nicolo kept that gold in the safest place in the dragon's underground lair.

If there is a God, then that was you and Doc vaporized up there, Nicolo. Bricker thought. *And I hope you both burn in hell.*

He took one last glance over his shoulder before the portal doors hissed closed and spotted a group of techs frantically scrambling around the weapon's control panel like drones. He could no longer discern the queen bee he had just been talking to from the similarly attired others.

"*Vaya con Dios*, Assholes!" He shouted as he broke into a full sprint down the cavernous hall way.

Tina, he thought to himself as he picked up the pace. *You may want to prepare a second place-setting at the celestial kitchen table tonight. I may be home for dinner.*

CHAPTER FIFTY-SIX
(Whitey)

I love this craft! Whitey thought to himself as he skimmed along the eastern Pacific Ocean towards the United States west coast. It was just the latest technological miracle he had experienced since he was first adopted into the Claire family of misfits over two Terran decades before.

When did I start calling Earth Terran? Whitey wondered.

"Shortly after you and the other humans were converted to hybrids on Centauri." Jayney responded aurally. "Sorry, but I'm all locked into you telepathically to assist you piloting the craft."

"No worries, I'm going to need all the help I can get."

Whitey thought back to that night, which seemed like yesterday, when he, Lenny and Eddie were summoned before the High Council and given the offer to transition. Jimmy and Gina had both lobbied for the opportunity, if only to reward us for our family service, and our assistance that night in recovering Stella and Apollo.

The other two leapt at the opportunity and joined the Nordic blue-eyed cult that very night. Whitey suspected they were both looking for a way to up their game with Petrichor and Dr. Nim, and maybe add a few years to enjoy themselves on their new home planet. He couldn't blame them. The Centauri women were beautiful, especially those two. And they were still human men when they arrived on Proxima-b, and human men always thought first with their dicks. Plus, doesn't every human boy want to grow up to be Superman?

It was different for Whitey, who was born a mutant. His mutation never garnered him any obvious benefits, other than providing a naturally superior physicality to his human form. The stress he suffered from his initial inability, post-puberty, to control his change into wolfen form forced him to self-isolate to keep his secret safe and prevent him from injuring anyone unintentionally. In high school he entered a trade program, despite the fact that he was a rising academic star when he first enrolled. He was also a natural athlete, who broke the varsity football coach's heart when he suddenly withdrew from the team.

The trade classes allowed him to work on projects alone and ignore the other students around him. It also allowed him to focus on what was right in front of him, and not subject himself to the emotional triggers from cliques and the expected interests in the opposite sex. Whitey loved human females, especially in the upper classes, who all sprouted into full-blown women hood overnight. But Whitey realized early on that any kind of physical sexual stimulation would literally bring out the beast in him. So, celibacy became his avoidance technique. And there were no girls in shop class.

When he told his parents that he was leaving high school after his junior year, they were completely understanding. His father had avoided winning the dominant wolfen gene lottery, and felt extreme guilt that Whitey was afflicted. They gave Whitey the money they had been saving as his college fund, and he invested it in a pickup truck, a complete set of every tool in the Stanley-Black & Decker Pro-line and used the rest to start up his local handy-man business. He chose northern Colorado as his permanent home because the people there were friendly enough to make daily business encounters pleasant enough, but respectful of his privacy outside of his professional life. Plus, there were lots of places he could hunt without interference.

His hybrid nature gave him the stamina to work without break from dawn until dusk. And his intelligence and craftmanship quickly established his reputation by word-of-mouth and kept him busy with as much work as he needed. On the bigger jobs, he would hire Latino day laborers, just so no one questioned how larger tools or machinery were moved or operated, when their specs called for more than one human to operate it. He paid them well and often sent them home early, just so he could focus on completing the jobs at his own speed and to his own meticulous standards. Still, Whitey paced himself so as not to arouse any suspicion from his local contracting competition. He didn't eat all the meat on the plate and left plenty of jobs to be fought over by whatever contractors were battling for the number two spot reputationally.

It was through a contracting job that Whitey was completing for Gina Moran on Casa Claire that he was introduced to a society of secrets, magic, and extraterrestrials. He was instantly welcomed with open arms into this group of mystical misfits by their ambassador, Claire the Mule, after she caught Whitey howling at the moon from atop a scaffold on a night he thought he was alone. Claire helped him realize that his secret was peanuts in comparison to those of the collective and that he was safe among them. Whitey embraced his new family from that initial magical exchange and had stood and fought beside them ever since. He even loved the pure humans, especially Lucian Benson, who had become a substitute for the son Whitey never had. Dying for them all would be no sacrifice because they had given him more love and excitement over the past decades than he had experienced his entire pre-misfit existence. He finally belonged. He had found his pack.

So, when Whitey needed to make his decision on whether to undergo Centauri hybrid conversion, he went to the family members who first provided him the opportunity to set foot on Casa Claire.

Gina Moran was completely human the day she hired Whitey to build her decks. She paid him his quote right up front and then left him to do his work without challenge or change. Whitey was left to proceed at his own pace. His only company on the job site were the two Moran dogs, Maeve and Blue, whom he easily befriended through shared telepathic communication. He thought it strange that whenever he was sharing thoughts with the dogs, who loyally never disclosed any of their family's secrets, he always found Claire within eye shot, watching him. He just figured she was lonely and maybe a little jealous of the attention he was showing the in-house pets. Little did he realize that Claire had been telepathically eavesdropping on their conversations. Once Claire had satisfactorily vetted him, she waited for the right opportunity to use Whitey's own secret as entre to her approach. Since that day, Claire had repeatedly demonstrated that she was not only the true brains behind this family, but its heart as well.

The night they all gathered to bury Claire's love, Mr. Rogers, was the night the family of misfits coalesced into the cohesive unit that had since expanded and evolved beyond all expectations. Part of that evolution was the hybridization of Jimmy and Gina Moran. Jimmy's transformation brought him back from the dead, which shredded Gina's heart, if only for that moment. Gina's involuntary transformation at Michelle's hands kept her from putting Jimmy through that same experience. So, she learned to accept it.

When Whitey approached Jimmy over the issue of submitting to the Hadron Distributor's rays, Jimmy gave him his very practical take on the matter. If Everett had not transformed him, Jimmy would never have had the one last chance to say goodbye to the love of his life. And Jimmy would have sold his soul to recover that chance. The resulting physical and mental upgrades were the icing on the cake.

Gina's perception of her own transformation was a little more troubled, given that she was struggling with deeply ingrained religious beliefs, that weighed against the desire she had to live as long as Jimmy in his hybrid form. She told Whitey that Michelle had done Gina the ultimate favor in forcing the conversion upon her. It not only allowed her to continue to share her husband's life on a whole different level, but it gave her the one thing that had been absent from her human existence. Their son, Apollo. So, while Gina explained that she would never tell another to undergo the change, she never regretted it being forced upon her. Apollo was her greatest gift and if she had to sacrifice her soul to get him, so be it.

And they were right. Whitey's Centauri hybridization had proven miraculous. Not only did it provide him with all the abilities of his

Centaurian cousins, but it even provided new expressions of his wolfen genetics. He could now transform partially, so that he could express the virtuoso tactical hunting and fighting abilities of his wolfen nature without surrendering his human control over that creature.

As he stood now at the holographic control panel of his ship, he called upon his alter ego to manifest so he would bring his apex predator to the fight he was about to engage in. His body instantly transformed into a larger, more muscular, and completely fur-covered creature, but he remained upright and the only change to his facial features was the enlarged teeth of a wolf.

Together this misfit crew had overcome the worst that Earth had to offer. Today, they were facing the worst the galaxy could throw at them.

Whitey, Eddie telepathically intruded on Whitey's reverie. *Check out the shitstorm ahead!*

CHAPTER FIFTY-SEVEN
(Everett)

In all the time I had lived among the Terrans, I had never seen anyone wielding a scythe before. I actually never saw one outside of Terran museums, although we once watched its interesting application in a human film. This poor bastard was stubbornly using one to beat the tall Colorado wild grass on his property into submission rather than slice through it. Given the small patch he had cleared, and the look of exhaustion on his face, the grass had quickly gotten the better of him. But he didn't quit. He just kept at it. It was him or the grass that would be the last left standing. I didn't understand at the time that I was witnessing what the human vocabulary referred to as a metaphor for the Terran I came to know and love, Jimmy Moran.

"Oh look, Ev!" Michelle said to me, given that she liked to practice aural communication, and she really had a lovely voice, "Someone finally moved into the Greer place. Stop and let's say hello."

Little did I know how that one particular exchange of human pleasantries would change the course of our two planets.

We had met a lot of Terrans since Michelle and I arrived on this planet in the first half of the last Terran century as part of our Centaurian portfolio. We were to do two things. First, observe and keep our race's genetically manipulated experiment from destroying their beautiful planet.

Second, divert any of their attempts to expand their manned space program beyond their moon.

No matter what happened, we had to follow the Prime Directive. Do nothing to alter their human evolution or directly intercede with their intra-Terran affairs.

Terrans were as fascinating as they were unpredictable. Their intellectual capabilities had been developing as expected according to the hypotheses of the scientists on Proxima-b. Over eons of Centaurian genetic tinkering, the human race had evolved from basic primates that had risen from this bountiful planet's primordial ooze into creatures fashioned in their own likeness. At some point hundreds of thousands of Terran years before, the leaders of the Centaurians fell in love with their creations and decided to end all active experimentation. A purely moral decision. The Terrans, as we called them, were to be left alone to progress at whatever speed their intellect and physical gifts would allow. The Centaurians withdrew from directly interacting with them, their role from that point forward being to just observe and protect them from destroying themselves.

Understandably, the emotionally abandoned Terrans filled that vacuum with religious beliefs. They sought a logical meaning for their existence. That kept most of them moving forward communally in peace and happiness.

They were right in their instincts. There is a higher power behind all that is or will be. It accounts for the existence of every sentient creature in the universe, and all creatures are sentient. And the fact that the Terrans may be the handiwork of the Centaurians, they were just an extension and continuation of the creative gifts and blessings bestowed as part of a ripple effect that continued ever outward from that original source of love. Pass it on.

But even Centauri's brightest scientists did not account for the passion of this genetically engineered race. Somewhere from within their junk primate genes evolved this wild card that made the Terrans wonderfully unpredictable. It heightened their emotions beyond anything the present day Centaurians had ever encountered or had long forgotten.

It allowed the Terrans to experience love, happiness, and anger on heightened levels that present Centaurians could not fully understand or appreciate. At times, it caused Terrans to bond with blind loyalty, or breach with each other with blind hatred. It invoked random acts of empathetic kindness, on one end of their emotional spectrum, and sometimes spontaneous, paranoidal violence, on the opposite end. Somewhere within the arc of this emotional pendulum, lay a sweet spot that made these creatures an absolute joy to walk among.

An interesting result of this continuing Centaurian experiment was that the Terrans' genetic predisposition towards acting on their heightened passion spread like a virus among their own race, which accounted for their centuries of war. What was completely unforeseeable was that the conflagration of passion could even cross-species, as it had now done with the Centaurians. Properly anticipated and considered, this outcome would have been predictable among the hybrids of their crew, but host-jumping to pure Centaurians like Everett, Michelle, and even Petrichor, could never have been fathomed. And yet, here we were.

Everett and Michelle had since manifested this passionate connection to their Terrans, especially Jimmy and Gina. It caused them to breach the Prime Directive that bloody night the mafia came calling at Casa Claire. Their reanimation of Jimmy was the first domino to drop in the line that ultimately led them to this moment. But Everett had no regrets.

Their exposure to this Terran emotional virus had also awakened Everett and Michelle's passion for each other. For this Everett was eternally grateful. For it was through this connection that Everett first understood what it was to really experience life and all its potential. He loved Michelle with every quark in his energy field.

And now this relentless emotional passion had them all hurtling towards engagement with an unforgiving foe that, by threatening one, had threatened all. Each one of their crew of misfits appreciated the one unacknowledged truth of their mission today. They would lay down their existence on this energetic plane for each other, and would, to their last being, fight to protect the Terrans.

We have a visual. Jayney advised all six of the team as Everett's screen brought up the three Draconian warships advancing westward across his adopted country.

Okay everyone, take out your targets and then help out as needed. Petrichor shared with the six on her team. *Come home safe and I'll see you all on the other side.*

Hey Ev, Michelle reached out to her mate directly.

Yes, dear?

When this is all over, I'm going to fuck your brains out.

Yes, please! See every bit of you on the other side.

"Jayney," Everett blocked his mind and whispered audibly. "Don't let anything happen to Michelle."

Jayney didn't respond. At that moment, she was fielding similar selfless invocations from all members of the misfit crew. She could not see the future, but her artificial and adaptive intelligence understood all the variables at play. If Jayney could have wept, she would have.

CHAPTER FIFTY-EIGHT
(West Coast)

Eddie reached into his tunic and pulled his dog tags outside, so it hung out on his chest like a necklace. He placed it in his teeth and rubbed the notch at its end with his tongue. He wondered if anyone would be around to jam it into his mouth when the time came.

"Jayney," he whispered. "This has been some fucking trip."

Eddie had been to war too many times. Each time he and his men stepped outside the wire during his deployments, could always be the last. As he did during those times, he ran a mental checklist of his few wonderful memories. Most seemed to fall after his reunification with his sister Bobbi, and his admission into Claire's crew of misfits.

He loved each and every one of them as the family they had become. He had already fought beside them twice. They were now blood to him, like those who had served with him in his unit overseas.

He knew he would readily die for them. And they for him.

Forever, a private person, Eddie never tried to develop his Centaurian hybrid mental abilities beyond the basics. He could get by in a pinch. He was far more interested in the physical upgrade that came along with the Hadron Distributor package, and his hybrid body now bore no signs of the scars or broken bones he had accumulated in his knock-around life. Even his liver was again pristine after the decade of drug and alcohol abuse he had subjected it to. The only downside to his new body was that his airborne tattoo disappeared with the scars. *You gotta take the bitter with the sweet.*

"Speaking of sweet." He whispered audibly.

Nim? He reached telepathically across time and space to the only female he had actually cared for since he had left the military.

Yes, Eddie. He felt her affection in her response.

Holy shit, it worked.

I've been waiting to hear from you, Nim replied. *I was worried but didn't want to intrude. Is everything okay?*

Eddie took a moment before responding. *Aldor's gone.*

Petrichor informed us, she replied. *Centauri mourns him as a hero.*

Good, Eddie responded. *He's a hero in my book.*

Eddie thought about all the negative shit he had been subjected to by the clueless young citizens he had once protected, upon his return from deployment. "Fucking sheep, bleating at their sheepdog." He whispered.

Everything all right? Nim asked.

Yeah, honey.

He could see Santa Cruz island in the distance. Beyond that, what he saw caught his breath.

Gotta go, honey.

Eddie, come home to me.

Top of my to-do list. He responded.

Eddie, Nim added. *I love you.*

Love you more. Eddie then blocked his mind. He had meant every word.

He focused on the task at hand. There right above the horizon, back lit by the approaching dawn, was the most incredible dogfight Eddie had ever witnessed. Six large Draconian ships hovered in a large circle over the last stretch of ocean between the Channel islands and Los Angeles. Around them buzzed about a dozen much smaller saucers firing impotent plasma bolts that couldn't permeate the aggressors invisible force field that extended in a 100-yard perimeter beyond the edge of the Draconian circle.

The Draconian ships began to move in a slow clock wise rotation while focused beams as bright as the sun began emitting from the front of each craft. With this one silent salvo, the saucers' numbers were cut in half. No explosions. When the beams found their mark, the mark totally disappeared, without sound or fury.

Whitey, Eddie reached out telepathically. *Check out the shitstorm ahead!*

Holy shit! Who are the tea cups?

Don't know, don't care. Eddie watched as the remaining saucers did their futile damnest to breach the shield wall around their enemy.

Engage at will. Stella instructed her team.

We need to draw the Lizards out of their cocoon. Whitey said as they drew closer. *Cull the herd.*

Eddie saw what he thought was an opening. *Going in.*

A new burst of plasma beams exited the slowly spinning Draconian wheel, eliminating the last of the circling saucers upon impact. Eddie's ship rose up from the water and fired a plasma bolt at a forty-five-degree angle towards the spot closest to his approach where one of the beams exited the perimeter. As the Draconian's beam hit its circular mark, Eddie's bolt passed through the same opening, entered the perimeter, and slammed into the next Draconian spoke in the wheel. The explosion that occurred was like a grenade going off in a crowded room, destroying the target and damaging the two closest ships. The perimeter defense shield shattered from the outward blast wave just as Eddie's ship was a quarter mile from ground zero. There were now only five Draconian ships in view. They were breaking formation. And they were pissed.

The Draconian that had provided Eddie with his opening went right after Eddie's ship, while the others engaged with the arriving Centaurian team.

Whitey, Eddie shared. *I'm leading this one away from the herd.*

Got him. Whitey replied in pursuit. *Fuck, they are fast. Eddie, get clear.*

Eddie rolled his ship to his right towards the coast line and there on his screen was an immense crater where LA once sat.

Jayney lock on. Eddie felt Whitey call as his own screen was consumed by a brilliant glow. A moment later, the glow dimmed and shrank to a circle of warm light at the end of a dark enclosure. A tunnel. He tried to maneuver his fingers on the template he knew must be before him to steer his ship towards the light but couldn't feel his hands. He saw the small silhouette of an equine taking form at the center of the light.

It's okay, Eddie. The sultry voice gently entered his thoughts. *I got you.*

* * * * *

"Aaaaarrrrrgggggggghhhhhh!"

Bobbi's sudden wail caused Renee to leap to her feet from her seat inside the protective circle. As she turned towards its source, the others had all scrummed around their lover, friend, and mentor, who sobbed with such force that the others throbbed outward in response.

"Eddie's dead!" Scarlett sobbed towards Renee through a tear shrieked face.

"There but for the grace of God." Renee whispered in response, reflexively tracing a sign of the cross in the air before her. "May God have mercy on his soul."

CHAPTER FIFTY-NINE
(East Coast)

Michelle watched her screen as the battery of SM-6s and Tomahawks rising from Southern Illinois that Scott Air Force Base launched were vaporized by three coalescing blasts from the three Draconian space crafts. The northern Draconian ship then took out the City of Chicago, leaving a huge crater that was rapidly filling with Lake Michigan. Everything just disappeared.

Stay close behind me lover. She shared with Everett, who was hovering in the craft beside hers. *Keep up!*

Michelle hurtled her craft Earthwards towards the three Draconian ships and fired a salvo of her plasma bolts at the one furthest south. She could feel the blowback from the resulting impact blast wave as the bolts struck the Draconian ship's overhead defense shield but did not breach the target. Everett followed directly behind her and unloaded sixty similar blasts towards the exact same target area. Finally, there seemed to be an alteration in the translucent shields, which now showed flashes at the impact zone that looked like sheet lightning as the energy holding it together became compromised.

It's weakening. Everett reported as he followed his spouse in an upward arc towards the atmosphere's canopy.

Nicely executed, Ev! Michelle responded as his ship joined hers at the apex. *Let's hit it again!*

Jayney, I need visuals on the other Draconian ships.

Everett and Michelle's screens went live with visuals of the two more northern ships engaged in battle with the other four Centaurians. A beam from their southern target just missed its mark, as its crossfire passed between Petrichor's craft and Lenny's, who were tasked with taking out the middle Draconian ship, while Jimmy and Gina were engaged with the northern most ship. The Draconians were covering each other's asses.

We need to get back down there. Everett shared and sent his ship into a leading free fall directly towards the southern craft. Michelle fell in right behind him.

The southernmost Draconian fired another beam towards the Centaurians engaged with the center ship. Everett unloaded his plasma bolts so quickly they looked like an unbroken energy beam all striking the same spot as before. This time the sheet lightning expanded all around the southern craft as Michelle released her barrage from a dozen meters behind and below her lover's ship, just as she passed over the impact zone. Michelle was so focused on observing the Draconian's energy field dissipate, she didn't see the blinding ray coming from the north until it struck Everett's ship.

Before her flash-blindness recovered, Everett was gone.

"You mother fuckers!" Michelle angrily sobbed as she dodged a second beam from her north. The sudden pain she experienced in her heart was almost debilitating, but the warrior in her held on. The southern craft, now without its protective screen, bolted forward in an upward arc, using its compatriot's beam as cover, and barely avoiding the next string of plasma bolts Michelle unleashed in its direction.

Michelle, help! Petrichor cried as the screen split and Jayney displayed the dog fights now occurring directly to Michelle's north. Michelle could only see two Centauri ships now caught in the upward cross fire of the Draconian warships.

"Sorry babe," Michelle whispered through tears as she ended the pursuit of her target and directed her ship northward. She immediately fired a salvo of plasma bolts towards the center ship, but it barely impacted its protective energy field. She repeated another relentless barrage towards the same mark hoping to take out the shield, which began to respond with the same sheet lightening show as the southern craft.

At that moment, the other Centaurians crossed directly between the two Draconian ships hoping to draw their crossfire beams directly at each other. Instead, the Draconians suddenly abandoned the battle, taking off in opposite directions. This forced the Centaurians to split into two separate pursuits, one-on-one. Michelle turned her ship back in the direction of her own target.

Jayney, Michelle demanded. *Who is left?*

Before Jayney could answer she forced Michelle's ship into a ninety-degree evasive turn, but it was too late. The brilliant light engulfed Michelle's chamber with such speed it looked like a flash. There was no heat, no pain, no sound. Just sudden darkness.

* * * * *

"Michelle, my love." Everette's disembodied voice reached out to her from within the darkness. "It's over."

A pin-point circle of golden light began to rapidly expand before her. She realized she was no longer in a physical body, but her senses continued to report vestigially. She felt Everett's love literally surround her and carry her consciousness in the direction of the light.

"Don't be afraid." Everett whispered. "I'm here."

Shapes began to form as she drew closer to the circle. A small gathering of shadowy figures parted to allow a large shadow to advance towards the edge of the light. Michelle recognized that silhouette.

"You're home Michelle," the sultry voice called out to her. "The battle is behind you. It means nothing here. Just let it go."

* * * * *

Gamma Draco stared at the spot on his screen where Michelle's ship had most recently appeared as the last of the particle beam he fired dissipated into the surrounding azure of the Terran atmosphere. This was his moment of glory. Indeed, if either of the two others Draconians faltered, Gamma could advance to the Beta, or even the Alpha position. He was ready –

-   Gamma never felt the spontaneous explosion that consumed him and his ship.

* * * * *

A large V shaped craft hovered over Central Missouri.

"Direct hit!" The petite Grey humanoid standing at the control panels confirmed to the slightly larger Grey humanoid sitting in a Captain's chair, studying the large screen before him.

"Should I pursue the other two Draconian crafts?" He asked the larger Grey.

"No, we need to head out to the west coast, where the rest of the battle is waging." The larger Grey responded.

The smaller Grey hesitated.

"If the Intergalactic Federation gets word that we are here at all, the Greys will be sanctioned. Maybe even driven out of the federation for good." The smaller Grey said.

"I know." The larger Grey said. "That is why I only brought my ship. Plausible deniability."

"Why are we here, Father?" The smaller Grey asked.

"*We* are here because *you* would not let me come alone." The larger Grey responded.

"Fair point," the smaller Grey responded, as he worked the control panel to adjust their ship's course. "Then why are *you* here?"

"Because those Lizards are trying to put down my cousin, Jimmy McCarthy!" The larger Grey replied, a palpable edge to his voice.

"The humanoid at the hearing?" The smaller Grey asked, incredulously. "But he identified himself as Jimmy *Moran* before the Intergalactic Federation."

"A shit by any other name would smell like home," Apples, the larger Grey, responded, his voice and cadence now shifting to a Manhattan patois. "Blood is blood. I'd recognize my cousin Jimmy even if you shaved his ass and made him walk backwards."

CHAPTER SIXTY
(Area 51)

"Okay, Jayney." Lucian said. "I'm taking us in over the Pahranagat Range, and then going for a deep dive."

"Jayney," Buck added. "How is this going to work again?"

"I'm just going to take a peek inside that mind of yours," Jayney replied. "All you'll need to do is look at the target and press that button on the holographic screen before you."

"Plasma torpedoes?" Buck asked.

"Close enough." Jayney responded.

"Will it take out their gun?"

"And then some."

"Big bang?"

"Big bang!"

"Okay," Lucian said. "Coming up on Hancock Summit. General, better get your hand off your cock and where it's supposed to be!"

"Don't worry about my hand, Loosh." Buck replied. "I got this."

"Cup and pucker, Buck." Lucian replied as their craft crossed into Area 51 airspace. "Jayney, lock onto their Plasma Gun."

Lucian's descent was traced by every munition the military could hurl in their direction. But Lucian played the keyboard like Billy Joel as he wove the craft past the tracer rounds at hypersonic speed down the mountain. At the half way point, Jayney shouted.

"Incoming!"

The first plasma bolt exiting Nicolo's cannon just missed Jayney's energy shield, taking a huge chunk out of the mountain behind them.

"Got 'em!" Buck shouted as he spotted the flash at the business end of the bore. "Pull up!" Buck slammed his fist on the control button just before the plasma bolt struck the right front of the ship.

"Energy shield is down!" Jayney shouted, as the ground where the plasma cannon had sat lit up like a MOAB impact.

Lucian tried to turn his ship eastward, but flack exploded in the sky everywhere around him. He managed to avoid five of the six Tomahawks.

"Jayney, wrap Buck!" Lucian shouted just as number six caught the back end of the craft. The explosion rocked them forward and sent the craft end over end hurtling towards the ground. Lucian fought to right it, just getting the nose up before it slammed into the giant salt lake, tearing a groove in the playa and leaving a trail of debris for a mile before finally coming to a rest.

Nothing moved in the darkness of the craft's cabin.

CHAPTER SIXTY-ONE
(West Coast)

It took a moment for it to register. There was no explosion, no dust cloud, nothing. Just a brilliant beam and Eddie was gone.

Whitey's kill was going to be different. His plasma bolts slammed into the rear of Eddie's assassin, who then made the mistake of trying to outrun the wolf. Whitey chased him south along the west coast line connecting with another hundred strikes before the Lizard's energy shield gave way.

The Lizard did his best in right angle maneuvers to shake Whitey's pursuit, but Whitey had crossed the red line and was in full hunt mode. The Lizard could not gain enough distance in order to turn and fight, so he headed back towards the dogfight off LA. Whitey sensed the creature's panic. The primal fear. He wanted this Lizard's last emotion to be his first taste of terror.

When Whitey saw the other ships battling in the distance, he knew he had to end it. He fired another fifty rounds of plasma bolts into the rear of the Lizard's ship and watched as the fireball at the front of the craft consumed the rest as it entered the conflagration. Whitey didn't peel off. Instead, he flew his craft through the center of the smoke ring from the ensuing explosion.

"Toasted Lizard smells just like chicken!" He shouted to Jayney.

As he reached where LA once stood, he saw both Stella and Apollo's crafts drawing the remaining four crafts into a Gordian knot through incredible maneuvers that prevented the Lizards from getting a clean shot without taking out one or more of their own crafts but allowing the Centaurians to fire short rounds of their plasma bolts that appeared to be weakening the Draconians ships' protective energy fields.

When two of the Lizards pulled out of the dogfight and positioned themselves in a hovering pattern to fire into the cluster, Whitey went for them. He fired his plasma bolts at the closest to the shoreline and before it could turn to return fire he had decimated its energy shield.

As he fired his kill shot, he howled as the Lizard's ship exploded, but before he could draw another breath, the interior of his ship flashed, and then his world went dark.

Whitey could not feel the contours of his body, but he sensed movement around him and knew he was no longer upright but racing forward shoulder to shoulder as part of a larger group, a pack. He sensed the energies of Blue and Maeve directly on either side of him, and so many other Canidae as they all sprinted through the darkness together. Whitey had never felt so free.

When a large energy drew up beside him Whitey quickened his own pace to keep up as it moved through the pack to the lead. Whitey felt the energies tighten behind them as the space seemed to compress into a bottleneck, and for the first time Whitey wondered where they were all heading.

When he spotted the golden circle in the distance, he felt his first moment of anxiety. But then he felt the love and heard the sultry voice emanating from the large form beside him.

"Don't worry Whitey, keep running, your friends are waiting." Claires voice sang out to him. "We are free to run forever."

CHAPTER SIXTY-TWO
(East Coast)

I had never seen anyone so beautiful. Lenny thought to himself, as he recalled the moment Petrichor had appeared outside her spacecraft on the tarmac in Oregon over two Terran decades before.

You would think that having just survived a firefight with dozens of mercenaries that night, and the onslaught of the U.S. military, that Lenny's mind would have been elsewhere. But Petrichor looked like she had just stepped off Olympus, or risen like Botticelli's Venus, fully formed, from the sea.

Lenny was once the ultimate romantic. He had loved his wife deeply for decades. Then one day she demonstrated her true colors and dumped him when the government made him a fall guy. He was banished from the most powerful city in the world to babysit ex-felons as part of WITSEC, the government's witness protection program.

Since Lenny's arrival in Northern Colorado in the early part of the Terran twenty-first century, he hadn't even looked at another woman. He showered his wonderful Am-Staff rescue, Maeve, with all his affection and spoiled her rotten. They were inseparable.

Otherwise, he spent most of his free time socializing with his best friends, Helen and Bobbi, a lesbian couple, after he helped Helen resettle in WITSEC to avoid any issues after testifying against the MS-13 gang members that murdered her Uncle Gus.

"Lenny's girls," as he liked to call them, gave him the best of all worlds. They provided him with a strong feminine energy, and actually cared about his welfare like a couple of doting sisters. They were lovely to be around, and their public expression of affection for each other was contagious. They were family.

Bobbi, a self-proclaimed psychic-witch, would even perform wonderful parlor tricks that left Lenny amazed and amused, and often confused, although he wasn't sure how much he believed in that hocus-pocus. And given that they ran one of the finest restaurants in the NoCo area, meant Lenny never went without delicious food in his belly. And those waitresses, the Sirens, who were way too young for Lenny but had an almost supernatural attractiveness that reminded him every day that he was still a man, provided regularly enjoyable moments on a purely aesthetic level.

Lenny was able to settle into a satisfactory, although emotionally isolated existence.

But then he met Jimmy and Gina Moran. Watching their interactions reawakened his desires for something more. Someone else. There were times during their regularly crowded gatherings at Casa Claire, when he would catch their shared glances, the brushing of their hands, their short-hand communications, even when they gave each other shit, when Lenny realized what was missing from his own life. He had made up his mind to start dating again. Lenny signed up for one of those on-line sites. But before he even got to swipe left, his entire world turned upside down.

Extraterrestrials and a talking-psychic mule named Claire were the catalysts that drew Lenny into a world where the totally unexpected became the new norm. Enter ghosts, witches, psychics, pixies and even a werewolf, add mafiosos, AI and wealthy evil geniuses, and finally sprinkle that with a corrupt world government, and you have the whirlwind existence that consumed Lenny's life over his last few years on Earth. Looking back, he wouldn't have changed a thing.

Enter Petrichor. Lenny was smitten.

Lenny spent the next Centaurian year following this incredible female around like a puppy. She refused all of his entreaties, and ignored every clever quip he could express during any gathering of their immediate crew or the pure-blood Centaurian people. Petrichor's inner circle was Michelle and Gina, which didn't provide Lenny with much opportunity to join in. So, Lenny decided to spend as much time as possible in the immediate social circle of Stella and Apollo, Petrichor's favorites, using the excuse of their continuing marshal training. He was happy to continue the tutelage he had started with them back on Earth, and he was happy whenever Petrichor stopped by to see them when they were in his company. He always used these opportunities to show off his wit and physical prowess, because his forged bond with the two children allowed Petrichor to experience Lenny through their eyes.

She never laughed at his antics, but the first time he saw her smile in his direction, his heart melted. But she still remained emotionally distant whenever they met publicly.

The night Jimmy Moran approached Lenny and the others with the offer to transform via the Hadron Distributor, Lenny was first in line. When he awoke after the event, he threw all caution to the wind, sought Petrichor out in her chamber and laid his heart on the line. This wasn't infatuation, he told her. What he felt for her was the real Terran deal, now nicely wrapped in a Centauri package.

Every dog has his day, and that day was all Lenny's.

To say that his first night with Petrichor was the closest thing Lenny had ever come to having a religious experience, would not do that night any justice. Lenny would have happily died that night in her arms, without regret. It was just that perfect. He even thought he had heard her giggle there in the darkness.

Given the added bonus that Centaurians needed very little sleep, Lenny had plenty of opportunities that night and every night since then to repeat that performance. He summoned up a clear image of the last time he saw her naked.

Is that all you ever think about? Petrichor intruded on just Lenny's thoughts.

I got no secrets from you, P! Lenny responded on the same closed telepathic channel. *Just seeing what's on the menu once we finish these Lizards off.*

Well, we better get that task out of the way then. Petrichor replied flirtatiously.

Okay everyone, take out your targets and then help out as needed. Petrichor shared with the others. *Come home safe and I'll see you all on the other side.*

* * * * *

Time to go. Petrichor again reached out to Lenny directly.

Right behind you. Lenny responded as he followed Petrichor's precipitous dive directly down upon the center Draconian craft which was at that moment firing one of its brilliant plasma beams in a southerly direction.

Lenny returned to the matter at hand and saw an image shared by Everett of repeated strikes on the Draconian's energy shield and the sheet lightening effect it was having before the telepathic line went dead.

Lenny followed in right behind Petrichor's dive over the top of the center Draconian craft and fired as many rounds as his mind could focus on that one spot where he had seen Petrichor drop her payload. Nothing.

As he turned the nose of his craft skyward, he watched on his screen as his lover's craft headed towards lower space. He caught his breath as she just avoided another beam emanating from the Lizard's ship. Lenny rolled right and turned his craft back towards his target and began firing towards the face of its craft, the source of that beam.

"No one shoots at my woman!" Lenny shouted into the ether.

* * * * *

Petrichor headed skyward, flustered that her plasma bolts had no effect on the Draconian vessel the way they appeared to have during Michelle and Everett's assault on the other craft.

Petrichor's ship was rocked by a blast wave coming from the south and as she recovered, Jayney shouted aurally. "Lenny's in trouble."

Petrichor reversed her course and checked her screen. There was Lenny heading straight towards the Draconian vessel which had just fired another plasma beam in a southern direction.

She pulled up a visual and saw Michelle's craft drop her pursuit of the third Draconian vessel and head in her direction. The rest of the southern sky was empty.

Lenny, pull out! Petrichor commanded.

Michelle, help! She begged her friend.

The simultaneous beams coming from the center Lizard ship and from its now returning compatriot struck Lenny's and Michelle's crafts within nanoseconds of each other. The two Centaurian ships were gone before the brilliant light dissipated.

Petrichor felt her knees weaken and start to give way. Jayney caught her with a captain's chair.

"Stay focused Petrichor!" Jayney shouted aurally in a perfect mimic of the Centaurian leader. Her own disembodied voice seemed to galvanize the Amazonian figure who leapt to her feet and began firing her plasma bolts at the closest craft that had just taken out Michelle. With no shields to protect it, it exploded in a fireball.

"That's for my girl!" Petrichor shouted, then turned her craft towards the center ship. "And this is for Lenny!"

Petrichor fired her weapon and thought the sudden flash that consumed her screen was the center ship exploding like the other, but there was no percussion, no blast wave, no Petrichor.

＊ ＊ ＊ ＊

I'm here, P. Lenny's voice reached her in a way that felt similar to their telepathic communications, but now she could also feel the warmth of his energy surrounding her in the darkness.

Are you all right? Petrichor asked. She tried reaching out into the darkness with phantom limbs and realized that she had left that energy plane.

Is this all there is? She asked, hesitantly.

No, my love, Lenny's thoughts responded. *Watch.*

A pin prick of light began to expand and approach from a distance. As it enlarged, Petrichor could see silhouettes start to take form on the edge of the opening, as Lenny's energy guided her consciousness in its direction.

A number of the forms in the center of the group started to resemble her Centaurian subjects in size and shape. She counted five but could not make out their faces.

The largest shape standing in the center of the group was unmistakable.

Lenny insisted on meeting you first. The sultry voice transcended her thought.

But the others, the children?! Petrichor responded.

Do not worry, Claire shared. *They have their journeys to complete. Your journey is over.*

CHAPTER SIXTY-THREE
(Area 51)

The pain in Buck's head was excruciating. He felt like he had just caught the full percussion from an M795 Howitzer shell landing beside him. The last thing he recalled was being wrapped in an invisible cushion by Jayney before the shit hit the fan. Then the tumbling began. He heard Lucian scream. Then darkness.

He was pinned face down on what felt like the curved ceiling of the ship's inner chamber. There was something on top of him.

"Loosh?" Buck's raspy voice called out. Nothing.

"Jayney?" He asked.

"Yes, Buck." Jayney responded, with a strange tone of bewilderment.

He freed his arms from beneath his chest and pulled himself forward until he got far enough out from under what had been lying atop of him. He turned his body around and sat up. He ran his hands over his head and chest to see if he felt any wounds or damage. Satisfied that there was nothing more than scratches and a few sensitive bruises, he ran his hands down his legs until he came to what had pinned him.

"Jayney, lights!" He shouted. After some flickering, enough of the cabin's ambient light returned. "Shit! Buck shouted.

There, lying across Buck's shins, was Lucian's lifeless body. Buck could see that the young man's left leg was twisted unnaturally, and there were rivulets of dried blood running from his nose and ears.

Buck reached for his carotid artery.

"Jayney, he's got a pulse." Buck said. "Do something! There must be something in your bag of tricks."

"Show me an image." She replied.

Buck had seen enough battlefield triage situations to visualize a rescue backboard, field cast, neck collar, intubation kit, oxygen and saline feed, and a morphine push to stabilize the wounded until you could transport them to a field hospital. He sat and focused as clearly as he could on each item as they would be applied by an experienced paramedic on the young man before him. Within moments, Jayney had stabilized Lucian just as Buck visualized.

"Now get us outside." Buck asked.

"You're in the middle of nowhere." Jayney responded. "He's not going to last long. Not sure he'll survive the transport."

Buck focused on the tarmac where his plane landed on the Groom Lake base weeks before.

"Take me there Jayney." Buck said, as he smoothed the hair back off Lucian's forehead. "I'm still a fucking General in what's left of this military."

A moment later, Buck was kneeling beside the stabilized Lucian in the same spot he had been standing when he first arrived at the Groom Lake airbase. The area was now filled with fire engines, soldiers and emergency service technicians and vehicles racing to deal with the outcome of the explosion of Nicolo's Plasma cannon. A line of armored vehicles loaded with soldiers were racing out in the direction of the salt flats.

Jayney, if you are still in my head. Blow that craft the fuck up. Buck shared. *I don't want these cocksuckers stripping it for parts.*

The huge explosion in that general direction told Buck his prayers were answered.

Given the catastrophic preemptive event that had just occurred on the base, no one seemed to notice one more soldier being triaged for injuries.

Buck spotted a military ambulance racing towards the outer gates to Nicolo's compound and stepped out in the roadway, his hands in the air, forcing the driver to jam on its brakes. It came to a stop just inches from Buck's chest.

"Are you fucking crazy?!" The driver shouted out the cab window as Buck ran towards the driver's door.

"*Are you fucking crazy, General?*" Buck barked as he pointed to his stars. Then he pointed to Lucian. "Get this hero to the base hospital, corporal, and do it yesterday!"

The driver hesitated just long enough to realize his future in the military was now hanging in the balance, and then called the EMS tech in the back of the vehicle to join him outside, stat!

Within moments Buck was on the bench in the back of the ambulance as it hurtled towards the base hospital. The General's fingers kept time on his knees with the soft beep of Lucian's heart monitor, and he felt himself willing Lucian's chest to keep inflating.

The EMS Tech checked the monitors and, satisfied he had done all he could, glanced over at Buck, studying the top of his scalp.

"Looks like you may need a few stitches there, sir." The EMS Tech suggested tentatively.

Buck glanced at the Tech's name badge. *Sgt. Raymond Keane.*

"Just worry about keeping this kid alive, Sergeant Keane." Buck said. "I want the best doctor on the base waiting for him when we arrive." While the Sergeant relayed the orders to the driver, Buck added. "And tell Colonel Smith that if he's not at the hospital to meet me upon my arrival, then he better be dead, or he'll wish he was."

"Yes, sir!" Sgt. Keane responded.

"And get me a satphone!"

CHAPTER SIXTY-FOUR
(Colorado)

Mac checked his watch. 7:45 a.m. During the hour since the general had left with Lt. Commander Benson, the world had changed forever. Mac had been fielding reports that every superpower was now leaderless, including the United States. The East and West coasts of his country were decimated. The military was now functioning as separate militias scattered across what was left of North America, including the Canadians, each imposing their own version of Martial law on the surrounding citizens. No one on the ground knew who was calling the shots. In the air, the invading UAP's had destroyed all air and sea support. Even Nicolo's RES squadron had been decimated.

The only hope left for the world was the rag-tag group of Aliens, and an ex-fighter jockey that had commandeered the general. From the reports Mac was receiving, things weren't looking good.

The satellite phone chirped on the general's desk causing everyone in Bobbi's circle to start.

"Major General Corry." He answered on the second chirp.

Bobbi, whose eyes were still red from her tears for her brother, was sipping some tea. She reached over and took Savanna's hand firmly in her own.

"Be strong," she whispered. Savanna pulled her hand free and called out to Mac. "What's happened?!"

"It's Buck," Mac said as he offered the satellite phone to Renee. "He wants to speak to you."

Renee closed her eyes and took a deep breath to settle herself before accepting the satphone.

"Yes Buck," she answered, barely able to suppress the smile that arose from the sound of his voice. She nodded a few times as she listened, glanced over at Savanna and her face sobered.

"Will do." She responded after a few more moments. She looked like she was about to hand the satphone back to Mac, then in a much softer voice, whispered. "Buck, I'm glad you're okay."

She placed the phone back onto the desk while she gathered her thoughts, then turned to the others. "There was a crash. Buck suffered a head laceration but is recovering." Renee hesitated a moment more, so Bobbi spoke.

"Lucian is in a medically induced coma," Bobbi poached her thoughts. "He's stable for now, but he's suffered three broken ribs, compound fracture to his left leg and a lacerated spleen. Then there's some swelling on his brain."

"Dear goddess!" Savanna shouted as Scarlett comforted her.

"Eddie says he's not with them. Not yet." Bobbi added, her eyes closed as she tuned in to the ether.

"Them?" Helen asked.

"Ev and Michelle... Whitey... Lenny... and Petrichor." Bobbi slowly relayed.

Helen dropped back into her chair, holding her face in her hands. Eileen placed her arm around Helen's shoulder.

"Gina and Jimmy?" Eileen asked, as the younger women's weeping was punctuated by deep sobs.

"Not yet." Bobbi responded.

"Stella and Apollo?" Helen added.

Bobbi shook her head. "No, they're not with Eddie."

Renee studied the group as they shared this incomprehensible information as if they were receiving it from a live voice on the other end of the satphone. What she had witnessed with her own eyes these past few hours had shattered the foundations of the science she had worked so hard to master. She felt a lot less confident about the universe she inhabited. And Renee did not care. She watched as each of this strange group did their best to console the others, she felt the love that bound them together and knew it would help them get through it all.

Renee watched Bobbi off by herself studying the others and realized that she had not gotten the opportunity to offer her condolences over the loss of Bobbi's brother. She walked over and gave Bobbi a hug. "I'm so sorry about Eddie." She whispered.

Bobbi placed her arms around her, and Renee felt a soft electric current coursing through her body. Suddenly, Renee felt an emotional release she had never experienced before and began to sob. Bobbi held her firmly and began to rock ever so slightly. Mother nature.

Then Bobbi whispered. "Don't worry, Buck will be fine."

"And Lucian?" Renee whispered back.

"That die is not cast."

Renee felt a warm tiny tongue flicker on her ankle, looked down and spotted Fergus. She released Bobbi, reached down, and scooped the pup into her arms, hugging him like an avatar of his caretaker, Buck. She thought about the others that passed and mentally recited a Methodist prayer she recalled from childhood.

Give rest, Lord Jesus Christ, to those who have died, and rest with you – where there is no more sorrow or pain, but life everlasting. Holy God, creator and maker of all; You are immortal; we are mortal, From dust we came and to dust we will return. Yet even at the grave, because you rose from the dead, we make our song: Alleluia!

"Amen." Bobbi offered to all. Hearing that affirmation, Mac reflexively blessed himself.

CHAPTER SIXTY-FIVE
(West Coast)

Now Apollo! Stella commanded, maneuvering her craft to avoid the percussion from the exploding Draconian ship to the east. She fired upon the Draconian ship on the tail of her brother, knowing he would crossfire on her pursuer. The impact of her relentless strikes caused sheet lightning to replace the translucent energy shield of her target. Apollo's ship passed within yards of hers, causing the two pursuing Draconians to swerve to avoid their unexpected exit from the aerial knot they had just tied.

Finish them! Apollo countered as the two Centaurian ships simultaneously fired again on each other's pursuers. Both found their mark.

The two Draconian ships exploded within nano seconds of each other.

Before Stella could reach out to her younger brother, her screen was filled with a brilliant light.

A moment later, she found herself staring at another screen showing her ship enveloped by a brilliant beam fired from the third Draconian's craft.

She was locked in someone's embrace.

"I got you." Apollo whispered in her ear. "Jayney, get us out of here."

At that moment another beam crossed Apollo's screen and the siblings watched as the last Lizard ship exploded. As Apollo's ship hovered, another large V-Shaped craft appeared on his screen.

"Who the fuck is this?!" Apollo said before transporting to his control panel, ready to fire.

Wait! Stella shared. *Jayney, is that Draconian?*

No. Jayney responded.

The large ship slowly turned towards the screen.

Sis, I'm taking this fucker out. Apollo shared. *You just saw what it did to the Lizard's ship. Right through their energy shield.*

"Hold on." Stella said aurally.

"They are Greys!" Jayney added.

A moment later, a humanoid face appeared on the screen. Its skin was light grey in color, almost white. Unlike other Greys Stella had heard of since her time back on Centauri, this one had a normal sized head and eyes, a nose, ears, and black, wavy hair, which was tied back in a pony tail. A smaller version of the same creature could be seen in the background. The main creature tilted his head and studied the female face appearing before him. There was a look of recognition.

When the creature began to speak, its voice had a slight, nasally tone but spoke in perfect English. It sounded like her father.

"Please tell Jimmy Moran that his cousin, Apples, heard the call of his Clan and came to join the fight. And as much as I would love to stay for the rest of this donnybrook, I've already placed my own people in the crosshairs of the Intergalactic Federation on this matter. But at least I could even up the odds. Tell him I'll be in touch once the smoke clears."

And with that, Apples stepped back from the screen so that his whole body was visible and moonwalked out of view, leaving just the smaller Grey staring apologetically at its cousins.

"And if the Intergalactic Federation does find out?" Stella asked.

"Well, as my father loves to say," the smaller Grey replied, now assuming a New York accent. "Fuck 'em if they can't take a joke!"

The screen reverted back to the hovering ship, which then disappeared.

Stella and Apollo, Gina's voice interceded. *If you hear me, help!*

Jayney, Apollo commanded, *find our parents!*

CHAPTER SIXTY-SIX
(Alpha)

That's right, chase me. Alpha thought as he led the last of two Centaurian ships away from the other. He didn't want to go too far, as he wanted a Centaurian witness to how a true warrior ends the battle. With any luck, Beta would play with his target long enough for Alpha to return and finish the job.

I hope Jimmy Moran is in one of these Centaurian ships.

Alpha knew from the telepathic silence that, beyond Beta, he had lost the rest of his crew. They had died in battle, an honor that had been in short supply since their warrior race were subjugated by the Intergalactic Federation. He would sing their songs of valor and bravery upon his victorious return to Draco. The Centaurians had proven to be far more skillful than he had expected, and the time had come for Alpha to end this game.

A barrage of plasma bolts slammed into the back of his ship, and his console warned of pending shield failure.

Alpha raised the nose of his craft towards the stratosphere in an attempt to get enough distance from his pursuer to turn and fire upon her. He was surprised that, despite travelling at his top speed, the craft behind him was closing in on him. He took his ship into a ninety-degree turn back east towards Beta.

Beta, lure your Centaurian west. Alpha commanded.

Within moments Alpha spotted the other Draconian ship on his horizon. The last Centaurian ship was not yet in sight.

That's right. Alpha shared. *Let's finish this together, Beta. Brothers in arms.*

CHAPTER SIXTY-SEVEN
(Jimmy)

Fuck these bastards are fast! Jimmy thought to himself as he raced to catch the Draconian after a series of brilliant evasive actions over the Atlantic left him scrambling to recover the chase. He really thought he had gotten the upper hand when the Draconian's energy shield dissipated in a flash just over Bermuda. But then the Lizard showed his flying chops that Jimmy just could not match.

Heading your way, Gina!

Jayney, throw on the afterburners, Jimmy begged as his fingers danced across the control keys.

No afterburners. Hang on! Jayney responded as the ship leapt forward under Jayney's support.

"You've been pretty quiet there, Claire." Jimmy called over his shoulder while he let Jayney play catch-up. When he didn't draw the expected sultry sarcastic response. Jimmy glanced back, but the chamber was empty. In the first time since he had faced down Dan Pearson's nine-millimeter, Jimmy felt very alone.

'Got him!" Jayney called out, drawing Jimmy's attention back to his screen. He spotted the Draconian ship growing larger on the horizon as Jayney closed the gap. His Lizard had just crossed back over the mainland

and the Draconian again went into evasive maneuvers which prevented Jimmy from taking his shot. Just as they reached Tennessee, Jimmy spotted the other Draconian ship approaching from the west directly on a bee line for its brother. It looked like they were playing chicken.

I'm coming, lover! Jimmy heard Gina's voice in his head.

CHAPTER SIXTY-EIGHT
(Gina)

I'm coming, lover! Gina shared with Jimmy as she saw his ship peek over the horizon, hot on the trail of the other advancing Draconian.

"I got you scumbag!" Gina shouted as she fired fifty plasma bolts at the Lizard a quarter mile in front of her. But her prey guessed just right and rolled downward left a nano-second before her bolts would have hit their mark. But it wasn't a complete waste, as the bolts slammed into the approaching Draconian ship dead center.

"Hard right!" Claire called from behind her. Gina's hybrid reflexes obeyed perfectly, just outrunning the impact wave from the explosion of the Lizard's craft.

Jimmy, I got him! She shared triumphantly as she looped her craft back towards the battle. She glanced back over her shoulder and spotted her wonderful mule staring back in her direction. There were tears on Claire's lashes.

Gina turned back towards her screen and saw Jimmy's ship pass through the dust ring left by the vanquished Lizard's craft and right into a brilliant plasma beam rising from the last Draconian ship, now climbing rapidly from below.

Thank you honey, Jimmy's voice resonated in her head.

Everything shifted into slow motion, and Gina thought her heart would explode.

Stella and Apollo, Gina's voice reached out into the ether. *If you hear me, help us.*

CHAPTER SIXTY-NINE
(Jimmy)

The fireball that consumed Jimmy's target ship directly in front of him blinded him long enough to miss seeing Gina's Lizard roll down to Jimmy's lower right. He saw Gina's craft pass safely off to his left as his momentum carried him into the dust ring.

Thank you honey, Jimmy telepathically shared with his lover, just as his screen was consumed by a brilliant light. Before he could close his eyes in avoidance, Jimmy found himself floating in absolute darkness. It felt just like his interdimensional transportation to the Intergalactic Federation, only this time Jimmy could feel his body. He wiggled his fingers and touched his own face as he hung weightlessly trying to get his bearings.

Then he smelled it. Lavender.

CHAPTER SEVENTY
(Stella & Apollo)

As their ship crossed Arkansas they spotted the flash on the eastern horizon. Within seconds they had reached the final battlefield over Tennessee. There, before them, were two ships, Draconian and Centaurian, hovering just a half mile apart. Nothing else moved in the sky.

CHAPTER SEVENTY-ONE
(Alpha)

What a glorious battle! Alpha thought to himself as he brought his ship to a standstill and hovered while he watched the ship of his last nemesis slow in response and hover so close he could feel the hatred from the occupant within. It was delicious. He only wished he could see who he was about to kill.

CHAPTER SEVENTY-TWO
(Gina)

Jayney, get that motherfucker up on my screen! Gina commanded.

"Gina," Claire whispered. "Run. Now!"

Gina ignored Claire, as her screen came alive with Alpha's face and upper torso. She could see the large cavern and the rippling light patterns in the background. The Lizard seemed almost surprised and studied her for a moment.

"I was hoping you were that insolent creature, Jimmy Moran," the Lizard hissed.

Gina glared back at the Lizard. She had never felt such hatred. The sound of Jimmy's name coming from those leathery lips enraged her even more.

"Sorry asshole, Jimmy couldn't make it." She hissed right back at him. "But he wanted me to make sure and give you this. Fuck you snake eyes!"

She slammed her palm down on the console and unleashed a stream of plasma bolts directly at the Draconian.

At the same moment, a brilliant light filled her screen, and she heard Claire's voice.

I got you!

CHAPTER SEVENTY-THREE
(Stella & Apollo)

Stella and her brother shared Gina's last visuals in their minds as they propelled their ship forward.

Stella cried out like a banshee as their ship's screen relayed how the plasma bolts fired by their mother were absorbed by the opposing brilliant beam of plasma that continued on its path and dissolved their mother's ship in a pool of light. It was over in a second. Stella's shriek continued unabated.

Apollo replayed their mother's last vision while focusing on the Lizard and its background until he drew enough information to form a clear visual of the location.

He opened his mind to his weeping sister as he dematerialized.

The next image Stella had was the back of the creature's head before Apollo spun him around to face him. The creature gasped as her brother grabbed his throat and lifted him into the air, his scaley hands desperately tearing at the skin on Apollo's hands and arm as he sought to free himself.

"This is how you die, up close and personal." Apollo whispered as he held the creature aloft. "That's for my father!"

Apollo slammed his other hand into the Lizards chest. Alpha's eyes bulged and he shrieked and wiggled, trying to free himself, until Apollo's sunken hand withdrew from the Lizard's chest cavity, and crushed the pulsating organ it took with it in a vaporous spray of green blood. "That's for my mother!"

A moment later, Apollo reappeared beside his recovering sister. He was glistening in green mist.

"Fry that fucker." He said, pointing for emphasis at the screen. The wounds on his hands were already healing.

Stella emptied a hundred rounds of plasma bolts into the now lifeless Draconian craft.

That's for the rest of the Berthoud crew," she whispered.

They didn't wait to see the explosion.

"Back to Buckley, Jayney," Stella commanded.

CHAPTER SEVENTY-FOUR
(Gina)

Holy shit, I'm in hell! Gina thought, as she attempted to adjust to the darkness.

No, sweetie, came the sultry thought from the ether around her. *You're going to get your wings.*

A pinpoint of light in the distance began to expand and Gina felt her essence being drawn towards it. While she could not feel the contours of her physical body, she nonetheless experienced the sensation of being lifted by something below her. She instantly recognized the holographic version of the strong back and broad shoulders moving beneath her, carrying her. She felt safe. She leaned forward and wrapped her energy around her friend's muscular neck, and while she could not discern any physical boundaries to her own energy, she sensed the warmth, even the feel, of Claire's mane, as this mystical creature carried her forward.

Claire?

Yeah, sweetie.

Is Jimmy here?

Not yet, sweetie.

Will he get here?

Eventually.

When?

Time is not really an issue here, sweetie.

The pinpoint had now expanded into a large opening with a soft golden light. As Claire carried her through the opening, Gina began to assume her memory of her best physical shape, now riding on the back of one of her dearest friends. There was a slight incline to what appeared as a bridge, or pathway opening before them. Gina could see silhouettes of human shapes, animals and other creatures forming further along that pathway.

The crew are all waiting for you. Claire shared. *Even Blue, Maeve and Mr. Rogers.*

Gina reached up and could now experience touching her own face. It wasn't a physical body as she knew it, but she could feel it. She felt the smile curling at the edge of her mouth and the tears that were coursing down her cheeks.

Claire? She asked her friend.

Yes, sweetie?

Do I really get wings?

She could hear Claire's Lurchy laugh rising up from below her.

No, sweetie, but you can fly. It's all done with a thought.

Gina liked that answer.

Claire?

Yes, sweetie?

Will Jimmy remember me?

Forever!

CHAPTER SEVENTY-FIVE
(Area 51)

Buck paced outside the glass encased treatment room in the Groom Lake medical center. Inside, a number of white coats and nurses checked gauges and readouts and double-checked a series of electrodes attached to various parts of the comatose Lucian Benson. The only part of the young man moving was his chest, that was being repeatedly pumped full of air by the ventilator. When a tall red-haired doctor exited the room, Buck stepped in front of him and placed his hand on the man's chest. The doctor attempted to look indignant until he saw the stars on Buck's uniform.

Buck checked the doctor's name tag.

"Okay, Doctor Kenneth Fischer," Buck began in a tone that telegraphed that he was not suffering any bullshit. "I need you to tell me who you are and what the fuck is going on with that young man in there."

The younger officer took a step back from Buck and peered at his iPad.

"I'm not going to sugar coat this, General." Dr. Fischer began. "Mr. Benson has suffered a traumatic brain injury causing a build-up of pressure on his brain. The neurologist has him on a propofol regimen to maintain a comatose state, and carbamazepine to prevent any convulsions. We also have him on diuretics to reduce the fluid buildup."

"Is it working?" Buck asked.

Dr. Fischer glanced away while he gathered his thoughts. Then he shook his head slightly.

"No," he said. "I'm the base neurosurgeon. While the buildup of pressure has slowed, it has not stopped, and there's been some clotting. I'm recommending a thrombectomy to remove some of the larger blood clots and to relieve some of the pressure."

Dr. Fischer glanced back at the young man lying in the bed. Then turned back to Buck.

"If he doesn't show any improvement," The doctor said. "I have him scheduled for surgery at 1200." He reached into his jacket and removed a card. "That's my cell number." He said, handing it to Buck and turning down the hallway, "If you have any questions, call me."

Buck slid the card into his pocket and leaned against the glass.

"Don't you quit on me now, flyboy," Buck whispered.

"General Sheridan!" Buck turned to see a harried Colonel Smith racing down the hall towards him, a nervous young Lieutenant followed at his heels.

"I told you I wanted you here when I arrived!" Buck barked.

"With all due respect General, there's a shit storm going on right now. On top of it being the end of the world, we're dealing with a major explosion over in the private sector–"

"Nicolo's shop?" Buck cut him off.

Smith started to stammer.

"Well, fuck Nicolo. I want your best platoon ready in ten minutes, locked and loaded. We're going in there to clean house. If I see one of his mercenaries go to scratch their nose, I want them neutralized. If it's Nicolo, I want a double tap."

Smith looked horrified. He couldn't give a shit about wasting a hired gun, but he knew what this meant to his post-retirement options in the private sector.

"Do you have a problem with that, Colonel?" Buck demanded.

"No sir."

"Good." Buck turned back towards the treatment room. "Ten minutes. At Nicolo's gate. Now go!"

* * * * *

Half-hour later, Buck stood gazing at the large pile of wreckage that used to be Nicolo's plasma cannon. He could barely hide his satisfaction knowing he had taken it off line from a spaceship of all places. His platoon had quickly rounded up the surviving mercenaries, who all surrendered without a fight. EMT's bagged and tagged the last of the toasted technicians that had been working the cannon.

There was a door half buried under rubble from the explosion at the back of the room.

Buck spotted Sgt. Keane trying to find an appendage on one of the crispy critters that didn't snap off when he tried to place the tag on it.

"Just toss it in the bag, Sergeant." Buck called to him. Then he waved him over and pointed to the large sliding doors. "What's through there?"

The sergeant checked the schematics on his iPhone and after double checking the room, shook his head.

"Sorry sir, those doors aren't on the blue prints."

"Go grab a couple of men," Buck ordered. "Let's go see what's behind door number two!"

* * * * *

It took another half hour to get the sliding doors uncovered and pried open. When Buck saw another set of similar doors waiting down the cavernous hallway, Buck turned to Sgt. Keane and said, "Get me an RPG. I'm not wasting any more time with this shit."

Suddenly the doors at the end of the hallway hissed and slid open and a stocky football player dressed like a dentist came walking out with his hands above his head.

Sgt. Keane trained a green laser point on his heart.

"Don't shoot General," John Bricker called.

Buck recalled the man who had been with Nicola the last time they met in his office at Buckley.

"Where's your boss and Ygor?' Buck called to him.

"I hope in Hell!" John called back to him. "They were in the saucer overhead that got lit up this morning. By his own fucking weapon. Irony is a wonderful thing."

"Good," Buck replied, smiling as he remembered the moment. "Now get over here and tell me what the fuck you are doing in there."

"I'll do you one better," John replied. "Come in and I'll show you how you are going to save the world."

CHAPTER SEVENTY-SIX (Colorado)

"They're coming back!" Bobbi shouted. "It's over."

"Who?" Helen asked.

"Stella and Apollo." Bobbi replied.

"Gina?" Scarlett asked.

Bobbi shook her head in the negative and the two sisters began to weep. Renee went to console them.

"Jimmy?" Eileen whispered.

"Don't know." Bobbi responded. "All I can say is that Eddie hasn't seen him."

"I want to go see Lucian!" Savanna declared.

"Do we have anything left that still flies, Mac?" Renee asked.

"There's the general's MH-6 Little Bird chopper on the north end of the base." Mac replied. "He never used it. Carries six. I can fly it. About 5 hours one-way."

"Five hours?!" Savanna repeated.

Suddenly two flashes of light appeared behind the general's desk and immediately transformed into the figures of Stella and Apollo. Stella looked drained. Apollo angry.

"You poor kids!" Bobbi said as she crossed the room and hugged both of them. Stella fought to keep it together. *Petrichor and Gina were goddesses. Still are.*

Scarlett walked over to Apollo and took his hand. "I'm so sorry about your mom."

He looked at his hand, the one that had crushed the Lizard's heart that still had the green blood coating it. He was touched that the gore didn't seem to bother Scarlett, who now cradled it in both of her hands, and held it against her chest. Her eyes brimmed with tears.

"Gina was like our mom," Scarlett offered. "She welcomed us into the family."

"Can you take me to Groom Lake?" Savanna suddenly asked Stella.

"Why?" Stella asked.

"Lucian's hurt."

He's in bad shape. Bobbi shared with the siblings.

"Let's go." Apollo said. "Ship is on the tarmac."

Stella took hold of Savanna's hand. Renee grabbed Stella's other one.

"Mac," Renee shouted. "Call Buck on the satphone and tell him to have Groom Lake stand down. We're coming in."

Apollo looked at Scarlett's hands still clutching his own. "I'm going to need that."

"I'm coming with you." Scarlett replied, a slight smile edging her lips. "Gotta keep an eye on my little sister."

A moment later, all five disappeared.

CHAPTER SEVENTY-SEVEN
(Jimmy)

Lavender. *Why is that so familiar?*

Something brushed Jimmy's fingertips.

Gina?

No Jimmy Moran, a beautiful voice filled his mind. *Gina is not here.*

Where am I? Jimmy asked.

I pulled you from your ship into an interdimensional portal. But you cannot stay here long in your bodily form.

Who are you?

An old friend. The voice replied. It was hypnotic in tone and cadence. It entranced him.

Jimmy now felt a warm hand take his own and lead him through the darkness. It felt comforting. Loving. Safe. The smell of lavender enveloped him, permeated his body. It was intoxicating.

Jimmy saw a pinprick of golden light in the distance off to his left as he was carried along in the opposite direction. He felt the urge to turn back towards the light.

No Jimmy, it's not your time. Your journey has not ended.

He could see he was being led towards a soft silverish glow. A portal. As he drew closer, the figure that was leading him by the hand came into focus in the dim ambient light. She was familiar. She was beautiful. Long black hair and olive coloring wrapped in a beautiful golden lamée tunic. As they drew to the edge of the portal she halted and pulled him to her. Her strength was uncanny. Her body was soft and exciting. Her lips gently brushed his own, and as she pulled away, he saw the most beautiful black eyes, one with a tear forming on its edge.

"Who are you?" he whispered aurally, as the taste of lavender danced on his lips.

"It does not matter anymore," she whispered back into his ear, a soft sob as punctuation. "Our time is done. You won't remember us."

The unexpected force of the shove that followed propelled Jimmy through the portal and back into darkness.

CHAPTER SEVENTY-EIGHT
(Lucian)

"Holy shit!" Sgt. Keane exclaimed as the five materialized outside Apollo's space craft on the tarmac in Groom Lake. When he spotted Renee, he saluted. "Lieutenant Colonel, General Sheridan ordered that you were all to come with me. He's waiting at the hospital." He gestured to the waiting Humvee.

Renee put her hand on Apollo's arm to calm him as he stared daggers at the squad of armed soldiers racing to encircle the craft. Stella scanned the young sergeant's mind and transported without a word to the shotgun seat, while the others trotted to and entered the vehicle the old-fashioned way. Apollo looked at the soldier closest to him and pointed to his ship. "There better not be a scratch on that when I get back."

Once Apollo had slid in the back door next to Renee, Sgt. Keane hopped into the driver seat and floored the vehicle down the tarmac.

"How is Lucian?" Savanna called out from the back.

Stella poached the young sergeant's thoughts as he considered the best way to respond. She experienced Lucian's condition through the young man's memory during transport in the ambulance and afterwards, hooked up to the monitors in the treatment room. She felt the man's empathy, his concern for his fellow soldier.

"Lieutenant Commander Benson is in critical, but stable condition, ma'am." Keane responded, doing his best not to sound like an automaton.

Renee sat quietly in the back between the sisters and Apollo. She caught Scarlett glancing over at the handsome young hybrid. She knew that look. She wondered how Buck was holding up.

* * * * *

Buck stood at the glass and stared at the young man lying comatose in the hospital bed while he did his best to wrap his head around everything that happened over the past 24 hours. The world he knew so recently had gone to shit. ETs for fuck's sake! Good and bad. And the alien technology Bricker just showed him, if the scientist was telling the truth, would generate unlimited free energy for the entire fucking world. With that endless resource, and the other alien tech toys Bricker demonstrated, there was nothing beyond humanity's reach. Buck was going to need Renee to translate it all, so his technically challenged brain could better understand it. According to Bricker, if Nicolo had it, there was a slew of other oligarchs hiding it for a century while the Earth went tits up. The old guard petrochemical barons and the greens were too busy at each other's throats to realize that both their positions on fueling the future of the planet were inadequate, indeed, incompetent. The oligarchs made sure there was enough money flowing to both camps to keep those fires burning, while they tried to figure out how to put a money meter on their stolen technology. Buck hadn't even begun to consider what was happening among the civilians beyond the gates of Buckley or Groom Lake with all the shit that had happened. Buck knew that it was now up to him to sort it all out. But that was tomorrow's problem.

Sudden activity by the nurses around Lucian's bedside, accompanied by a rapid increase in the sounding chimes and fluctuating neurologic and cardiac screens in the room, drew Buck's attention back to the here and now. Buck recognized panic in the faces of those trained not to. A team with a crash cart flew past him and when Buck tried to follow them into Lucian's room, one of the nurses firmly shoved Buck back into the hallway, while the rest of the medical team frantically went through their motions to save the young man they didn't know. When the screens and tones all flat-lined, the team stepped back while one young black doctor made Lucian's body arch under repeated attempts with the chest paddles. After the third unsuccessful try, an older doctor placed his hand on the young doctor's shoulder and gave him the cut-off sign. The older doctor glanced at his watch and called the time of death. Twelve noon.

Buck pounded the glass with his fists with such force that the entire trauma team looked over in alarm. The door of the room flew open, and the older doctor walked out without a hint of sorrow. Another day at work. Before Buck could say anything, the older man held up his hand and delivered his worn-out bromide. "We did all we could." Then headed off down the hallway.

Buck entered the room while the nurses performed their routine clean up in aisle five, detaching the electrodes, shutting down the monitors and removing the respirator. When Buck reached the bedside, he found the young black doctor standing beside Lucian, holding one of Lucian's hands. The doctor's eyes were closed, and a tear trickled down his cheek. His lips were mouthing a simple prayer. When he finished, he blessed himself, opened his eyes and looked at Buck. "I'm sorry, sir." The young doctor said, his baritone voice sad, yet rich in empathy. "I did my best."

"I know," Buck whispered back, checking the doctor's name tag: Dr. Emile LaFond. "Thank you, Emile."

The doctor slipped past Buck and exited the room with the last of the trauma team. A lone nurse began shifting the monitors back along the far wall, leaving Lucian lying peacefully alone in his bed, like he was asleep. The general leaned over, brushed the hair off Lucian's forehead, and whispered, "It was an honor to serve with you, son." Buck wiped away his lone teardrop that splashed on Lucian's cheek.

"Buck!"

The general spun around just in time to see Renee and the rest of the crew racing down the hallway and into the room.

"Oh, my goddess!" Savanna shrieked when she saw Lucian. She threw herself across his lifeless chest and started to weep while Scarlett glanced at the battered and bruised face of the fallen hero and did her best to console her sister.

Buck motioned for the nurse to leave the room.

"Are you all right?" Renee asked, embracing Buck in a full hug, burying her face in his chest.

Scarlett turned to the hybrids who stood back by the entryway. "Do something!" She demanded.

Sis, Apollo shared. *Your hands.*

Stella's hands began to glow with a bright white light. She approached the bed while Scarlett pulled the still sobbing Savanna out of the way. Stella gently placed her hands on Lucian's forehead and heart, as the light intensified until it had created an aura that encased Lucian's entire body.

Stella's own body began to shake as she focused on the young man in the bed. Suddenly, the light went out and Stella faltered. Apollo transported and steadied her.

Lucian did not move.

"I'm sorry." Stella whispered. "I've never brought anyone back from the dead."

Savanna engaged in a new series of banshee wails. Scarlett turned to Apollo and took his hand again. "Everett brought Jimmy back from the dead!"

Apollo's eyes lit up as he recalled the memory of that event Jimmy and Gina had shared so many times with them as children.

"Sis," Apollo whispered, "The Hadron Distributor!"

"We can't," Stella said.

"You can, and you must!" Scarlett shouted in a tone that was not open to debate.

Stella met the other woman's eyes and nodded. She patted her tunic and then reached in an appearing opening and withdrew the small silver cylinder that Michelle had handed her the day she left Proxima-b.

The others stood back as the young hybrid pointed at the object and concentrated.

Mom, Stella shared silently with the ether. *I need your help.*

Suddenly, a golden beam shot out of the business end of the cylinder and struck Lucian's torso and head. His body lurched as it did under the paddles and then settled peacefully back on the bed.

As the group watched, the injuries to Lucian's face started to disappear. A moment later, the young man bolted upright in his bed and shouted, "What the fuck?!"

"Jesus Christ!" Buck bellowed. Stella returned the Hadron Distributor to her tunic.

Savanna threw herself on Lucian and began showering him with kisses. Scarlett threw her arms around Apollo and whispered into his ear. "Thank you, thank you, thank you."

Renee ran out of the room, and a moment later, returned with the young black doctor, who, astonished, raced over and began checking Lucian's vitals. As he checked Lucian's pupils with his pen light, he said. "You're a blessed miracle, Lucian Benson. When did your eyes turn blue?"

At the sound of the doctor's voice, Lucian finally spoke.

"I heard your prayers, Doc." Lucian whispered in a raspy voice. "Thank you."

CHAPTER SEVENTY-NINE
(Colorado)

Eileen lay with her eyes closed across the office settee with a sleeping Fergus cuddled in her lap. The dog snored softly in rhythm with his caretaker.

The satphone chirped and while Mac went to answer it, Bobbi's face lit up.

"Lucian is alive and well," she whispered to Helen.

"Yes Buck, that's great news," Mac said into the receiver. "I'll tell -"

He looked over and saw Helen and Bobbi excitedly embracing.

"Wait?! I think they already know."

Mac looked over at the sleeping pup.

"Fergus," he called softly. The dog perked up and looked over at Mac. "Your daddy wants to talk to you."

The dog scrambled across the room and leapt up on Buck's desk. When Mac put the phone to the pup's ears, his tail gyrated like a metronome. After a moment, the dog barked and then leapt off the desk and back onto Eileen's lap, which woke her. The dog started licking the woman's face.

"Eileen," Helen shared. "Lucian is going to be all right!"

"Jesus, Mary and St. Joseph," Eileen replied, with just an ancestral hint of a brogue as she came to full consciousness. "Thank God for small miracles!"

CHAPTER EIGHTY
(Home)

Jimmy awoke to find himself lying on a compressed bed of wild grass, in the middle of a tall thicket of high stalks. He could see the bluest sky he had ever witnessed and white clouds passing over the body sized opening above him. He was completely disoriented. Despite this, the view bore a feeling of familiarity.

As he rose to his feet, he tried to recall his last memory, but his mind felt muddled. The grass was too tall to see above, so he carved a narrow path following his hands clasped in prayer before him. He must have traveled five yards before he exited the path from the thick foliage, and onto a large, nicely mowed field. He turned to the grass and took a few steps back to get perspective. It was a large cylinder of eight-foot-high vegetation rising out of the center of an even larger field. The grass and other wild vegetation swayed in the gentle breeze. It almost seemed alive.

As he tried to get his bearings, Jimmy spotted a large pond. There were a couple of Canadian ducks taking turns dunking for bugs beneath the surface between some cattails. He saw two large mounds rising from the Earth in the field and when he walked closer, he saw the names "Claire" and "Mr. Rogers," respectively, on the wooden crosses at the head of the mounds.

His head started to spin as images filled his mind. A large mule appeared in his thoughts and said, "Jimmy, go up to the house."

I must be tripping, Jimmy thought to himself.

He performed a slow hundred and eighty degree turn and there, in the distance, was a house, sitting on a rise in the property. He slowly made his way in that direction, and as he did he noticed that he was wearing strange clothing. A one-piece, blue jump suit with matching boots.

As he got closer to the house, images began to flash before his eyes. Gatherings of people, eating, drinking, and laughing. He knew them. He could see the mule that had just appeared to him standing among the people and joining in their festivities. Then another image flashed, of a beautiful brunette sitting on the back deck with two beautiful children, both with burgundy colored hair, playing peek-a-boo and laughing. The name Gina flashed into his mind. He felt a palpable ache in his chest.

Then he had an image of a foreign world, on a distant planet, and a tall, blonde goddess sitting on a large throne-like chair. This felt familiar as well.

His mind swam while he fought to make sense of these images, as more started to appear and connect. By the time he had reached the house, it was all beginning to make sense.

"I am Jimmy Moran," he whispered.

He slid open the basement door and called out, "Gina?"

There was no answer, so he entered and followed a memory that led him to an inside stairway. He called again. "Gina?" He could hear his voice echoing throughout the upstairs of the house. Still no answer. As he climbed the stairs, his memories flooded with images of the beautiful brunette, laughing in the kitchen, sipping wine on the back deck, lying naked by the roaring fireplace. An image flashed of her standing over him, a look of horror on her face. Jimmy reached up and rubbed a small spot on his upper chest, but there was nothing there.

He reached the first floor and called out one more time, "Gina?!" He performed a circuit of that floor and with each room his memories continued to return and coalesce. Closeup images of his friends returned as he visualized them around the tables and sitting on chairs on the deck and in the back yard. Their names appeared in no particular order, and he realized that these people were his family.

The two children now preoccupied his mind as he recalled their various stages of development. He recalled them doing amazing things. He recalled memories of their playing, as they dematerialized and reappeared throughout the house. He could now see them as adults, wearing similar clothing to what Jimmy had on. He felt how much he loved them.

When he reached the stairs leading to the top floor of the house, he recalled lying in the king-sized bed next to the beautiful brunette. He recalled the smile she wore when she showed him what he now remembered was a pregnancy test. He closed his eyes and an instant later found himself sitting on the bed, in the same spot, without ever touching the flight of stairs.

Then Jimmy remembered a council of strange creatures standing before him and the large Reptilian who grabbed him and lifted him off the ground.

"I'm coming, lover!" He recalled Gina saying to him. But she wasn't talking. He could hear her thoughts.

He was in a spacecraft. His friends were dying.

Then there was a flash of light. Then blackness. *What happened?*

Jimmy? It was that mule's voice in his head again. Claire.

Jimmy felt drawn to the living room. A moment later, he was standing in the center of that room.

His memories were now all coming together. He remembered who he was. And now he remembered where he was. Home.

And there before him stood his friend, Claire the mule. His mind compared his earlier images of her with the holographic version that he now saw. There was a translucence, where you could almost see through her. But she had physical form. She leaned in and nuzzled his chest, and he reached up and scratched her ears. He felt her love and she felt his.

"What happened, Claire?" Jimmy asked.

"The world almost ended, Jimmy," she responded in her Lauren Bacall voice. "We stopped that from happening."

Suddenly, Claire was back in his head downloading all the missing pieces, except one.

"Where's Gina?" Jimmy asked, his voice cracking just a little.

Claire tried to avoid Jimmy's glance. He could see tears forming on her eyelashes. Jimmy reached down and took her chin in his hand and raised her face to his.

Claire showed him Gina's last memories and then shared Stella's and Apollo's memories of her last moments on their ship's screen. Then she showed him Claire's memories of escorting Gina through the final portal.

Jimmy began to weep and soon was sobbing uncontrollably. He dropped to his knees, trying to catch his breath, but the pain was overwhelming. Claire extended her neck over his shoulder in an attempt to cradle him to her chest.

Moossha, moosha, moosha, Claire whispered as she tried to console him.

"I need to see her, Claire," Jimmy begged through his tears. "One more time."

Claire closed her eyes and mentally reached across the veil. A moment later, the image of Gina appeared in Claire's mind. She was in perfect form. Claire shared this image with Jimmy, who suddenly smiled despite the ravages of pain on his face.

Jimmy, Gina shared. *I'm sorry, honey. I thought that bastard had killed you. I wasn't thinking straight. He got the jump on me.*

No, Jimmy responded, *it's not your fault. Are you all right?*

Never better, Gina responded, she tried to smile. *The whole gang's here, even Whitey, although he likes to hang with Mr. Rogers and the dogs. Do you know you can fly up here? Don't even need wings.*

Jimmy wouldn't engage in Gina's attempt to console him.

I can't live here without you, Jimmy sobbed.

Oh, don't be an asshole, Jimmy, Gina said with mock sternness. *It's not your time. Those are the rules, right Claire?*

Claire nodded her head.

And you gotta look after those kids. Ya' hear me. Gina continued. *They have to step up and run Proxima-b. You have to be around to help them. That's your journey.*

Jimmy began to weep again. He wasn't listening.

Stop that right now, Gina said, fighting back her own tears. *You gotta be strong.*

I'm not strong. I'm nothing without you.

Gina shook her head and looked like she was hearing something Jimmy couldn't.

Listen, honey. I gotta go. She whispered. *I'm sorry.*

No, Gina, please! Jimmy pleaded.

Don't worry, Gina said, doing a terrible job at masking her own sorrow. *Your brothers taught me how to keep an eye on you. So, I'll be watching... and waiting. I love you, Jimmy!*

Gina's image dissolved. Jimmy howled like he was being eviscerated while Claire did her best to comfort him. They rocked for a few minutes together. Then the image of the Three Witches suddenly appeared in Claire's mind, just as Jimmy dematerialized.

* * * * *

"Don't do it, Jimmy."

Claire appeared at the top of Mt. Elbert, ten feet from where Jimmy balanced on the edge of the precipice overlooking the fourteen-thousand-foot drop before him.

"Gina will never forgive you if you leave those kids without their father." Claire added.

"They'll be fine." Jimmy replied sullenly, without looking back at his friend.

"They're stuck helping rebuild this planet from practically scratch while also running Proxima-b, and they'll be fine?" Claire demanded. "All their hybrid family is gone. You going to leave them all alone?"

Jimmy continued to stare into the abyss. He kicked a small stone over the edge and watched it drop. *Just that easy,* he imagined.

"I never thought I would ever say this, but you are one selfish prick." Claire spat out. "Go ahead, jump. But I ain't walking you through the gates if you do."

Jimmy spit off the cliff, and the wind blew it right back into his face. He slowly turned around and stared at his best friend, with a fresh loogey hanging off his nose.

"Message from beyond, Jimmy." Claire said, trying not to smile. "Better heed it."

Jimmy studied Claire's face. He focused on her deep brown eyes. They reminded him of Gina's eyes, when she was pissed at him, before they turned Centaurian blue.

"You know Gina will make your afterlife miserable for eternity if you test her on this!" Claire added.

Jimmy thought this last statement over for a bit. Then he looked at Claire and smiled.

"Eternity is a pretty long time to be on Gina's shit list." Jimmy said.

"I'd rather be in hell." Claire responded.

"I thought there was no hell." Jimmy countered.

"You just went through it." Claire responded. "Come on, let's go home. The rest of the crew will be arriving shortly."

Jimmy walked back from the ledge and wrapped his arms around Claire's neck. He whispered in her left ear, rubbing its bent tip as he did so.

"You weren't going to really let me jump, were you?"

"Fuck you, Jimmy."

Then they disappeared.

EPILOGUE
(The Prometheus Project)

Apollo spent the rest of the afternoon walking John and Renee through each part of the alien technology in the large cavern, including alternative energy devices. He even helped John engage one of the zero-point energy field generators, the size of a car battery, with the energy grid for the military side of Groom Lake. He explained to Renee how the generators could be scaled to operate any size electrical equipment and anti-gravitation engines. He also taught them the process of creating purified alloys so that the generators could be mass produced and shared with the world. Renee took copious notes on her iPad.

Apollo destroyed anything left in Nicolo's collection that could be used to wage war. He instructed Renee on how to pursue developing holographic control mechanisms for their RES program, and promised he would continue to assist them in the future once they had mastered zero-point energy and disseminated it across the planet.

While this knowledge transfer was a much slower process than just downloading the information, Apollo was impressed with both John's and Renee's ability to assimilate, process, and apply what he showed them. He would make each of them repeat what he taught them, like his aunts Bonnie and Tessa used to do when they tutored Apollo and Stella as children, to ensure they understood. He promised them he would return to Groom Lake every six earth-months to check on their progress.

He left John in the lab, tinkering with replicating and down-scaling one of the energy generators to the size of a pack of cigarettes, to be used in a motor vehicle. Bricker was like a kid at Christmas.

At the end of the afternoon, Apollo extended his hand to Renee and said, "Come on, let's go find Buck." As soon as she took his hand, they dematerialized.

John looked over at where they had just been standing.

I got to build me one of those!

* * * * *

Stella was impressed by Buck's leadership skills. In the few hours it took the now hybrid, Lucian, to be ready for discharge, the general had fired the old doctor that hadn't given him the time of day and installed Dr. Emile Lafond, the young black doctor, as administrator of the Groom Lake hospital. Buck had Sgt. Keane escort the old prick to the gate.

Stella noticed Sgt. Keane sneaking glances in her direction while Buck issued his orders. She loved how he blushed when she met the last glance. She almost blushed when she peeked into his thoughts. She made a mental note to follow up on that once she got everything sorted with Buck.

Buck sent his soldiers into the surrounding area to reestablish order among the still terrified civilians. He was in equal parts pleased and concerned to learn that Las Vegas hadn't even registered that an alien invasion had occurred until their energy grid failed, and their slot machines shut down, long after the battle had been won. The casinos wisely opened the bars to placate their customers until they could get a better sense of which direction their dice were going to roll once civil order was reestablished. Buck instructed Bricker to install a zero-point energy generator to power up that city as soon as possible.

With Stella beside him, Buck first briefed General Dowling at Luke AFB in Phoenix on the latest developments, and promised to fly Bricker down to her base to install an alternative energy device before her conventional petrochemical resources were depleted. He was fascinated by how quickly General Dowling accepted the short-hand explanation Stella provided about the who, when and why of what had just changed the world over the past two days.

The general informed Buck that all the California military bases had been compromised, and that Los Angeles was now a bay from the Pacific Ocean. They made plans to reach out to the other military bases, first among the remaining western states, and then working eastward. They would reestablish order and protect the citizenship until they could sort out a more permanent solution. In the meantime, they would immediately cede power to the state governments still functioning, and protection to the local civilian police and fire departments, until a more comprehensive plan could be established. Buck's primary goal was to ensure that this new energy resource was publicly disseminated without any interference from the Davos crowd or the military industrial complex. Their reign was over.

Until then, they would use all existing petrochemical resources. You don't shut off the house lights at night until you have that working flashlight in your hand.

When Apollo and Renee materialized in the office Buck had commandeered from Colonel Smith, who was now leading the small contingent to maintain order in Las Vegas, just because Buck didn't want him anywhere near a serious posting, Stella was thrilled to see Buck take Renee in his arms and kiss her. She was doubly thrilled when Renee kissed Buck back, with twice the passion. They reminded Stella of Gina and Jimmy.

By the time the two military lovebirds came up for air, Apollo had disappeared and reappeared, holding a frantic Fergus, who, upon seeing his human caretakers, leapt out of Apollo's grasp and into the delighted general's arms. The dog then shared frantic facial tongue lashings equally between Renee and Buck.

Apollo walked over and took Scarlett's hand. Stella reached over and grasped Lucian's hand, completing his chain with Savanna.

"Pay attention, newbie," she said to her latest hybrid cousin.

I'm not kidding, Stella shared.

"Holy fuck!" Lucian responded. "I heard that!" Savanna gazed at Lucian with even more wonder in her eyes.

Lucian looked over at the general, nodded and said, "See ya, Buck!"

Both Renee and Buck were in mid-salute when the five of them disappeared.

* * * * *

Mac was standing at Buckley's northernmost tarmac, as instructed by Bobbi, along with the three Sapphic sisters, when Stella's craft arrived. Apollo materialized outside of the craft and walked over to the now Lieutenant Colonel.

"Congratulations on your promotion, Mac!" Apollo said as he reached in and gave the surprised soldier a hug which lifted the human off the tarmac.

"So, you're running the place?" Apollo asked.

"For now." Mac said proudly.

"Well, I think Buck made the right choice," Apollo patted him on his shoulder.

"Are we going to see you again?" Mac asked.

"Mac," Apollo smiled. "you're family now. I'll be stopping by for the occasional holiday meal. Until then, take care of yourself and keep the lights on."

Apollo winked and turned to his three Clan Aunties, who stood in a line, clasping hands. "Ready ladies?"

"Bye Mac!" the three chorused.

Apollo took Bobbi's hand, completing their chain. Then, they all disappeared.

Mac watched as the craft lifted a few feet off the tarmac and hovered for a few seconds.

His eyes couldn't follow its lightening ascent as it lifted into the sky.

* * * * *

"Who the fawk are you?" Brian Erickson demanded when he opened the front door of Casa Claire and found Jimmy sitting at the front window, sipping a coffee, and watching some bunnies playing among the gnomes on the hill on the front property.

"You've done a nice job keeping the place up." Jimmy responded. "I'll make sure you and Janice get a huge bonus at Christmas!"

"What are you, a wise ass?" Brian responded, just as his wife followed him through the front door.

She looked over at Jimmy and shouted. "Holy shit! You're Jimmy Moran! I've seen you and your wife's photo up in the bedroom."

"Who the fawk is Jimmy Moran?" Brian asked his wife.

"Not sure," Janice replied, "but he once owned the place."

Just then Stella's space craft dropped out of the sky and hovered in the front yard.

"Jesus Christ, the aliens are back?!" Brian shouted.

"That's my ride," Jimmy said, with a wink. Then he disappeared. A moment later, he was standing out on the front lawn with the rest of his family of misfits, who instantly appeared from inside the craft. They all embraced him in a scrum and shrieks of joy and laughter could be heard from the crowd.

"We're going back to Bawston," Brian declared, as he stared outside at the joyous mayhem .

"Sorry, sweetheart." Janice responded. "The aliens nuked it."

* * * * *

Jimmy spotted Lucian and gave him a big hug.

"Look at you," he cried. "You've changed!"

You don't know the half of it! Lucian shared telepathically. Jimmy grabbed the young man's face and stared into his Nordic Blue eyes.

We were going to tell you, father. Stella shared.

Are you coming with us? Jimmy gestured to the ship.

Lucian gazed over at Savanna and shook his head.

"Nah," he said aurally. "I think I'm going to hang here."

"And I'll be back regularly," Apollo added with a wink at Scarlett. "To show him the ropes."

Stella materialized beside Lucian and slipped the Hadron Distributor into his jeans pocket.

"If the time ever comes," she whispered. "Just ask Apollo how to use it."

Stella now turned to the group and shouted. "All those leaving on the Centauri express, better be boarding. Take off in two minutes and counting."

They all formed a cluster of rotating hugs and tears and then the mystical humans and their newest hybrid started to back away.

Jimmy walked back over to Helen and gave her a final hug. She started to weep.

"I'm so sorry about Gina," she whispered between sobs. "Bobbi says she's doing well, although her potty mouth still gets the best of her."

Jimmy extended the hug for a few extra beats.

"I think I'm going to miss you most of all," Jimmy whispered back.

Time to go. Stella shared.

"Hold on!" A sultry voice shouted as Claire galloped from around the side of the house and then stopped for a moment before the remaining crew. "I was just taking a last stroll around the property. She nuzzled Scarlett and Savanna, and then turned to them all and declared. "Ladies, and gentleman," she said with a nod towards Lucian, "I'll be back!"

Claire then joined Jimmy and his children, and with one final group wave, they all disappeared.

PROLOGUE
(New Beginnings)

Bobbi, Helen, Eileen, Scarlett, Savanna, and Lucian stood equidistant from one another in a loose circle surrounding the tall cylinder of vegetation on the back property of Casa Claire. They all held white tapers, their golden tips, dancing in the night. The Hunter's Moon had reached its apex in the October night sky.

"Make a wish!" Bobbi shouted and pointed to the arcing trail of the shooting star across the Northern horizon. "Here, where the ley lines meet!"

They all gazed heavenwards and offered their silent aspirations.

Suddenly, three tiny, winged creatures rose from and above the center of the circle and then swooped down and rotated widdershins around the heads of the group's members. They chirped as they gently tapped the top of each head. On their second pass, they all collected in front of Scarlett and chirped in unison.

"Holy shit!" Scarlett shouted. "It's Aine, Breena and Cirrha, Bonnie's Sprites."

"Since when do you speak Sprite?" Savanna asked.

"Don't know," Scarlett replied. "But they need our help!"

NEVER THE END

ACKNOWLEDGEMENTS

First and foremost, I must thank my inner circle of readers, Eileen Cotto, Anna Hillman, Yvette Benson, Renee Clarke, Pete "Buck" Sheridan, Mike Abramson, Janice Erickson, Anne Rifenburg, and Jim Kelly for accompanying me on this last installment in The Claire Saga. I so admire your patience in reading this one chapter at a time and giving me your thoughtful critiques in real time. I also appreciated it when you each picked something to challenge me on and fought me to a happy compromise. All the newbies in this group make an appearance as characters in the novel. You are all in The Claire Saga (and back story) forever.

I also appreciate the discerning eyes of the cold readers Tom Kojac, Mike McBride, Maura McLoughlin, Marissa Banez, Anne Rifenburg, Kerry F. Freeman, Rebecca Peacock, and Adrienne Williams Stucki for generously giving me the time to sit and read through that complete first draft of the book. Marissa, I appreciate the redline. I received the needed overall impression of the book, characters, and story, to make sure it satisfied you all as supporters of the prior four books. This gave me the confidence that I got it right.

To my wife, Lisa, children, Luke & Georgie, Jackie & Zack and Mark & Sara, and grandchildren, Lucian, Scarlett, Savanna, and Stella, I love you all more than life itself. Magic makes the world so much more fun. Never forget that. May you never have a dream that does not come true. Thanks for putting up with me Lisa.

To the McCaffrey Clan-siblings, Veronica, Eddie, Bernie ("the Ginger") and John-and all of your respective spouses and children, their spouses, and grandchildren, with a special mention of Barbara Frank. Family is everything. To my nephew Malachy, I loaned your nickname to the character "Mac." Thanks to my cousin Jimmy "Apples" (RIP) and his wife Connie (RIP), and to his sister Christina Jubak, and to all of their respective and collective descendants. I love you guys. Apples, I'll always remember stargazing on summer nights in the back yard on Mosholu Avenue, looking for aliens. Now they're here. Grey suits you. And shout out to all of my other McCaffrey and Frawley cousins.

To the amazing writers Joe Barrett, S K Murphy (Sis), E.H. Wilde, and David Buzan, thanks for the awesome cover blurbs. Kerry F. Freeman for the amazing introduction. Colin Broderick, thanks for cheering me on throughout *The Claire Saga*, giving me blurbs and being the go-to writer friend that shared only great advice and a lot of laughs. May all of your books sell millions of copies and all of your films be blockbusters. Christy-Cooper Burnett, the female half of my brain and personality, you rock.

To Lonnie Bell, Kyle Dooley, Jen, John McBride, and all the wonderful crew at Mike O'Shays in Longmont Colorado. You need a bigger bookshelf.

To the Wallen Witches and all of their family members, thanks for the continued support. Thank you Mark Wallen (RIP) for being such a cool character in life and literature. Thank you Dina for reading my *WTLLM* draft. Thanks Beau for reading *WTLLM*. I want to be you when I grow up. Congrats Tyler and Elizabeth, and welcome Grayson Tatum Sacca into this wonderful clan.

To Everett and Michelle, my favorite extraterrestrials. Never leave this earth without me.

To the OFC–Brian "BC" Corry (and Nan), his wonderful younger brother Doug Corry (RIP), Joe "Bam-Bam" Serrano (and Donna), Mark "Lenny" Lenahan, Mike "Stein" & "Disco" Augustyni (and Delia) and Eileen "Bubbles" Cotto (née Collins). Without you guys I would not have one story to tell. Love you all.

To Mike Kojac. I told you I would put you in. Rock that hat. Couldn't get Tommy in but I did acknowledge his cold read.

To Fergus, a dog for the ages.

To Ralph and Debbie Droz, Jackie and Sue Vaughan, Robin and Peter Vaughan, Big Jack (RIP) and Connie Vaughan, Tommy (RIP) and Ann McQuillen, Mary Moran (my dear SIL), Tom Delaney (RIP), Dr. Martin Stransky, Russell Jones (the strongest guy I know), George Silver, Danny Cahillane, Terry Hughes, Ken Hart, Jackie Hart, Pete Flanagan, Mariann

Galdi (and the rest of CSHS Class of '74), Lori Zeh, LT John Sheridan "Jack" Lawlor, USN, Colleen Joanne Lawlor (and all of her friends at Compassion Café on LBI and the Squat N Gobble in Bluffton, SC), John & Christine (RIP) Bricker, Dr. Frank Neeson, Terry Collins, Tommy O'Hagan (RIP), Sergeant Brian Gallagher and Tricia Gallagher, Peter and Raymond Smith, Johnny Carey (his lovely wife Helen and kids and grandkids), Maggie Dowling Steinberg, Lesley Romani, Jimmy, Stevie, Peter, Ebby and Matthew Betz, John Hughes, Denis "Murray" Collins (RIP), Jimmy "Schwartz" Whitelaw (and wife Jaysree), Pete Lenahan, Karen "Cruiser" Anderson, Chrissy and Kathy T, Rev. Gregory McNeil, Rosemary McBride, Elaine Staltare, Theresa Daly, Sue Woebke, Mike Daly, Chris Goldberry, Maura McLoughlin, Tricia Gallagher Hempel, Packi Jo Gilheany, Mike Keegan, Matty & Kerry Burke, Mary Young Cooney, Phil Taylor, Jerry Fall, Phil Boyle, Steve, Marty and Annemarie Quinn, Patty Gannon Tyler, Liz (Morin) & Tanner, Bill Campion, Rosie Lambeau, Paul & Richie Gray, Gregory Grey (RIP), Mike McBride, Mark Wallen, Bob Mahoney (and his lovely wife and children), Mike Mahoney, Marissa Banez, Mark Lafayette, Neil & Marci Ross (and Hugo), Bernie Yee, Charles Sullivan, Bob Mulvey (RIP), Debra Mayer, Marna Brown-Krauz, Mark Diller, Margo Scott, Howard Weller, Mark Diller, L. Londell McMillan, Gillian Lusins, Paula Guibault, Rob Margolis, Marna Brown, Debra Mayer, Londell McMillan, Mark Eisenberg, Amy Lippman, Linda Yassky, Minna Ferziger Felig, Emile Lafond, Nelson Bogart (RIP), Michael Manuellian, Alan Friedman, Paul LiCalsi, Jane Stevens, Christine Lepera, Tom Farrell, Mike McLaughlin, the rest of the Collins' Clan, Billy Dinome and the entire DiNome Family and anyone else I might have forgotten that may even in the slightest way possible resemble any of the characters mentioned herein, I thank you for your past friendships and the roles you have all played in this journey.

To my ever expanding circle of dear writer friends David Buzan, Sheila E. Young, Stefanie Barnfather, Andrea Couture, Maria Rojas

Tamay, Don "Donny-O" O'Connor, J.G. Macleod, Ismael S. Rodriguez, Jr., CS Hughes, Kerry Frye Freedman, Jessica Tate, Haris Orkin, Margaret Reyes Dempsey, Nikki Rodwell, Ivy Logan, Melissa Quigley, Nicky Shear, Jupiter Rose, Raelle Logan, Aleksandra Tryniecka, Vincent van Zandvoort, Rebecca Peacock, The Ancient Millennial, Writer Rob (from Colorado), LadyofLakes57, Dragonrok007, MindytheMenace, the Poet, Rachel (the poet), Terry – Greenhills, Witch, SweetieJassi, Rev Kristen, Sean Armstrong, Cellyhikes, Elena Ruiz, Michelle Caffrey, Cam Torrens, and Brian Fitzpatrick. I strongly recommend their books and on-line creative postings. I love the fellowship and the support. I wish you all nothing but success.

To my first official street fans – Carole and Ron Becker - who staked out a place I said I was going to be, waited patiently, and when I arrived, asked me to sign a copy of The Wise Ass. Congrats Tyler Sacca and Elizabeth Monaghan on the birth of your beautiful son, Grayson Tatum Sacca. You too, grandpa Terry Sacca and Grandma Michelle Sacca (RIP).

Must not forget my first Book Fair fan, Jasper. You rock.

To Richard Lamb. Your covers are magical and amazing. Thank you for making Claire iconic.

To the real Jimmy Moran. Love you brother. Love to Liz and all the family, Dana, Kevin & Brooklyn, Sara & Mark, Jackson & Ella. RIP Frances Mahoney.

To Bob Kunisch, my invaluable accountant and dear friend. Never die. Ever. And my best wishes to your lovely wife, Renee. To my wonderful barber Anna, thanks for making me look almost human.

To Jimmy and Kathy Fronsdahl, I appreciate your continuing support. Stay well. Love you both. Claire sends her love.

To Dan Pearson and his family. As always, with all due respect.

To my dear friend and law partner, Robert "never Bobby" Meloni. I love you, no matter what. Also love to your family, your spouse, Adrienne, your lovely three daughters, and siblings, especially your sister Lisa Meloni Ragusa.

To Helen (BFF), Bobbi & Eddie Roelle, Kim & Anthony Russo, Katherine Glass, and Dee Krauer (RIP). You all prove there is magic in the world every day. Love you all.

To every friend and family in Riverdale (Bronx). It is as magical as Middle Earth and Hogwarts.

To all my Berthoud friends and neighbors. Pay attention to those Ley Lines. You are the best.

To Reagan and Minna Rothe and the entire production, sales, and PR teams at Black Rose Writing, here goes number 5. Thanks for this continuing opportunity and all of your patience and support.

To all members of the Military, Police, Fire, and EMS departments throughout the country, thank you from the bottom of my heart for your selfless service. You are all loved and respected.

Thank you Tommy "Rocky" O'Hagan, Bill McGinn, Orio Palmer, and all of those first responders and other men and women who sacrificed their lives on 9-11-01. To Luke's buddy, Chris Kirby. You will never be forgotten. And finally, a nod to Fr. Mychal Judge, the patron saint of everyday heroes.

To Claire, who continues to share this amazing journey with me. You are my dragon.

I am forever in your debt. You, of course, carry this sequel
and all of its characters to the very end. Thank you.

And much love to my mini-mule, Claire's PA and little sister, Honey.

ABOUT THE AUTHOR

Tom McCaffrey is a born-and-bred New Yorker who, after a long career working as a successful entertainment attorney in Manhattan, relocated with his wife to a small town in Northern Colorado to follow a road less travelled and return to his first passion, writing. Both Tom and Claire and the gang are thrilled at this finale of *The Claire Saga*.

THE WISE ASS

TOM
McCAFFREY

"This is Grisham, on mushrooms."
—Colin Broderick,
author of
Orangutan
and
That's That
and
writer/director
of Emerald City

NOTE FROM TOM MCCAFFREY

Word-of-mouth is crucial for any author to succeed. If you enjoyed *Where the Ley Lines Meet*, please leave a review online—anywhere you are able. Even if it's just a sentence or two. It would make all the difference and would be very much appreciated.

Thanks!
Tom McCaffrey

We hope you enjoyed reading this title from:

BLACK ROSE
writing™

Subscribe to our mailing list – *The Rosevine* – and receive **FREE** books, daily
deals, and stay current with news about upcoming
releases and our hottest authors.
Scan the QR code below to sign up.

Already a subscriber? Please accept a sincere thank you for being a fan of
Black Rose Writing authors.

View other Black Rose Writing titles at
and use promo code
PRINT to receive a **20% discount** when purchasing.